NORTH

NORTH

JAMES B. HENDRYX

Originally published in 1923.

Published by Wildside Press.

Visit us online at wildsidepress.com.

CHAPTER I
BURR MacSHANE

IT WAS JUST BEFORE Christmas, and into Dawson, a straggling camp of tents and log cabins, the sourdoughs were drifting from the outlying creeks and washes. It was in that portentous year of the Yukon when in August, Henderson's strike on Gold Bottom was followed immediately by Carmack's strike on Bonanza, and the men of Fortymile and of Circle looked into the blowers and saw coarse gold that had been panned from the grass roots. Whereupon, claims paying "better than wages" were abandoned, outfits hastily thrown together, and in poling boats and in canoes, the sourdoughs stampeded up river. The traders, the saloon keepers, and the girls from the dance halls followed the gold hunters and on the flat in the shadow of Moosehide Mountain the camp of Dawson was born of the life blood of Circle and Fortymile.

But, from the first the new camp differed essentially from the older camps where it had been the wont of the sourdoughs to foregather for a winter of idleness and revelry. For, close upon the discovery of gold in the upper country, came the discovery of the process of "burning in," and in that year the Yukon saw the first winter mining of her history. These were the days of the unspoiled Yukon, before the stampede from the outside filled the valleys and the creek beds with its hordes of tin-horns and *chechakos*—the days when a man's word was as good as his pile and a card would be turned unquestionably upon a finger bet for thousands.

But with Christmas hard upon them, despite the fact of the new found winter mining, and despite the fact that the sourdoughs were gouging in gravel richer by far than the gravel of their fondest dreams, one by one the fires were allowed to die out in the shafts along the creek beds. The sourdoughs were drifting into the new camp. For Christmas is Christmas—and what is a week or two of work, when the bulk of the winter is still ahead, and when each test pan shows coarse gold and more of it than the luckiest of them had ever taken from many test pans? And what is a week or two of work when the white lights are calling—the clang of the dance hall piano, the feel of a woman held close, the smooth purr of the wheel, the run of the cards at the poker tables, the warm grip and glow of the liquor, and the comradery of men who thudded heavy sacks onto the bar from the mouths of which coarse gold was shaken onto the scales?

There had been no prearranged plan for a general celebration at Christmas—no looking forward in anticipation of a grand hurrah. But the spirit of Christmas was in the air. And each sourdough, independent of his neighbor, harnessed his dogs and silently hit the trail, knowing instinctively that at the end of the trail he would find his neighbor. For man is by instinct gregarious, and he will travel far to answer the primordial call of his kind. For a month, a year—longer, he may remain alone. But the passive act of remaining is a distinct effort of will, a continued and continuous throttling of desire, until at last the time comes when desire may no longer be throttled. A man may remake himself, may completely change the sequence of act, the sequence of thought, that has differentiated him from other men, he may thus change what men are pleased to call his nature. But, the fundamental law that has decreed him a social animal he cannot change—and remain a man. The fugitive from justice, though he know himself to be beyond thought of capture in some far fastness of the wilderness will, when the time comes, count prison bars, and even the hangman's noose, as naught, and will deliberately risk capture in seeking the society of his kind. And the man of the far North will brave the hardships of the long trail, will laugh at the strong cold, will bore through the blinding blizzard, will risk thin ice, and uncomplaining accept the gruelling labor of the snow-trail for no other thing than that he may intermingle with his own kind. It is the law. Men have broken the law and have paid the fullness of its fearsome penalty. The brain that makes man man explodes, and the man of a moment before is a raving insentient brute which in a fume of unreasoning fury seeks only to destroy until in a final paroxysm of malignity he destroys himself. Or, the dissolution of the brain may come gently and the breaker of the law of kind, maundering, and prattling, and babbling, may live on, and on, and on.

A short distance above the mouth of a dry wash that emptied into the wide valley of Bonanza, Burr MacShane threw the last shovelful of gravel onto his dump and methodically kindled his fire on the iron-hard gravel at the bottom of his shallow shaft. An enormous malamute turned with a sneeze of disgust from his contemplation of the shaft as the acrid smoke filled his nostrils, and MacShane laughed: "Surprised as hell, ain't you, Highball, that fire gives off smoke? Every day you stand there an' get a noseful, an' then down goes your tail an' you sneeze out the smoke. You act like a fool pup—an' you the best trail dog in the North!" At the words the tail of the great dog snapped erect, and rearing upward he placed two large forefeet upon the man's chest. The ensuing tussle during which each tried to put the other in the snow was interrupted by the tiny tinkle of bells. Man and dog paused to watch an outfit pass the mouth of the wash far out on the trail. MacShane grinned: "Headin' for Dawson," he confided to the dog, "That's the sixth one in three days, an' the Lord knows how many that we didn't see. An' in a week or so they'll be headin' out again. Ain't men fools, Highball? They ought to stay with the gravel."

That afternoon MacShane cut cordwood and from the vantage point of the rim saw three more outfits pull by. When it was too dark to see he descended to the cabin, built a roaring fire in the stove and proceeded to fill a tin boiler that had originally been a petrol can, with ice.

"Kind of like to hear how the rest of 'em are makin' it," he muttered to himself while the ice melted. "I'd kind of like to know if any of 'em have struck bed rock. That's what's goin' to tell the story of this strike: What's on bed rock? This shallow gravel is sure shot full, but the real stuff will lay where it can't work down any farther."

The ice melted, he added more, and when the tin boiler was half full of water he stepped outside and carried in a piece of old tarpaulin onto which he had shoveled a hundred pounds or so of gravel from the morning's digging. The gravel was frozen into a solid mass and he set it beside the stove while he stripped off his clothing and took a bath, using the water sparingly. Dressing himself, he proceeded to wash his discarded underclothing, shirt and socks in the boiler. Hanging these garments on the drying rack, he produced a pan and when the gravel had thawed sufficiently, dumped in a batch and filled the pan from his wash water. Squatting upon the floor close beside the lamp which he moved to the edge of the table, he began to work the pan with a peculiar circular motion that threw the lighter dross splashing over the edge onto the floor. The coarser gravel he removed with his hands, tossing it aside. As the gravel and water lowered in the pan he examined the residue carefully until with a final flirt he ridded the pan of the last remaining bit of muddy water. Then he turned the contents onto a piece of wrapping paper spread out to receive it, and sorted the gold from the remaining dross. Flour gold, dust, and nuggets, that single pan weighed in at one hundred and forty dollars! MacShane rose, carried the tarpaulin with the remaining gravel out to the dump and with the water that remained in the boiler he washed his floor. Crossing to his bunk he withdrew from beneath the blankets a buckskin pouch and pouring its contents onto the paper, sat for a while and looked at the yellow pile. He consulted a memorandum book, and added a notation.

"That makes close to eight thousand dollars out of the test pans," he figured, "an' at that rate there's over a hundred thousand on the dump, an' God knows how much on down. This is sure some strike! Wait till the news of it gets outside! I would like to have a dance or two. I guess most of the girls have hit the new camp by now. This new strike sure raised hell with Circle an' Fortymile!" As the words unbidden expressed his trend of thought, the man's fingers abstractedly separated the larger nuggets from the little pile of gold. He returned a handful to the sack and dumped the coarse gold and the dust in after them. Then he prepared his supper and as he ate it he cooked up a meal of tallow and rice for his seven dogs.

"I expect Horse Face Joe come up along with the rest," he mused as he washed and dried his dishes, "He sure is a doleful bird, but he can make the piano talk. Reminds a fellow of—I don't know—sort of just lifts him up an' out of it all. From about the fourth drink on, he's a wonder. It's a gift—music like he makes is. When he's feelin' right he can just play on an' on, makin' it up as he goes, an' all of it's better than anything that's be'n wrote down—somehow it gets right to a man." He apportioned the dog food into seven separate dishes and carried them out the door, then he returned and lighted his pipe. "Noticed the tea was gettin' a little low, an' another hundred of flour wouldn't hurt. She was two dollars a pound when I come in, chances are she'll go an ounce to the pound by spring." Ensued a silence during which MacShane's pipe went out. "That mitten I burnt the end of ain't goin' to last long either. Horse Face would be just about hittin' his gait by now." He stepped to the door and glanced toward the mouth of his shaft where the red glow proclaimed that it was time to throw on more wood. Closing the door he put on cap and mittens, but instead of going to the shaft he pulled off his mittens, filled his pipe and sat down. "They're sayin' that this is the last big strike," he mused, "That when this peters out there won't be any more poor man's gold—but hell! There's always another strike. There always has be'n, an' there always will be." He jerked the cap from his head and tossed it onto his bunk. "To hell with the fire! I'll pull in the mornin'. Got to get that tea, an' flour, an' another pair of mittens. You can't trust burnt moosehide." He fired up the stove and put on another batch of dog food. "I'll hit the trail early tomorrow, an' I'll burn her up!" While the dog food cooked, MacShane sat and stoked the fire and thought. Most men would have passed the time by reading, but not Burr MacShane. He preferred to think, to envision long trails—trails he had mushed alone with his dogs, and trails no man had ever mushed.

Just turned thirty years old, he was chiefest among all the sourdoughs of the mighty North. And he knew the North as no other man ever knew it. Cabin boy on a whaler, he deserted at the age of fourteen at St. Michaels, and for several years he knocked about the Russian settlements and the Eskimo villages of the lower Yukon, gradually widening his circle of adventure until in the eighties, and early nineties, men who thought they were exploring virgin territory were continually crossing his trail. Indians who had seen no other white man knew him by name, and little, isolated tribes there were who years afterward still called all white men Burrmacshane, believing it to be the name of the whole white race. He was the first white man to explore the Kuskokwim, and the first to traverse the mighty waste eastward from Kotsebue Sound up the Kobuk and down the Koyukuk to the Yukon. Always he played a lone hand, and among the sourdoughs he was regarded as a super man. No boasting of adventure where men foregathered but what some adventure of Burr Mac-Shane out-topped them all. Yet, of these adventures MacShane, himself, never talked. For no adventure could there be in the North of which MacShane had not tasted the fullness. He had fought starvation, strong cold, blizzard, thin ice, rotten ice, fire, famine, water, and disease, and always he had won. By the very force and indomitable nerve of him he had won, and by the strength of his iron-hard frame. Every camp in the gold country had at some time or other boasted his habitat, but none had boasted for long. The wild, restless spirit of him forever goaded him on. The long trail beckoned, and he would hit the long trail. The strong cold descending upon a camp would drive men to the shelter of their fires, and MacShane, defying the strong cold, would throw his outfit together and mush a thousand miles. Men whispered that every safe in Alaska and in the Canadian Yukon held some of MacShane's gold. But not for his gold was he held in regard, for no man ever thought of MacShane as rich. His deeds outshadowed his gold—in a land where gold is God.

So MacShane mused, half dozing by the fire while the dog food cooked. "She's a great strike, all right, but she ain't the last great strike—by a damn sight. An' next year this country won't be fit to live in. When the news gets outside there'll be fifty thousand *chechakos* pilin' in here. The damned fools! Most of 'em will go broke, an' a lot of 'em will die, an' a few will take out some dust—but what good will it do 'em? They'll go back outside an' buy 'em a chicken ranch. The big country will never get to 'em. They'll think they're *skookum*, but it'll all be luck. The strike's be'n made, an' all they got to do is shovel out the gravel. I'd rather be a Siwash than the best of 'em—a Siwash has got a chance to see something new, to follow a trail that ain't packed, to tear his meat from the teeth of the land, an' not buy it at the tradin' company's store. Damn *chechakos*! But I won't be here to see 'em. There ain't anyone tried the Colville river yet, an' even the Koyukuk ain't be'n scratched. God, but she's bleak up there, with the long night, an' the strong cold. But she ain't b'en scratched, an' combed, an' raked, an' the cricks ain't be'n punched full of holes. I've got a hunch. North, it says. North!" and with a smile on his lips the man removed the dog food, blew out his light, and rolled between his blankets.

CHAPTER II
IN THE BIG CAMP

IT WAS DAWSON'S FIRST Christmas eve. The Golden North Saloon was a blaze of light. Sourdoughs from the creeks crowding the bar kept weighers and bartenders working as they had never worked before. For in the new order of winter mining, the sourdoughs were bent on crowding a whole winter's hilarity into the space of a few days and nights. Sound filled the air, the blare of the dance hall piano as two step and waltz crashed forth under the sure touch of the nimble fingered Horse Face Joe, and the screech and scrape and moan of the accompanying violin. With punctuating stabs sounded the voice of the caller as, at someone's vociferous demand, the music swung into a square dance. All this was the crescendo of sound. But other sounds there were, audible, distinguishable, blending a minor theme into the wild harmony of the whole. The soft scraping of moccasined feet on the floor boards, the clink and tinkle of glasses, the crackling rustle of silk petticoats as some sourdough in a sudden excess of exuberance swung his partner high in the air, the drone of voices, the purr of the wheel, an occasional burst of laughter. It was a good night—as nights go—for the pervading spirit was Fun. And the men from the creeks had earned their fun. By the gruelling toil of their two hands they had earned it, by the chopping of cordwood, the tending of fires, and by the gouging and hoisting of frozen gravel from the black mouths of shafts. It was their night, and in the fullness of their several capacities, they were enjoying it.

At the bar the talk was of gold. "I've cleaned up more than an ounce to the pan—not once, but a dozen times," said Moosehide Charlie.

"I took five ounces out of a test pan, an' didn't get all the flour gold, at that," interrupted Camillo Bill, "an' I'm bettin' my whole dump will run better than an ounce to the pan."

"I'm tellin' ye," said Old Stuart Gordon, "Ye're goin' to see a hundred dollars to the pan before this winter's out."

A general laugh followed: "Have another shot of hootch, Old Timer, an' make it two hundred, an' we'll all get rich!" bantered Ace-In-The-Hole Brent.

The old man wagged his head sagely, and redoubled his prophecy: "Aye, an' ye'll see two hundred to the pan before bed rock is reached. I'm tellin' ye we're right now ridin' the biggest strike the world ever seen. But don't let me hinder the orderin' of the round of drinks. A wee bit tipple on a night like this hurts no man. Don't the Gude Book say 'take a leetle wine for thy stomach's sake'? An' the wine not bein' handy, we'll have to make whusky do."

The men laughed and drank, and the glasses were refilled, for Old Man Gordon, as he was called by the men of the Yukon, was a general favorite among them. He was not old, probably in his early fifties, but his grizzled beard and grey hair made him appear a veritable patriarch among them. For Dawson was a camp of young men. But grey hairs were not his sole distinction. He was the only man in camp who had brought his family with him. Originally a Hudson's Bay Company employee, he had married the daughter of a factor in the Mackenzie River country, and several years before, bringing his wife and little daughter, had built a cabin on Birch Creek. When news of the up-river strike reached him, he abandoned his claim, loaded his family into a poling boat and was among the first to erect a cabin in the new camp. Another thing that differentiated him from the general run of his associates was his religious turn of mind. The deep-rooted Calvinism of his ancestors had taken firm hold of his rugged nature. No provocation could wring an oath from his lips, and his conversation was liberally besprinkled with quotations, and misquotations from "the Gude Book." Strangely enough, this strict Calvinism, while it held him to a certain stern code of morals, seemed to take small offence at his occasional lapses from sobriety. He never gambled, but there were those who laughingly whispered that his natural Scotch canniness, more than his religion, was responsible for his aversion to the gaming tables. Be that as it may, gamble he would not, and the suggestion of poker or roulette generally called forth a vehement discourse upon the frivolity and worldliness of "riskin' gude gold on the turn of a card or the spin of a wheel!"

"An' so ye think," continued the old man, warming to the liquor "that I'm touched i' the head wi' my talk of a hundred, an' two hundred dollars to the pan?" He paused and glared a challenge into the faces of the five men grouped about him.

Camillo Bill laughed: "No, no, nothin' like that, Gordon! Only if this here camp ever feels the need of a booster's club, I'll sure nominate you for the first president of it."

"You said we was goin' to see two hundred dollars to the pan before we struck bed rock," reminded Moosehide Charlie, "What's she goin' to run when we do hit the bottom?"

"Ye'll see four and five hundred dollars weighed from a single pan when bed rock is reached," replied Gordon, "Ye think I'm crazy—but, wait an' see."

"Mebbe bed rock will be a solid floor of gold, an' we can just blast her out in chunks," suggested Stoell, the gambler. "It'll sure be hell on the mahogany when the boys get to tossin' them big chunks across the bar."

"Whoopie!" cried Bettles, "Five hundred to the pan? I sure feel rich! Come on, boys, liquor up so I can spend some of this here fabulous wealth! You'll do me a favor by helpin' me lighten my sack. I feel weighted down with gold, an' that's a hell of a fix to be in."

"It's my turn to buy," interrupted Camillo Bill, "Here you, Jack, shove out a bottle! Hold on!" he cried in mock solicitude, as the bottle thumped down on the bar. "You'll sure have to learn to set them glasses an' bottles down careful. Old Man Gordon, here, has got gold comin' in chunks so big you'll have to cover yer bar with boiler plate to keep her from wearin' out."

"Have yer fun, ye addle pates!" grinned the old man, "But the days ain't far off when ye'll be sayin' how Old Man Gordon was the only one that could see ahead of his nose. An' speakin' of b'iler plate, I wish I had a good b'iler here right now."

Shouts of laughter greeted the announcement. "Give him a boiler for his, Jack. It's my treat!" snickered Camillo Bill.

"He's goin' to melt ice an' run a winter flume."

"He's goin' to rig a steam h'stin' derrick to lift them big chunks of gold out of his shaft."

"Borrow the boiler out of the steamboat fer the winter. They won't need it till spring."

"Dogs can't pull no such output of gold, nohow. He's figgerin' on startin' a steam sled line out to his claim."

And so it went, one preposterous suggestion followed by a more preposterous one. And in the centre of the group, Old Stuart Gordon poured his drink in owlish solemnity, and let them rave.

"I believe they're jokin' at you, Gordon," said Bettles, with solemn countenance, "But, layin' jokes aside, what in thunder do you want of a boiler?"

"To thaw out the gravel wi' steam," and undisturbed, he waited for the laughter to subside. "Ye'll see it done," he continued, with conviction. "Ye'd of all laughed an' babbled yer brainless jokes last winter if anyone told ye there'd be winter minin' on the Yukon. An' now ye're used to the winter minin' by thawin' the gravel wi' cordwood fires, an' ye think it'll always be thawed that way. But it won't. It's a waste of wood, an' a waste of time, an' a waste of hard labor. Wi' a b'iler, now, an' a steam hose runnin' to the bottom of the shaft, ye could thaw the muck an' gravel faster, an' use half, an' less than half the wood."

The door opened and a man entered in a cloud of steam that swirled about his knees. Shaking his hands from a pair of heavy fur mittens which dangled upon their thongs, he fumbled at the tie strings of his cap. He was a lean man, with the rugged leanness of perfect health, and he advanced into the room with the springy step that bespoke perfect coordination of tireless muscles.

"It's MacShane!" cried Moosehide Charlie, and instantly the name passed from lip to lip throughout the length and breadth of the room. Men called greeting from the poker tables, the dancers paused amid the whirl of a waltz to wave a hand at him, and the onlookers at the wheel and the faro layouts crowded forward to the bar. The newcomer was deluged with invitations to drink. For in the camp of the sourdoughs, the name of MacShane was a name to conjure with.

"Merry Christmas, you trail-mushers an' sourdoughs!" he called, "Merry Christmas, you frost-hounds, an' dancin' girls!"

McCarty, owner of the Golden North Saloon rapped loudly upon the bar: "The family's all here!" he cried, "An' the house buys! Mush up, an' name yer liquor. We're goin' to drink to a Merry Christmas—an' many of 'em!"

The music ceased abruptly in the middle of a dance. The girls crowded forward on the arms of their partners, shouting greetings to MacShane, who called most of them by name as he returned the pleasantries. As the glasses were filled, MacShane was busy greeting old acquaintances, recalling with unfailing accuracy the last place he had seen them. It was: "How's everything at Nulato?" "When did you quit the Tanana?" "How's everyone at Eagle?" "What's doin' on the White River?" and so on, until McCarty interrupted, holding his glass aloft.

"A Merry Christmas!" he cried, and "Merry Christmas!" arose from the throats of the crowd in a mighty surge of sound.

"Come over here, Horse Face!" cried MacShane, when the empty glasses had been returned to the bar, "I figured you'd be here. One drink calls for another, an' while you're all bunched up handy, you'll drink with me." He nodded to McCarty. "Have the boys fill 'em up again," he ordered, "an' we'll drink to the luck of the camp! I want Horse Face right here beside me so I can see that he gets a good sizeable noggin', 'cause he's sure got to make that old music box talk this night." He paused and looked around: "All set?" he asked, "Here goes, then: 'To the luck of the camp!'" And once more a mighty surge of sound filled the room: "To the luck of the camp!"

Someone else wanted to buy, but MacShane laughingly shook his head: "Not too fast!" he cried, "We all have got a day or two yet, or a week for this here jollification, an' we don't want to get drunk to start off with, 'cause if we do we'll have to either stay drunk or feel sick, an' I don't aim to do neither one. An' besides, Christmas ain't till tomorrow, anyhow."

A few ordered drinks, but for the most part the crowd, with the words of approbation on its lips, went back to its cards, and its dancing. MacShane joined the little group of sourdoughs, who still stood at the forward end of the bar: "How's everything?" he asked, "How you all makin' it?"

The answers were unanimously optimistic, and Camillo Bill laughed: "But you ought to be'n here a while back an' heard Old Man Gordon speak his piece."

The old Scotchman interrupted, stepping forward: "Ye're Burr MacShane, I take it? I've crossed ye're trail, but I never had the luck to meet up with ye."

MacShane laughed: "I'm Burr MacShane," he answered, "an' where was it you crossed my trail?"

"It was two or three years back, an' the trail was three or four years old, then—but still fresh."

Moosehide Charlie grinned: "That's the way with Old Man Gordon," he explained, "He mostly talks in riddles—when he ain't prophysin' some fool thing or other."

"'Tis no riddle at all, but clear as the spoken word to any man blessed wi' better than a louse-sized brain. Ye'll recollect an' old Injun named Amos, that lives way up on the head of the Porcupine, where a little swift river piles down out of the Nahoni Mountains?"

MacShane nodded: "Yes, I believe I do."

"Well, there's where I crossed ye're trail." He turned to the others. "Amos broke through thin ice. A minute more an' he'd of be'n caught by the suck of a rapids when MacShane went in after him. He went in all over, an' it was thirty below, an' no camp made!"

Exclamations broke from the lips of the men of the North as their eyes sought MacShane's face.

MacShane laughed: "You don't want to believe everything an Injun tells you. Mostly, they're lyin'."

"This one wasn't," answered Gordon, with conviction. "An' that's what I meant by sayin' yer trail is fresh yet on the Porcupine. An' Injun never forgets."

"Hell! Thirty below ain't so cold," answered MacShane, with just a trace of annoyance in his tone. "We got a fire built right away, an' in half a day we was dried out an' good as ever. But, what's doin' on the creeks? How far down you got, an' what does she show?"

"I'm lookin' to sluice out big in the spring," offered Camillo Bill. "Took five ounces out of one pan."

"I've took better than an ounce out of a lot of pans," said Moosehide Char-lie, "an' I know I ain't into the good stuff yet. I ain't only about ten foot down. But, you'd ought to heard Gordon! He says we're goin' to be takin' out a hundred dollars to the pan—"

"He said two hundred, before we struck bed rock," interrupted Bettles.

"And five hundred dollars on bed rock," added Ace-In-The-Hole.

"An' wood firin' has got too slow for him," supplanted Camillo Bill, "so he's honin' fer a boiler fer to thaw out the gravel with steam!" A general laugh followed in which Burr MacShane did not join.

Camillo Bill was the first to notice that the newcomer's face had remained grave. "What do you think?" he asked, "You know more about the game than all of us put together."

"Has anyone hit the bottom?" asked MacShane.

"No one that I've heard of, an' I reckon us fellows right here would be down as far as any."

"But, it's all damn foolishness to be talkin' about a hundred, an' two hun-dred, an' five hundred dollars to the pan," broke in Moosehide Charlie. "Of course we're ridin' the biggest strike yet—any strike is plumb out of reason that pans an ounce. But they ain't no call to go boostin' it like Gordon. What do you think?"

"I think," answered MacShane, "that Gordon has hit it about right."

A long moment of silence greeted the announcement, during which the sourdoughs stared into each other's faces, and into the face of the speaker.

Bettles was the first to speak. He cleared his throat harshly: "Jest say that again, will you?"

"Sure I will. I say, Gordon is right. You'll all see it—an' it won't be long till you do. I took one hundred and forty dollars out of a single pan last evening—an' I ain't anywhere near to bed rock."

Again, dead silence greeted the announcement, until suddenly Moosehide Charlie, filling his lungs, let out a whoop, and tried to clamber onto the bar. Bettles and Camillo Bill jerked him back.

"Keep still, you fool! Do you want to make a panic? Let 'em go ahead with their cards an' their dancin'. What they don't know won't hurt 'em none, an' what we do know that they don't, may do us a lot of good."

Moosehide subsided, and the few who had paused to glance toward the group, resumed their play with remarks about "Moosehide feelin' his oats."

Where the prophecy of Old Man Gordon had met only with laughter and derision, the same words from the lips of Burr MacShane were accorded noth-ing but respect by the men of the high North. For these men knew MacShane. His spoken word carried weight. And when he said that they would see from two to five hundred dollars taken from a pan, not a man who heard the words but believed implicitly that he would see from two to five hundred dollars taken from a pan.

"God," breathed Bettles, and there was a nervous quaver in his voice, "then we're a bunch of millionaires, right here!"

MacShane nodded: "There's men in this crowd that'll clean up more than a million—maybe double, and treble a million. But you want to remember that the gravel is spotted. It ain't all rich. The first hole I put down didn't show anything better than wages at twelve foot. A thousand foot from there I panned out one hundred an' forty dollars at five foot. An' I took out a half an' ounce at the grass roots."

Camillo Bill stared at Gordon: "You old son-of-a-gun!" he grinned, "Was you guessin'? Or, how did you know?"

"It was a hunch," replied the old man, "I could feel it. As the Gude Book says, it was a vision."

Camillo turned to MacShane: "But about the boiler?" he asked, "There ain't nothin' in that boiler business, is there?"

"I don't know anything about boilers," admitted MacShane, "I do know that winter minin' is so damned new that we'd be fools to think we've learnt all there is to know about it. You can bet that if steam thawin' will work, an' will save time an' labor, it's bound to come. Trouble with us is we're plumb ignorant. We've got a thing here that's so big we don't know what to do with it. We can't even realize the bigness of it yet, let alone how to handle it. Why, I ain't even begun to think, an' I can see a hundred ways to clean up big without ever puttin' a pick in the gravel."

"What do you mean?" they cried, crowding close.

MacShane laughed and waved them back: "Look a here you all malamutes an' sourdoughs! What do you think this is, a business meetin'? This here is Christmas eve, an' we're here to celebrate it. I'm goin' to have another drink, an' then I'm goin' to dance! Horse Face ain't woke up yet. Plenty time to talk business after a while. Let's get Horse Face where he belongs, an' whoop her up!"

Someone called for the drinks, and Old Man Gordon drew on his mittens: "I'm goin' home," he announced. "Ye young devils can go ahead wi' ye're hullabaloo. Tomorrow is Christmas, an' I'm goin' to be sober. The wife an' kid, ye know."

"Wife an' kid!" exclaimed MacShane, "You got a wife an' kid here in this camp? A kid, did you say? A real honest to God little kid?"

"You bet he has!" cried a chorus of voices, "Purtiest little thing you ever seen," announced Moosehide, "'Bout so high, ain't she, Camillo?" He held his hand about four feet from the floor.

MacShane was looking off across the dance hall. "A little kid!" he muttered, "Well, what do you know about that?"

"She's eleven," informed Gordon, "An' she can handle a canoe, or a team of dogs like a man. Good night, boys, I'm goin' home. See ye tomorrow."

CHAPTER III
CHRISTMAS

WHEN THE DOOR HAD closed behind Gordon, MacShane drank with the others, and when the glasses were returned to the bar, he asked: "How many more kids is there here in camp?"

"No white ones, except Gordon's," informed Camillo Bill, "There's a bunch of Siwashes, mebbe a dozen or two, countin' the ones in the camp about four miles down river."

"White ones or red, it's all the same," answered MacShane, "What's the matter with this camp? Where's yer Christmas tree? Yer all dead four ways from yer belt! All you're thinkin' about Christmas is to get a bellyful of hootch an' raise hell! Christmas is, first and foremost, for kids!" He vaulted lightly onto the bar and roared for attention. The card players paused and the dancers stopped in the middle of a waltz. "Come up here, you all!" he called, "An' get you an earful!" The crowd surged about the bar, for when MacShane had words to say, it was worth their while to listen. He stood looking down into the upturned faces, some laughing, others waiting in eager expectancy for what was coming. For MacShane was not given to theatricals. Had anyone else mounted the bar the act would have received no more than passing notice. But MacShane—. He walked the length of the board, his moccasins leaving tracks upon the polished mahogany. "Tomorrow's Christmas," he began. "There's kids in this camp! Real, regular kids—one white one an' a lot of Siwashes! What are we goin' to do about it? Come on, speak up! Are you goin' to let Christmas pass 'em by like any other day? Not by a damn sight you ain't! This here camp's got to start right! This is its first Christmas, an' she's goin' to be a regular Christmas!" Here and there in the crowd men voiced approval.

"Now you're talkin', MacShane!" cried a girl, in a low cut gown of red silk. "Tell us what to do!"

"A Christmas tree!" suggested some one.

"What would we put on it?" yelled another, and a babel of voices broke out, hurling questions and answers.

MacShane held up his hand for silence: "Where's McCarty?" he asked.

"Right here!"

"McCarty, tomorrow mornin' this dump ain't a saloon. It's a town meetin' house, an' there'll be a Christmas tree in the dance hall for kids! We'll start in at ten, an' we'll be through by noon, an' after that we'll hit the high spots! How about it?"

McCarty caught the spirit: "She's yours!" he cried. "Go to it!"

"So far, so good!" cried MacShane, "An' now for the program: Who'll go out an' get a tree?"

Every man in the house volunteered with a whoop. MacShane laughed: "Too many trees! Here you, Camillo, an' Moosehide, an' you two over there by the door, you go get a tree, an' make it as big an' bushy as will set up in this room. How many stores is there? All right, you Ace-In-The-Hole, an' Bettles, you go down an' find out what they got in the way of toys an' candy."

"They're closed up!" ventured someone.

"Unclose 'em, then! Tell 'em MacShane says to open up an' stay open till we get this thing fixed up."

Other arrangements were discussed, suggestions and counter-suggestions coming in an indistinguishable jumble of words.

A wave of fog rolled into the room as the door opened: "There ain't a damn toy in town!" cried Bettles from the doorway, "An' only a little candy," supplemented Ace-In-The-Hole.

MacShane leaped from the bar and made his way to the door, the crowd parting to give him room.

"Come on, half a dozen of you packers," he called after him, "We'll look around a bit."

Pushing into the first store where the sleepy proprietor grinned a welcome, MacShane opened up: "What kind of a dump you runnin' here? No toys! Who in hell ever heard of a store without toys at Christmas? What have you got? There's cranberries! Give us ten quarts. An' all the candy you've got. Twenty pounds of sugar an' some chocolate. We'll set some of the girls makin' candy. Got to have dolls. The girls can make 'em, give us some cloth, an' somethin' for waddin'—an' they've got to have dresses. Give us a bolt of cloth for dresses—not no squaw cloth, some honest to God silk. Ain't got it! What's that hangin' up there?"

"Them's silk skirts. The girls buys 'em."

"Give us a bunch, assorted colors—red an' pink, an' blue. Is that all you got? Ain't you got nothin' for boy kids? Give us some tin pails, then—they can pound on 'em for drums. What's in them fancy bottles?"

"That's perfumery for to sell the girls."

"Give it here!" demanded MacShane, "Sell 'em a bath tub, an' they won't need this. Kids like the smell of it. Oh, yes, an' some candles."

"If you want 'em fer a Christmas tree, I ain't got none of them holders."

MacShane thought a minute. "Give us some clothes pins, we can rig 'em on with them. An' a can of red paint, an' yellow, an' blue."

"I got red, an' black, an' white. No yeller, an' blue."

"Give us them, then," ordered MacShane "an' when you figger up the bill send it to me."

Back to the Golden North hurried the men, bearing their booty in their arms. Depositing it upon the bar, MacShane mounted beside it. "Now girls, it's up to you! Those that's handy with needles get busy an' make up a dozen or so of dolls. An' rip up these here silk skirts an' make clothes for 'em. An' then make some socks an' bags out of what's left to hold the candy. A couple of you cook up a batch of candy—here's sugar an' chocolate. That'll keep you all busy. Here you Sourdoughs—some of you borrow needles an' thread from the girls an' string these here cranberries. The rest of us has got to whittle out circles, an stars, an' horses, an' dogs, an' men, an' we'll dip 'em in paint an' hang 'em on the tree. They won't be fit to handle tomorrow, but they'll shine up bright! Come on up, now—one more drink, an' we'll all fly at it. When we git the tree rigged, we'll go ahead an' dance till daylight. After that there's nothin' goes on here till noon, except it's for the kids."

Laughing and talking, they crowded the bar, and MacShane who had leaped to the floor, motioned to Horse Face. "Come here an' open your sack," he said. Whereupon MacShane shook some coarse gold from his own sack into the other. "You're on shift tomorrow mornin' to play tunes for the kids," he commanded, "an' make her talk, Horse Face, make her talk!"

The men returned with the Christmas tree which was soon braced and wired into place at one end of the dance hall. The dancing girls brought their sewing materials down stairs. Someone rustled a big pine packing case which was promptly knocked to pieces, and the boards distributed among the men, who got out their knives and proceeded to whittle grotesques shapes of men and fearsome beasts, of stars, and crescents, and circles, and hearts, which were fantastically painted and hung, by bits of cord, upon the tree. Cranberries were strung in long ropes that festooned the tree in loops and graceful curves of gleaming red. And the dolls! There were dolls made and dressed that night that would have done credit to an artist, and there were dolls as ugly and distorted as the lines of a heathen god. But the spirit of Christmas was there. Men and women did their best, and laughter reigned supreme. At the piano Horse Face Joe's untiring fingers swept the keys in crashing volumes of sound that roared and reverberated through the room like volleys of mountain thunder, to sink suddenly into the softest murmurs. Little tinkles and trills of purest melody would almost imperceptibly swell into rich chords and dreamy soul-gripping strains that momentarily stilled the laughter so that men and women, with pressed lips, fixed their eyes upon their work, or lifting them, stared long at blank walls. The mood would change and a galloping, romping air would suddenly crash forth to run its course and blend into the solemn strains of some half forgotten hymn. It was Horse Face Joe's inspired night. Never before had the like been heard, and never again would Horse Face duplicate the feat, as with closed eyes he sat and toyed with the hearts and the souls of the men and the dancing girls who were putting the best that was in them into the fashioning of playthings and gewgaws that on the morrow would delight the hearts of one little white girl and many Indian children. On and on he played the music that had never been written—music fashioned in his own warped brain even as his fingers flew nimbly over the keys.

In and out among the workers moved Burr MacShane and McCarty, praising, encouraging, good-naturedly ridiculing and bantering the workers as they collected the finished products and piled them at the foot of the tree. At length the job was done. The last doll was finished, the last grotesquely whittled totem received its splotch of color, and the last gay candy bag was filled. Horse Face broke into a wild whirling fanfare of sound, weird as the scream of a Valkyrie, wild as the wolf's long howl. The music ended suddenly in a crash that threatened to tear the strings from their moorings, and once more laughter reigned supreme, for as MacShane and McCarty, standing upon chairs, hung the toys, and decorations, and candy bags upon the tree, each offering was greeted with loud-called words of praise accompanied by boisterous hand-clapping, or with howls of derisive laughter as some particularly grotesque or misshapen object was displayed to view.

MacShane glanced at his watch. "Four o'clock!" he cried, "Swarm to the bar, I'll buy! From now till eight o'clock everyone's time's his own—except this—no one gets drunk! Anyone caught drunk between now an' afternoon's goin' to settle with me! After the kids get theirs will be time enough for us. At eight o'clock we all hit out an' begin to gather kids! Come on, now!" he raised his glass aloft: "Dawson's first Christmas! Drink her down!" He emptied his glass at a gulp and grabbing the girl nearest him threw her onto his shoulders and made for the dance hall. "Speed her up, Horse Face!" he cried, as he set his partner upon her feet, "Come on, girl, we'll show 'em how to dance!"

Horse Face "speeded her up," and MacShane led off in a dizzying, whirling waltz that swung the girl from her feet before half the length of the room had been covered. Laughing and shouting, others joined the sport, and for fifteen minutes the room was a gyrating riot of color as the men outdid themselves to whirl their partners clear of the floor, the strongest among them, like Mac-Shane, spinning them high above their heads as they rotated with incredible swiftness. Dance followed dance in a bewildering turmoil of fun. There were not girls enough to go round and men tying handkerchiefs about their sleeves, took the part of girls.

When a man paired off with one of these pseudo girls it immediately became the aim of each dancer to whirl the other down, that is, to whirl so rapidly that the other, losing all sense of balance, when suddenly released, goes staggering foolishly to a fall. Many such tilts there were, to the intense delight of the spectators, the vanquished one crashing to the floor amid cries of "Loser buys! Loser buys!" And the loser bought, albeit with one accord they drank sparingly, for most of them were light drinkers by habit, and of those who were not, none cared to be called upon to settle with MacShane. For there had been occasions when men had tried conclusions with MacShane at close quarters, and rumor of them had travelled the length of the river.

At five minutes to eight, MacShane whirled down McCarty in the last dance of the orgy. Interest centered at once upon the two, and soon they had the floor to themselves as faster and faster they spun round and round to the galloping music of the piano. Both were strong as oxen, and both were past masters at the game, and when at last MacShane suddenly released his grip and staggered backward, the crowd burst into a wild yell of acclaim, as McCarty, his arms clutching at the air like flails, reeled half across the room and sprawled his length at the feet of Horse Face Joe.

"Come on, you snow hounds!" cried MacShane, "Out with you! It's every man out doors! Grab every kid you see—big an' little, red, white, black, an' yellow! Down the river an' up the river an' get back here by ten! Bust into the cabins an' tepees! You've got a free search warrant for kids! Wrap 'em up good, an' bring 'em along. Tell their folks to come too, if they want to—but every kid within five miles has got to be brought! Dump 'em in here when you catch 'em, an' go an' get more. The girls will herd 'em till time for the show to start. Vamoose, now! Hit the trail!"

CHAPTER IV
A GAME OF CRIBBAGE

THE INDIANS OF THE Yukon are a gentle folk, else that early morning raid of the sourdoughs had produced a war. Pouring through the door of the Golden North Saloon the men, shouting and laughing, dispersed in every direction, and in twos and threes invaded the habitations of the Indians, who had not yet crawled from between their blankets. For eight o'clock in the morning in December is not yet dawn on the Yukon.

Few of the men could speak or understand the Indian tongue, and few of the Indians could understand English. Vociferous explanations were as futile as were the half-hearted, wondering protests of the Indians as their children were seized, wrapped warmly in the first blanket or robe that came to hand, and carried screaming and fighting out into the sub-Arctic night. Only slightly reassured by the laughter and evident good intentions of the invaders, the parents hastily arrayed themselves in their outer garb and followed as rapidly as they could, being guided through the darkness by the howls and screeches of their kidnapped offspring.

A stoic your Indian unquestionably is under adversity, and much of his life is lived under adverse conditions, but the stoicism does not begin at the cradle, or more appropriately, at the moss bag, nor yet does it begin in early youth, as the men of the Yukon learned, when they unceremoniously dumped their squirming, squalling burdens upon the dance hall floor. And the dancing girls learned it also, as in vain they tried to quiet the little savages, and to bring about some sort of order from the chaos of blankets and robes and screaming babies and fighting children. In fact, they even added their bit to the general din: "O-w-ow! You little devil! Look out, girls! They bite like a malamute pup!"

It was Horse Face Joe that finally solved the problem, as seating himself at the piano, he struck up a rollicking air that stilled most of the voices in wonder, and drowned those it did not still—Horse Face, and the arrival of the Indian parents, who quickly reclaimed blankets and offspring, and huddling at the farther end of the room, listened to the music in dumb fascination.

It was nearly ten o'clock when the last cabin had been searched and the last protesting child deposited upon the floor. Gordon, with his wife and little girl, occupied seats of honor near the piano, and Burr MacShane, through an interpreter, who had been discovered among the Indians, stepped onto the floor and endeavored to explain what it was all about. Then Horse Face Joe struck up an old melody, someone started the words, half familiar, half forgotten, others joined in, and before they knew it every white man and woman in the hall was singing as they had never sung before. Louder and louder swelled the mighty volume of sound until it overrolled and drowned the voice of the piano. Reaching swiftly down, MacShane picked up little Lou Gordon and stood her upon the top of the instrument. Men and girls naturally gravitated toward the music and soon Horse Face Joe and his beloved piano with the little girl standing on its top like a queen looking down with shining eyes into the upturned faces of her subjects, were the centre of a close standing group.

"Give us another!" came the demand from a dozen throats, as the last strains trailed into silence. And Horse Face did give them another, and many others. Never was the like seen north of sixty, a hundred men and women close crowded about the piano singing at the top of their lungs, and at the far end of the room the silent, half-frightened Indians—and the dance hall floor between. While overtowering all presided the great Christmas tree, majestic in its sweep of dark green branches, resplendent in its outlandish and grotesquely painted images, its brilliant hued dolls, its long festoons of gleaming red cranberries, and its blazing candles whose yellow flames wavered and flickered in the billowing waves of sound.

The last song was sung. The last crashing note was sounded upon the piano, and with one accord, laughing and jesting among themselves the men and the girls made descent upon the tree, and amid shouts and laughter began to distribute presents from its bountiful branches. With his own hands MacShane picked out the most beautiful doll with its dress of flaming red silk, and its cap of blue, and its tiny mukluks of yellow, and the biggest bag of candy and carried them to little Lou Gordon, who, with eyes round with delight, viewed the proceedings from her point of vantage on top of the piano. Not a child, even to the tiniest baby but what received its present and its box of candy, nor were the older Indians forgotten, for when MacShane and McCarty saw the influx of parents that followed in the wake of their protesting offspring, they quietly slipped out and made further purchases at the store, with the result that every man received a gift of tobacco, and every woman a small package of sugar or tea.

Twelve o'clock struck and the children's celebration was over. The Indians were herded from the room, and just as Horse Face Joe sank wearily upon his piano stool to strike up a lively dance tune, MacShane stayed him with a wave of his hand. Advancing to his side he demanded his gold sack into which from his own he shook a liberal portion of dust, then, with Horse Face's sack in hand, he passed around among the men, and when he returned it to its owner it was bulging with dust and coarse gold. It was Horse Face Joe's great Christmas—and his last. He mumbled awkward words of thanks, and struck into a galloping waltz as men sought their partners and hurried onto the floor. That dance was never finished. The music lagged slower and slower to the end in a low rumble of protesting chords as the body of Horse Face Joe sagged forward upon the keyboard in a deep sleep.

They carried him to his room, and one of the girls took his place. Hours later he awoke, and with his bulging pouch made a beeline for the bar. As it had been Horse Face Joe's inspired night, so also was it his swan song. Never again did his fingers sweep the keys of a piano for with the proceeds of his bulging Christmas sack, he stuck steadfastly at the bar. Night and day for six days he remained gloriously drunk, and upon New Year's night, which was Dawson's coldest night that winter, he was picked up half buried in the snow on Front Street—a rigid corpse of ice.

Christmas night the same group of cronies foregathered at the forward end of the bar, Bettles, Camillo Bill, Moosehide Charlie, Ace-In-The-Hole, and Old Man Gordon, and with them was MacShane.

"What was it you started in to say last night, MacShane?" asked Camillo Bill, "About a man's bein' able to make his everlastin' stake right here without ever puttin' a pick into the gravel?"

"Sure he could," answered MacShane, with conviction. "I could clean up a million here in this camp within the next two years, an' never touch a pick or a pan, or chop a stick of cordwood. Anyone of us could do it, but I doubt if anyone of us will—I know I won't. It's simple as A B C spells cat. Take town lots, for instance, right here on the flat. Have you stopped to figure what's goin' to happen next spring, an' next fall? The news of this strike has already hit the outside, and in the spring there'll be the doggondest stampede into the Yukon that anyone ever saw. Fifty thousand men will come boilin' in here crazy for gold. They've got to be fed an' housed. Lots that you can buy now for a few dollars will go to thousands. Buy lots, that's one way. Buy flour an' sugar, an' bacon. Ship a sawmill in here an' go to loggin'. Lumber will bring anything a man's mind to ask for it next summer. Buy a steamboat an' run between here an' White Horse. This stampede's comin' down the river. Go up to Lindermann an' build polin' boats, an' buy up all the canoes in sight. An' when you get that done, buy claims an' sell 'em to the *chechakos*.

"I'm tellin' you a man can clean up ten dollars for every dollar he puts in, an' turn his money over a dozen times in a year. The chances are here, plenty of 'em, an' someone is goin' to cash 'em in, but I doubt if it will be any of us. Trouble with us fellows, we ain't business men—we're gamblers, or we wouldn't be here. I know how it is with me, always wantin' to see what's just beyond. I'd rather make a new strike on some crick that no one had ever prospected than stay here an' work the richest claim on Bonanza, or Gold Bottom, or Eldorado. Go to it, now! I've told you how. An' likewise I've told you that there ain't a man here that will turn real estater, or storekeeper, or logger, or steamboat man. We're prospectors, that's what we are—gamblers. An' speakin' of gamblin' how about a game of stud?"

"Give us a drink," demanded Ace-In-The-Hole of the bartender, "A drink, and a deck of cards."

The men drank, and as Old Man Gordon set down his glass, he regarded the others with a frown. He had imbibed rather freely during the afternoon and early evening, and the strong liquor had loosened his tongue: "Ye'll not get me to risk gude gold on the flip of a card!" he exclaimed, with asperity. "Ye're onregenerate sons of Belial! Ye waste ye're substance wi' riotous livin' an' harlots, agin the command of the Gude Book, an' I'll have none of it!"

"Give it to him, Gordon!" laughed Camillo Bill.

"Tell him where to head in!" cried Bettles.

"He's a sinful man, ain't he, Gordon?" encouraged Moosehide Charlie, "I bet he ain't got no soul left to speak of!"

"Who be ye, to be passin' judgment on a man's soul?" cried Gordon, turning on the speaker, to the huge delight of the others. "Ye're all tarred wi' the same brush, as the Gude Book says. One of ye is no better than the others, if as gude! Ye're empty sepulchres full o' dead men's bones! Ye're rushin' hell-bent fer destruction! Ye're a generation of vipers!"

Ace-In-The-Hole turned gravely to the bartender: "Don't give him any more to drink," he warned, "He's seein' snakes!"

"An' who could see aught else, lookin' at the likes of ye?" retorted the old man, "Snakes an' serpents ye are, layin' in wait to sting the unwary wi' the turn of a card!"

"You're a gambler yourself," grinned MacShane, "Or you wouldn't be here. You're bettin' your life against the gold you expect to take out of the gravel."

"Wise ye are, Burr MacShane, in the ways of the trail, an' a man 'tis gude to know. But ye're philosophy is but the babble of a child. 'Tis no gamble—the gold ye take out of the gravel. 'Tis fairly earnt by the sweat of the brow, an' by the work of the brain. Ye're poker is a gamble, pure an' simple. The pot ye rake in is not come by by the sweat of ye're brow, nor is it earnt by the work of ye're brain. 'Tis luckily won by the foolish turn of a card."

"I've dealt till I sweat," retorted MacShane, "An' I've sure worked my brains overtime tryin' to dope out whether to call, or raise, or throw 'em away."

"Blither, an' blather!" cried the old man, thoroughly roused, now, to his subject. "Give us a drink, barkeep, till I blast through the bed rock that these skulls are made of, an' see if there's a bit of a brain below!" He turned again to MacShane, "Poker is a gamblin' game, d'ye hear!"

"I've had an inklin' that such was the case," grinned MacShane.

"Ye've admitted it, then? There's hope for ye, which is more than I thought. Bein' a gamblin' game, it's riotous livin' for to play it, as the Gude Book states plain. It's a gamblin' game because ye've got to have the cards to win. The cards is got in the luck of the deal, an' no amount of work ye can do, or thinkin' ye can do will change the fall of the cards."

"Then, if a man's got brains enough, an' is slick enough with his hands to deal crooked, that's all right?" cut in Moosehide, "I s'pose then, he earns what he gets?"

Gordon favored him with a withering glance of scorn: "That's plain thievery," he roared, "an' lower in the scale even than gamblin'. Poker's gamblin', because if ye ain't got the cards ye can't win," repeated Gordon, with conviction. "Cribbage, now, is different. In cribbage the best man wins. Ye've got to put brains into cribbage, an' if ye win, ye've earnt what ye win by the work of ye're brain."

"Poker's gamblin', but cribbage ain't," laughed MacShane, "Is that right, Gordon?"

"That's right, an' gamblin's an onchristian pastime, but it ain't onchristian to earn gold by the honest work of the brain."

"You're crazy as hell! If you don't get the cards in cribbage you can't win any more than you can in poker!"

"Crazy as hell, am I?" cried Gordon, exasperated to the point of smiting the bar with his fist, "An' if ye don't get the cards ye can't win! Young man, if ye played cribbage, I'd bet ye a thousan' I can beat ye, come the cards as they will! It's brains wins in cribbage, not cards."

"Well, I play cribbage a little. I'll take you up."

"Come on, then!" cried Gordon, "Just the two of us. Give us the cards. I ain't a swearin' man, an' I would not swear at any man of my own word, but, Damn ye! as the feller says, I'll make a Christian of ye, if I have to play cards to do it!"

The two seated themselves at a table, and the others crowded close, bent on watching every play of the game. "Old Man Gordon's playin' cards, an' he's bet a thousand," the word passed from lip to lip and others joined the group, until the table was rimmed with spectators, for never before had any man seen Gordon touch a card.

The game was finished and MacShane won. "What did I tell you?" he said, "I got the best cards, so I won."

Gordon scribbled the amount of the bet upon a leaf from a small note book, tore out the leaf and tossed it across the table: "Ye had no better cards," retorted the old man, "Ye outplayed me! Ye only beat me by two points, an' 'twas my own fault. I should known better than pair ye're nine spot, on the second deal, I might have known ye had the third. Come on, play again—two thousan' this time!"

MacShane shuffled the cards without a word, offered the deck for the cut, and the second game began. This game, also, MacShane won. And again he called attention to the fact that it was because he had held the better cards. But the old man refused to admit it.

"'Twas my own bad playin' done it!" he retorted, gruffly, "I ruint a sure ten hand to hold for a possible twenty-four, an' I didn't get the turn so I only counted four. Ye beat me by five points. If I'd played my sure ten, I'd have won by a point. We'll play again." Pausing abruptly, he produced his note book and tearing another leaf from it, passed it across the table. Then he consulted a penciled memorandum. "Ye've won three thousan'," he said. "I've still got five hundred in dust in McCarty's safe, an' about two hundred in my pocket. We'll play for seven hundred. I owe no man, an' I'll not go in debt."

MacShane leaned back in his chair and shook his head: "Why can't you be reasonable, Gordon? The cards are runnin' against you. Anyone can see that. I don't want your dust."

The old man glared wrath fully across the table: "An' why don't ye want my dust? Ain't my dust as gude as any man's? Come, play! 'Tis my deal, an' ye won't be quittin' wi'out giving me a chance to win back what ye've won from me!"

MacShane shrugged: "Deal," he said, tersely, and picked up the cards as they fell.

MacShane won, this time by a wide margin, and Gordon tossed his gold sack onto the table, and with it an order on McCarty for the last of his gold in the safe. Then, fixing MacShane with an angry glare, he leaned half across the table: "I'll play ye for the claim!" he cried. "What'll ye put against it?"

"Not one damned cent!" cried MacShane. "I'm done."

"Ye'd win a man's dust an' not give him a chance to get it back?" taunted the old man. "'Tis not what I expected from a man that's known as the best man in the North! Put up ten thousan' against the claim. It's worth more than that, from top indications. An' we'll play for it." There was dead silence among the spectators that rimmed the table as they watched with breathless interest the two who faced each other across the board.

It was not the size of the stakes that interested them, for in the early Dawson days, before the inrush of the *chechakos* and tin-horns, big games were the order, and thousands of dollars in dust and markers passed almost nightly over McCarty's tables. The interest was in the fact that Old Man Gordon was playing, and that in a sudden abandon of profligacy he was risking all he owned upon a game of cards. For, not a man among them but had listened to the old man's oft repeated tirades against the vice of gambling. The interest lay in this, but to even a greater extent, it lay in MacShane. For the unwritten law of the Yukon was plain, needing no interpretation of court to make it understood. If a man sat in a game of cards he stated no limit of liability. "Table stakes" and "limit" games were unknown. A player stood to lose all he possessed. He must not bet beyond the limit of his property without the consent of the other players. And should a pot in which he was interested be forced beyond the value of his property, he could call for so much of the pot as had accumulated up to that point, all subsequent bets being considered as between the other players only. Also, in all fairness, the law decreed that a man should be given the chance to win back what he had lost. The practice of "making a killing" and quitting a game was brought in by the tin-horns, with their "table stakes" and "limit" games.

Old Man Gordon was demanding to be allowed to win back his loss. And breathlessly the onlookers watched MacShane, for not a man among them would have had the nerve to refuse to play. Yet, every man among them knew that MacShane did not want to win the old man's claim. It was up to MacShane. The law was plain, and no man would have blamed him had he played and won. But MacShane, veriest sourdough of them all, chose to disregard the law, and the fact that men knew him for what he was gave approval to his decision.

"This game is over, Gordon," he stated, quietly. "I'm quitting." And with the words, he pushed back from the table and stood up.

The old man leaped to his feet and faced him, shaking with rage: "Ye're a quitter! The great Burr MacShane is a quitter! Bah! Ye've be'n a big man hereabouts, an' throughout pretty much all the North—but it took Old Man Gordon to find ye out! Hereabout, men know ye now for what ye are! Ye've won thirty-seven hundred in gude gold from me—but ye've lost more than I have, Burr MacShane! I bid ye Gude Night!"

MacShane listened to the tirade without a word, and when the door closed behind the old man, he strolled to the bar and presented his slips. McCarty weighed out the dust, which was in several small sacks. MacShane gathered up the sacks, added the one Gordon had tossed across the table, and slipped them into his pocket.

Over a round of drinks, Moosehide Charlie voiced the general opinion of the camp: "You done right, MacShane. There's no fool like an old fool. You done it for his own good—but, at that, there ain't many of us would have wanted it to do."

Later, MacShane called Camillo Bill and Moosehide to one side: "Where's this claim of Gordon's," he asked casually.

"It's up the river a little ways, on a crick that runs in from the north."

"Does he live there?"

"No, he's got a cabin here in camp. He's got a little shack on the claim where he stays part of the time."

"I want you boys to come with me."

"Where to?" asked Moosehide, quickly.

"To Gordon's claim." A moment of constrained silence greeted the announcement, during which Camillo Bill regarded the speaker with steady gaze. The more mercurial Moosehide, shifting his weight from one foot to the other, was the first to speak:

"What for?" he asked.

"Just want to look it over," answered MacShane.

"Well, talkin' about me I'm too busy," retorted Moosehide. "I got you wrong, a while back, an' I guess there's lots of others did, too. You kin save yerself that trip, though. There's plenty of us here that will take Old Man Gordon's word that his claim's worth ten thousan'. If you want to give him a run fer his money tomorrow I guess he'll be able to stack up the dust agin yourn." And so saying, he turned abruptly away.

MacShane listened in silence, not a muscle of his face changing, and when Moosehide had mingled with the crowd, he turned to Camillo Bill: "How about you?" he asked, in a voice that gave no hint of anger.

Now the first thought that leaped into Camillo Bill's head at MacShane's words was the same thought that Moosehide Charlie had expressed. But whether it was because he was slower to jump at conclusions or because the thought could not be made to tally with his own estimate of MacShane, which was, he knew, the estimate of the North, is immaterial. Camillo Bill withheld judgment.

"What do you say?" insisted MacShane, with just a trace of impatience in his tone.

"Let's go," answered Camillo, bluntly, and together the two passed out the door.

CHAPTER V
NORTH

THE JOURNEY TO THE Gordon claim was made in silence, and in silence MacShane pushed aside the poles that covered the mouth of the shaft against snow, and dropped lightly in. Peering curiously over the edge, by the light of the glittering stars, Camillo Bill saw MacShane drop to his knees, thrust a hand into his pocket, withdraw a sack of dust and methodically sprinkle it into the gravel at the bottom of the shaft. Another and another sack followed until all the gold he had won from Gordon had been returned to the gravel, then, with the aid of the windlass rope, he drew himself from the shaft. As he stooped to fasten the thongs of his snowshoes Camillo Bill's mittened hand descended upon his shoulder with a thump that threatened to send him sprawling into the snow:

"Well, I'll be damned! MacShane, I—I—Oh, hell! I'll be damned!"

"Um-hum," grunted MacShane, regaining his feet, "I reckon we all will—accordin' to the preachers. But there ain't no call to go braggin' about it."

"You son-of-a-gun!" rumbled Camillo Bill, admiringly, "Gawd, I'm glad I ain't Moosehide!"

MacShane regarded him with a twisted grin: "Moosehide's all right, accordin' to his lights," he said, "I ain't blamin' him none—an' you ain't got any call to blame him. You thought the same as he did—only you took the trouble to make sure. You don't need to say nothin' about this. It ain't no one's business but mine. It was the woman an' the kid—they need the dust, an' I don't. Hope the old man learnt his lesson, though."

"The hell I won't say nothin' about it!" cried Camillo Bill, "The hell I won't! It's too good a one to keep. Jest wait till the boys hears about it! Moosehide's prob'ly spilt it all over the place that the reason you wouldn't give Old Man Gordon a run for his money was because you wouldn't take his word that his claim was worth what he said it was worth without slippin' up an' seein' for yourself. You wait an' see. I'll bet you the drinks you won't be near so pop'lar when you hit the Golden North as what you have be'n."

"I don't give a damn what they think," said MacShane, "Only don't go gettin' excited if Gordon comes rompin' in the first time he mucks out his shaft, claimin' he washed four or five hundred dollars out of a pan. I tried to salt her even, but I reckon maybe she's spread a little thick in spots."

"Maybe you don't care what they think, but I do. It ain't you they'd say much to, nohow. There ain't many of 'em would be huntin' fer a chance to mix it up with you. But, me, it's different. Whenever you wasn't around they'd be damnin' you off amongst theirselves, an' knowin' what I know an' they don't, I'd jest naturally have to sail in an' knock hell out of some of 'em an' there's some of 'em that could knock hell out of me if I tried it—an' there you are!"

MacShane laughed: "You're all right, Camillo. But, anyway, don't say anything about it till I'm out of the country."

"Out of the country!" cried Camillo Bill, "What do you mean—out of the country?"

"Plumb out of the Yukon," answered MacShane, "I'm hittin' the trail. You know how it is with me, Camillo. I kind of get tired of a place. An' besides it ain't goin' to be anyways fit to live here as soon as spring comes, with the *chechakos* pourin' down the river, an' swarmin' all over the country."

"You're hittin' the trail," breathed Camillo, dumfounded, "An' only last night you was tellin' of washin' a hundred an' forty dollars to the pan! Be you plumb crazy, or what?"

"No, I ain't crazy. Leastwise I don't call it that, an' I'm the only one that wins or loses by what I do. No, it ain't craziness, it's jest naturally a honin' I've got to hit the trail—to go places an' see places, that other folks ain't be'n to an' seen. It's—say, did you ever hear the *opposite* word to homesick?"

Camillo shook his head.

"I mean, it's like this, some folks get homesick, just get to pinin' an' mopin' to get back to the place they call home, an' when they get that way, an' get it bad enough, there ain't no place else looks good to 'em. They'll quit any job, or whatever they're doin' an' hit back home, an' it don't make no difference if home is a mud shanty. I knew an Injun once, he was a harpooner on a whaler, an' he drawed down more money at the end of a voyage than all the rest of the Injuns in his tribe thought there was in the world. But he got homesick an' quit cold when we run in to Valdez one time. Three or four years later I run onto him way back in the Kuskokwim country, an' he was dryin' whitefish on a rack—but he was happy. He was home, an' his home was a caribou hide stretched over a couple of willow sticks. Well, that's the way with me—only just the opposite. I never had any home that I can remember. I run away from a foundlin' home when I was somewheres around eight or nine, an' I've be'n goin' ever since. I reckon at first, I kep' on the move because I didn't want 'em to get me an' take me back there, an' after a while it got to be a habit. Till now it's got so that after I've be'n in a place a while, I get homesick for someplace I ain't never seen. I used to try to buck it, but it wasn't any use. I've be'n in a lot of good places—places that ought to satisfy any man, but I've never be'n satisfied, an' it ain't long till I'd hit the trail."

"But, man, the gold! A hundred an' forty dollars to the pan an' you ain't nowheres near the bottom! There ain't nothin' like it ever be'n heard of before! Where in hell are you ever goin' to make another strike like that?"

"Maybe I won't," replied MacShane, gravely, "An' then, again, maybe I will."

"There ain't nothin' like it in the world!"

"Maybe that's true, an' maybe it ain't. There ain't no one can prove it. A year ago there wasn't any such thing as a hundred dollars to the pan in the world. Next year or next month, I may be takin' out a thousan' dollars to the pan, a thousand miles from here—an' I may not be takin' out wages."

"Where you goin', an' when?" asked Camillo Bill.

"North," answered MacShane, "That's all I know about it myself. The hunch I've got now says North, an' North I go—North to God knows where!"

"When?"

"Tonight!"

"Tonight! Ain't you going back to yer claim?"

"No. The hunch is pullin' strong. I didn't know when I left I wasn't goin' back or I'd have brought along some more stuff, but, shucks, there ain't nothin' there that I can't get somewheres else, so I'll let her stay."

"What you goin' to do with your claim?"

"Sell it."

"Who to?"

"You, if you want it. I'll give you first chance at it. I figure there's over a hundred thousand in the dump, an' a lot more in the ground—maybe half a million, maybe two million, I don't know."

"What do you want for it?"

"Five hundred thousand."

"That's more than I can swing," said Camillo, regretfully.

"How much you got?"

"Nothin' to speak of, right now. My dump has got a lot of good stuff in it, but I can't get it out till spring. An' my claim is good for a whole lot more. But dumps an' claims don't do you any good."

"None whatever," laughed MacShane, "Tell you what I'll do, we'll go pardners. Bunch the two claims an' you work 'em an' we'll pool the dust."

"Mine ain't as good as yours," said Camillo Bill.

"I know it ain't," agreed MacShane, "But, you've got the work an' worry of gettin' out the dust, an' I ain't. The difference in what they're worth will be your salary as manager of the concern, see?"

"Suits me if it suits you," grinned Camillo Bill, "But, at that, I think I'm gettin' the best end of it."

"You're welcome to it."

"Where North you goin', MacShane?" asked Camillo Bill as they drew into the outskirts of the camp, "Beyond the daylight?"

"Yes beyond, an' way beyond. I'll most likely hit up the Chandalar an' cross over to the Koyukuk, an' maybe I'll stop there an' maybe I'll keep goin'. There's a river north of there yet, the Colville, where there ain't no one ever be'n. When your hunch says North, you might as well go good an' damn North."

"You've took a hell of a pick when it comes to places to go," grinned Camillo, "Up there all alone in the dark, an' the strong cold, an' prob'ly north of timber."

"I'd just as soon be alone, an' I ain't afraid of the dark, an' I don't mind the strong cold, an' I don't aim to do any loggin', so it won't be so bad. Maybe that's where I'll find my thousand-dollar-a-pan strike."

"Damn sight more apt to freeze to death an' feed the wolves," replied Camillo Bill, lugubriously. "Why in hell can't you let well enough alone an' stay with yer claim?"

MacShane smiled: "I just told you why—or, tried to tell you. I didn't expect you'd understand exactly. No one does. I don't understand it myself. All I know is, that when a hunch comes to hit the trail, I hit the trail—an' that's all there is to it."

"Where you goin'?" asked Camillo Bill in surprise, as MacShane paused and held out his hand before the door of the Golden North.

"I told you, I'm goin' North," answered MacShane, "So long!"

"But, ain't you comin' in? Ain't you goin' to say goodbye to the boys?"

"The boys won't be particularly glad to see me. Moosehide has talked before now. No, I'll just slip down an' get my outfit an' pull. So long, pardner, I'll see you again—sometime!"

"So long!" cried Camillo Bill, his hand meeting MacShane's in a mighty grip, "But, you better wait till tomorrow, or today, rather, it's most two o'clock, an' you didn't get no sleep last night, an' you ain't had none tonight."

"Plenty of time to sleep where I'm goin'," laughed MacShane, "up there it's *all* night."

"Good luck to you, you damned old sourdough! If I ain't here when you come back, your share will be in McCarty's safe."

MacShane waved his hand, and after watching until he was swallowed up in the gloom, Camillo Bill opened the door and entered the Golden North where he was at once greeted by Moosehide Charlie:

"Where's MacShane?" he enquired.

"He pulled out," answered Camillo Bill, shortly.

"Pulled out! Then, he never aimed to give Old Man Gordon a run fer his money?"

"No, he didn't."

"Did he go up an' snoop around Gordon's claim?"

"Yup."

Moosehide sniffed contemptuously: "Ain't that the damndest thing you ever seen a man do?"

"It were."

"Well, I don't know as I blame him none fer pullin' back to his claim after the way he done—an' that's the way most of the boys looks at it. I don't savvy it. If it be'n anyone else but MacShane! He's counted the best man in the North. Bettles says the only way he kin figger it is that playin' a lone hand as long as he has, it's mebbe got to him, here." Moosehide touched his forehead significantly with his finger.

"Mebbe it has," commented Camillo Bill, his eyes sweeping the room, "Where's everybody?"

"Most of 'em's gone to bed," Moosehide replied, "An' I ain't goin' to be far behind 'em. Two nights hand runnin' is a little too strong fer me. I got to sleep now an' then."

"Me, too," agreed Camillo Bill, and together they left the saloon.

CHAPTER VI
CAMILLO BILL AVERTS A STAMPEDE

LATE THE FOLLOWING AFTERNOON the festivities at the Golden North Saloon were once more in full swing. The moccasined feet of the dancers softly scraped the floor, there was not an empty chair to be had at the poker tables, and the crowd that encircled a certain table at the back of the room bespoke play of more than passing interest at the roulette wheel. Horse Face Joe clung with one hand to the bar and voiced in maudlin tones his desire that the other occupants of the room should each and several join him thither.

The door swung violently open, and into this moil of frivolity burst Old Man Gordon, his eyes wide with excitement, his long woolen scarf trailing the floor in his wake, his coat open, and one mittened hand clutching in a vicelike grip a small mooseskin bag. So precipitous had been his entry that he had not stopped to remove his snow shoes, the tails of which dragged noisily across the wooden floor.

"Shut the door!"

"Was you raised in a saw mill?"

"He was raised on a side hill where the doors shut theirselves!" These, and other railings from the assembled crowd fell unheeded upon Gordon's ears. Someone else closed the door as the old man clattered to the bar.

"What did I tell ye?" he cried, his voice pitched high with excitement, "What did I tell ye right here in this room? Crowd up here ye malamutes an' look at gold!" As he spoke his mittened hand brought the sack down upon the bar with a thud, "Weigh her up! Weigh her up an' tell me I ain't dreamin'! Thirty-two ounces, my scales says—five hundred an' twelve dollars! Every grain of it out of one pan, an' I ain't only six foot down!"

Chairs overturned as the players of poker leaped from their seats. The music stopped and men and women surged in from the dance room, and from the roulette wheel, to crowd excitedly about the bar. McCarty, himself, weighed the gold.

"Thirty-two ounces is right," he announced, in a voice that despite himself, trembled slightly. Silence greeted McCarty's words, a silence that the heavy breathing only seemed to accentuate, as three and four deep, the men and women crowded the bar, their eyes on the yellow gold. Of all the people in the room, only Camillo Bill remained in his chair at a poker table, a grim smile upon his face as his fingers idly riffled a deck of cards.

The voice of Horse Face Joe broke thickly upon the silence: "What in hell y'all gawpin' at? I got more dust'n that. Here, Mac, weigh mine up. An' I'll spend 'er too. Ol' Man Gordon, he wouldn't never set 'em up to the house."

The silence broken, a perfect babble of voices burst forth. Everyone was talking at once, and above the din rose the strident voice of Gordon: "An' only last night I offered to risk the claim agin ten thousan' dollars! Where's MacShane?"

"How'd you happen to be workin' today, anyhow," inquired Ace-In-The-Hole Brent, "Was it a hunch?"

"A hunch! A hunch, d'ye say? Aye, it was a hunch! A hunch that said I was broke, an' if I wanted maybe a wee bit tipple, or a bite to eat for the woman an' the little lass, I'd better be gougin' gravel."

"Hell, man, you could have got all you wanted in dust or liquor right here!" exclaimed McCarty.

"Aye, Mac, I know," retorted the canny Scot, "But, 'twould have to be paid back. 'Twould be burnin' the candle at both ends, as the Gude Book says. If I was here borrowin', I'd be loafin' an' spendin', an' if I was out there in the gravel I wouldn't be spendin' an' what I got would be mine, an' nothin' to pay back later. As it is, I owe no man."

"Go on! Go on!" came from a dozen throats, "It ain't a sermon we want, it's facts!"

"An' so," continued Gordon, without deigning to notice the interruption, "I hit out gude an' early this mornin' for the claim, hopin' to pan out an ounce, maybe two, afore night. I built a gude fire in the shaft, an' in the shack I melted the ice, an' it was along about noon I brought up my first bucket of gravel and carried it into the shack. But 'twas not till I finished washin' that I had any idee what I'd got!" His voice, which had subsided into something of its normal tones as he talked, again leaped into the falsetto of excitement. "Ye should have be'n there to see for ye're selves—when the last bit of muddy water sloshed from the pan! There was no gravel to be seen. Yellow gold—spread even, an' thick! 'Twas like peerin' into a firkin of butter! Losh! I squatted there like a daftie, starin' down into the pan—a minute—ten minutes—mebbe an hour. I had no heed of time. Then I weighed up, an' my hands was shakin' so at first I bungled the job. There was flour gold in that pan that I didn't get. It's layin' back there on the floor of the shack. I got what I could in the sack at last, an' then I started fer here. I'd got mebbe it's twenty rod before I bogged down in the snow, an' I noticed I'd forgot my snowshoes, an' I had to waller back an' get 'em."

Across the room Camillo Bill paused in the riffling of the cards, and regarded the close-packed crowd with a twisted grin: "You c'n take 'em off now, Gordon. Mac's floor is toler'ble solid. You won't bog down here."

"An' only last night," quavered Gordon, "I offered to risk the claim agin ten thousan'! Where's MacShane? Where's the man that wouldn't put up ten thousan' agin a claim 'twould have paid him out in the first twenty pans?"

From his seat at the table Camillo Bill surveyed the scene with interest. He noted that no one was paying any attention to Gordon, now. Noted, also, a certain restlessness, a tenseness that seemed to fill the air, and manifested itself in the quick tying of cap strings, and the nervous buttoning of coats. Several of the girls who had slipped away unobserved, reappeared at the foot of the stairs, dressed for the trail. Here and there, men were drawing on parkas.

"I'd ort to let 'em go ahead an' stampede their fool heads off," grinned Camillo Bill to himself.

"'Bout half of 'em thinks MacShane played it low down on Gordon, an' it would serve 'em right."

There was a sudden concerted rush for the door, a rush that seemed to include every man and woman in the room except Gordon, and Horse Face Joe, who, clutching the bar, blinked in maudlin solemnity as he vainly tried to sense the purport of what was going on about him. Even the bartenders had torn off their white aprons and were frenziedly donning coats, caps, and mittens.

"*Hold on!*" The voice of Camillo Bill rang sharp as the crack of a dog whip. At the door the leaders paused, and as a man, the crowd whirled to face the speaker. Camillo Bill was standing, now, and the twisted smile had widened. The voice of Old Man Gordon cut the tense air thinly:

"'Twas the hand of God rewardin' me for tryin' to bring the Philistine into the fold, even though I failed."

"It was the hand of Burr MacShane!" roared Camillo Bill, "Tryin' to learn you to leave cards to them that knows somethin' about 'em! You won't wash no ten thousan' out of yer first twenty pans, neither. You'll wash thirty-seven hundred out of 'em—that's what you'll wash—besides what little was in the gravel before MacShane salted it."

"Salted it!"

"What d'you mean—salted it?"

"What in hell's comin' off here?" The crowd surged back, only this time Camillo Bill, and not Gordon, was the center of interest.

"What are you talkin' about?"

"Speak up, can't you?"

"What in hell was MacShane doin' saltin' Gordon's claim?"

Camillo Bill's eyes caught the eyes of Moosehide Charlie. For a moment their glances held, and in that moment, the latter seemed somehow to shrink back, as though he had suddenly divined what was passing in Camillo's brain.

"I would shrivel if I was you, Moosehide. But, MacShane ain't holdin' it against you. He's too big a man fer that. It'll learn you mebbe, not to go off half cocked, the same way it'll mebbe learn Gordon that gamblin' is gamblin' whether it's poker or cribbage." He paused and allowed his eyes to sweep the crowd of faces before him. "Most of you thought like Moosehide, that the reason MacShane wanted to hit out for Gordon's claim was so he could size up whether she was worth ten thousan'. Instead of that, he drops down into Gordon's shaft, an' he pulls out them sacks, an' goes to work an' salts every last speck an' grain of the dust he win from Gordon back into the gravel. 'It's fer the woman an' the little kid,' he says, 'They need it, an' I don't.' That's what he says. An' then he says, 'You don't need to say nothin' to nobody about this. Only don't go bustin' up here on no stampede if the old man claims he's washed four or five hundred dollars to the pan.'"

In the silence that followed, Moosehide Charlie started for the door.

"Where you goin', Moosehide?" called Camillo Bill.

The other turned: "I'm headin' fer MacShane's," he answered.

"An' I'm with ye!" cried Gordon, who had listened, open-mouthed, to the recital, "Losh, what a fool a man can make of himself onct he gets started!"

"I'd ort to let you both go," grinned Camillo Bill, "The trip would do you good. But, the fact is, MacShane ain't out to his claim."

"Ain't to his claim! Where is he, then?"

"He's hit the trail. He's kissed the Yukon good bye. Last night while *chechakos* like us was sleepin' MacShane was a-borin' a hole through the dark."

"Gone!"

"Pulled out!"

"An' him takin' out over a hundred dollars to the pan!"

"Where's he gone?"

"You don't mean he's gone—outside! MacShane quit the North?" Questions and exclamations hurled themselves at Camillo Bill from half a hundred throats, so that it was some moments before he could make himself heard; "No, he ain't gone outside. MacShane won't never go outside. He just naturally got homesick for to hit the trail, an' he pulled. It's gettin' too crowded for MacShane down here. He hit North."

"But his claim?" cried Bettles, "What about his claim?"

"We pooled our claims before he left," said Camillo. "I'm workin' 'em both. We're pardners."

CHAPTER VII
THE GORDONS HIT THE TRAIL

WITH THE SPRING BREAK-UP the men of the creeks abandoned their shafts and turned their attention to sluicing their dumps. The Northland knows no gradual merging of Winter into Spring. One day it is Winter, and the next day it is Spring—unequivocally, and undeniably Spring. Here is no half-hearted surrender of the Frost King after weeks of dawdling effort to maintain his sway. For here he fights in his own fastness—fights with unabated fury to maintain his iron grip on the frozen land—fights to the last gasp with no sign of weakening. For only at the point of utter annihilation does he yield up his sceptre to Spring.

Water from melting snows trickles down the sides of the mountains, pours from the mouths of "dry washes," and rushes in leaping torrents over the surface of ice-locked creeks. The thick creek ice, loosened by the torrent, lets go in places and allows the surface water to get beneath it. Scattered cakes float down on the flood. More cakes, and more, until the whole surface becomes a mass of grinding, whirling cakes. Jams form at bends and upon the shallows, ice cakes up-end, leap clear of the water to be forced higher and higher by the grinding, battering impact of other cakes. Behind these jams the water rises, bursting from the creek beds in a hundred places, overflooding lowlands, cutting new channels, but rising always until at last the high-flung mass of cakes can no longer withstand its weight, and with a mighty roar the jam lets go, the whole mass of grinding, crashing cakes rides the crest of the suddenly released flood to crash into the next jam.

It was after the run-out of ice cakes that the work of sluicing began. The men of the creeks worked that spring with an air of tense expectancy. What would the "clean-up" show? Men knew that the strike was rich, the test pans had showed that. But, how rich? All day long, in rapidly lengthening days the sourdoughs toiled wet to their middles in snow water to answer that question. For the "clean-up" is the harvest of the gold diggers. And the clean-up that year was big. Work on the frozen dumps had scarcely started before men knew that the prediction that they were riding the richest strike yet made was an established fact. Rumor piled upon rumor as the dust poured into the camp. Dawson real estate increased in value by leaps and bounds. McCarty, his safe full to overflowing, was forced to decline storage room for the dust that poured in from the creeks.

Summer brought the first rush of the *chechakos*. Down the Yukon they came in canoes, in boats of every shape, kind and description, on rafts and on anything that by any possible act of manipulation could be made to float. They swarmed the camp and spread out into the hills. Stampedes were of daily occurrence. Every creek, and feeder, and pup was staked from rim to rim—and still they came. Although wages were high, few of that first onrush were content to work for wages. They heard the stories of gold, gazed with blazing eyes upon coarse gold in the scales, saw men shake raw gold from the mouths of sacks in payment for drinks at the bar, and straightway they headed into the hills. It was pitiful, but there was none to pity. The newcomers looked on and did likewise, and the sourdoughs looked on, and grinned. Their fortunes were assured, and they knew that in the fall laborers would be plenty.

As MacShane had predicted, however, not all of the sourdoughs sluiced great wealth from their dumps. A few there were who struck it big, counting their dust in hundreds of thousands, many counted in thousands and tens of thousands, and many more found that their dumps had yielded scarcely better than wages.

Among these latter was Old Man Gordon. The pay streak on his claim turned out to be all in the grass roots, that is, the only gravel that was really worth working lay close to the surface. His whole dump averaged better than wages, but the lean gravel thrown from the deeper half of the shaft showed that the pay streak would peter out long before bed rock was reached.

By the time Gordon discovered this fact the *chechakos* had already staked the country for miles around, and although he located several new claims, he failed to strike anything that showed.

For three years he stayed by his claim, getting what there was on the surface by top stripping, and only now and then sinking a shaft in hope of hitting a lucky spot on the lower level.

Then, he sold out for a few hundred dollars to a *chechako* and procuring a poling boat drifted northward down the great river. For another year he sniped on the Birch Creek bars, and then hearing whispers of a strike on the Koyukuk, he once more loaded his wife and child into a poling boat and, dropping down the Yukon to the mouth of the Koyukuk, spent an entire summer in ascending six hundred miles of its course that lay between the Yukon and the newfound placers.

It was gruelling and laborious work, track lining and poling the heavily loaded boat against the swift and treacherous current of the Koyukuk. And it was work that all three shared equally. For Lou, a lithe bodied, rather ungainly young miss of fifteen, who seemed somehow to be mostly legs and arms, and the legs and arms all muscle, did a man's work every day. Nor was her mother far behind her in the matter of handling a pole or paddle, or pulling on the track line. They were in the land of the midnight sun, now, and the continuous daylight was a source of never-ending wonder to the girl. Nor was the actual visualizing of the phenomenon any the less wonderful because she could demonstrate the text book explanation for it. For, despite the fact that her life had been spent entirely in the remoter outlands, yet she had suffered not one whit in any detail of her education. For her mother had been an apt pupil of a famous old mission school on the Mackenzie, and she took a great pride in passing the education she had gained on to her little daughter.

They were a happy family—the Gordon's. Simple and God-fearing in their belief, and simple and contented in their manner of life. For them the semi-nomadic life of the Northland was no hardship. It was merely the accepted fact of a normal existence. When the luck of the early Dawson days piled up a small surplus of dust, they accepted their good fortune with unboastful equanimity, and later when the claim petered out, and the high prices drained their little surplus, they accepted the reverse of fortune with philosophic stoicism. As their daily lives were sternly ordered by the vicissitudes of a stern land so was their religion a stern and unflexible code of laws. The much thumbed Bible that Gordon read daily was the dictated word of God, and as such was to be believed literally, word for word. The code of law set down in the Gude Book was the code of law subscribed and authorized by God. Any act not in accordance with this code was therefore sanctioned and authorized by the devil. Gordon feared God, and hated the devil. Yet, such was the austere honesty engendered by this implicit belief in his austere code, that had necessity compelled him to have had any dealing with the devil, he would punctiliously have rendered the gentleman of darkness his due, even to the uttermost farthing. For it was his pride, and the pride of his wife, and the inborn pride of his daughter that they owed no man. At least, this had been their pride up to the moment that Camillo Bill told him that MacShane had salted the gold he had won at cribbage into the gravel at the bottom of the shaft. From that moment Gordon knew, and his wife knew, and in a vague sort of way, the little Lou sensed, that no more could they say they owed no man.

Not that they considered themselves debtors to MacShane in the sum of the thirty-seven hundred dollars which he had won, and had seen fit to return.

The dust was his to do with as he pleased, and the fact that he had pleased to return it to its original owner created no obligation on the part of that owner. No, it was no money debt—this debt that the house of Gordon owed to Burr MacShane. It was a moral debt.

When Gordon had denounced MacShane, as he rose from the card table and refused to continue the play, he had honestly believed that MacShane was deliberately refusing him the chance to win back, "earn back," as Gordon would have it, the money he had risked in an honest endeavour to show that same MacShane the error of his ways. When Camillo Bill's explanation of the sudden wealth he had found at the bottom of his shaft, had convinced him of MacShane's honesty in his refusal to continue the game, and his subsequent generosity in the disposal of the dust, even in the face of public denunciation and insult—from that moment Gordon found himself obsessed by a sense of debt. He owed MacShane an apology. And until he should meet MacShane and offer that apology, he was MacShane's debtor.

With the words of Camillo Bill ringing in his ears, Gordon had that evening quitted the Golden North Saloon, and had gone straight to his cabin, and had laid the whole matter before his wife and daughter, nor had he spared himself in the telling. What one Gordon owed, all Gordons owed, therefore his debt became their debt. From the cabin he had returned to the Golden North and publicly had denounced himself even more bitterly than he had, the previous evening denounced MacShane. Thus, having made all amends within his power, with a clear conscience, he bided the time when he should meet MacShane. Nor was he lacking in diligence in his endeavor to locate him. No traveler from the North crossed his path, but was asked the same question: "Have ye run acrost Burr MacShane?" And, always the answer had been, "No."

It was the same as he floated down the Yukon, and while he worked the Birch Creek bars, always the same question, and always the same answer, and it was the same upon the Koyukuk.

Small chance for inquiry though, they found upon the Koyukuk, two prospectors at the mouth of Hog River, and another one further along, were working the bars with indifferent success. One of these, the lone prospector of the upper bar, an old man, had known MacShane years before on the Kuskokwim, but had not run across him since. At Bergman the Commercial Company's agent had known him on the Lower Yukon. At Moses's Village, the largest native town on the river, several of the Indians knew him, but could not, or would not, give any information as to his present whereabouts. At Bettles, the head of shallow-draught steamboat navigation the Gordons remained for three weeks, the women resting while Gordon prospected several likely looking creeks. But the creeks had all been prospected before, so the laborious up-river journey was resumed, with the new camp of Coldfoot as their objective, seventy-five miles to the northward.

CHAPTER VIII
COLDFOOT

AT LAST, AT THE end of a long day's toil, the trio beached their boat on the shallows, and pitched their tent on the outskirts of the new camp that had sprung up on the flat at the mouth of Slate Creek. They had arrived at Coldfoot, the most northerly gold camp in the world.

Supper over, Mrs. Gordon surveyed the cluster of low log buildings, and canvas tents: "Surely, Stuart," she said, reflectively. "We'll find Burr Mac-Shane here."

Her husband shook his head: "An' why d'ye think we'll be findin' him here?" he asked.

"Why because Coldfoot is the very last camp. If he headed North, he's bound to be here. There is nothing beyond."

Gordon smiled: "Aye, but ye do not know MacShane. Camps are nothin' to him. He knows the North as no other man knows it, an' always he plays a lone hand. 'Tis not because he does not like man, or the company of his kind, for he does. Everywhere, by white men, an' by red men alike, he is held in regard. An' when he foregathers with men he is the life of the camp. It was him, d'ye mind, that planned an' carried out the Christmas ye had that year in Dawson." He turned to the girl who had been listening. "An' 'twas him that lifted ye in his two hands to the top of the piano, the better ye could see, an' 'twas him that give ye the doll, the prettiest doll of the lot it was, an' he picked it out for ye."

Lou smiled, "I have the doll yet," she said, "And I remember that a big man picked me up and stood me on the piano, but I can't remember his face. It must be awfully lonesome for him—to be always alone."

"It is too bad he has never married," said Mrs. Gordon. "A man like that would make some woman a good husband."

"Losh, woman!" cried Gordon, "An' who would he marry? Who are the women he knows—Injun squaws, Eskimo klooches, an' the strumpets of the dance halls! MacShane would have none of them. For, he's clean."

"He must get his supplies at Coldfoot," said Mrs. Gordon, "There is no place else."

"Aye, but ye must remember there was no Coldfoot when he passed this way, if he ever passed."

"What do you mean, if he ever passed?"

"I mean that the Koyukuk is not the only river that lies North from the Yukon. There are many. An' knowin' MacShane by his reputation on the trail, he may be this minute anywhere between Hudson Bay an' Bering Sea. An' even if he traded in Coldfoot today, he might do his next tradin' at Fort MacPherson."

"Oh, I wish we could find him and thank him for—what he did."

"Aye, woman," answered Gordon, heavily, "I've sought him this long time. My humility weighs heavy upon me. But, as the Gude Book says, 'Everything comes to him who waits.' 'Tis doubtless the Lord's will I should carry my load long."

Inquiry at the Commercial Company's store revealed the fact that only two months before MacShane had come into camp from the northward, remained for several days, and purchasing supplies, had suddenly pulled out.

"An where did he hit for?" asked Gordon.

"Lord knows, I don't. Myrtle Creek, maybe. That's where most of 'em are hittin' for now. There has be'n some pretty good sacks of dust brought down off of Myrtle this summer. Goin' to locate?"

Gordon nodded: "Aye. An' can ye tell me how I'll reach Myrtle Crick?"

"Sure, just follow up Slate Creek, an' it's the third creek that runs into it."

"Maybe it's all staked?"

"No, it ain't, there's plenty of room there yet. They ain't so many of us up here, you know. It ain't like the Yukon. The *chechakos* an' the riff-raff don't hit Coldfoot. This here country is a heap too *skookum* fer their blood. Bettles catches about the last of them, an' they don't stay there long. They hit back to the Yukon where they got more chanct of winterin' through. They ain't got no guts fer the long night an' the strong cold. This here is a man's country."

"An' Myrtle Crick," persisted Gordon, "Is there timber for cabin logs?"

"Yes, plenty timber for cabin logs. It ain't what you'd call big timber or nothin', an' it's kind of scatterin' like, but you'll find patches here an' there that'll do. Now, how about your outfit?"

"I'll be needin' grub," answered Gordon, "The rest I brought with me. I came up from the Yukon in a polin' boat."

"In a polin' boat!" exclaimed the trader, "Alone!"

Gordon smiled: "No, there's three of us, my wife an' daughter."

"Wife an' daughter! An' come clean up from the Yukon in a polin' boat!"

"Aye," answered Gordon, "'Twas a considerable chore."

"An' he calls it a chore," muttered the trader, "Like feedin' the dogs, or cuttin' firewood! An' a hell of a lot of 'em thinks they be'n somewhere's when they come up to Bettles on the steamboat an' shove a polin' boat the rest of the way!" He suddenly thrust out his hand, "Crim's my name, old timer, an' I'm proud to meet you. The boys'll all be proud to know you, here on the Koyukuk. You're our kind."

"Mine's Gordon," replied the Scotchman, and for the next hour Gordon and Crim were busy with the grub list. When the last item had been stacked up and the list checked, Gordon drew out his gold sack. "We thought prices was high in Dawson," he said, as he balanced the sack in his hand, "But nothin' as high as here."

"No. Coldfoot's the farthest north gold camp in the world, an' she's the most expensive. These here shallow-draught steamboats that runs up as far as Bettles can't fetch up no hell of a load of freight, an' they ain't afraid to charge fer what they do haul, an' on top of that it's all got to be man-hauled in summer, an' dog-hauled in winter fer the seventy-five mile between here an' Bettles. An' all that freightin' has got to be added onto the Yukon prices." The man paused and his glance traveled from Gordon's gold sack to his face. "You can put that up," he said, "These goods is charged."

"But—you don't know nothin' about me. An' besides, I don't like to be in debt. There's dust enough here to pay."

The trader nodded: "There is. But how about dogs? You didn't bring dogs, did you? An' as fer the rest, I know all I need to know about you. That's what the Company pays me fer—to size up men. This here will run you till Christmas, then you can come back fer more. An' remember this, Gordon, the Koyukuk diggin's is spotted. You might strike it lucky the first crack out of the box, an' you might prod around fer a long while 'fore you strike it, but it's here, an' sooner or later you'll win."

"How about MacShane?" inquired Gordon, "Has he struck it, yet?"

"MacShane," the other smiled, "You can't never tell nothin' about Burr MacShane. I know'd him, it's years ago on the Lower Yukon. He might of mushed five hundred mile to get that grub. MacShane ain't on Myrtle. It's a way I've got—not tellin' a party where another party is, till I've got the party sized up. But, fact is, I don't know where MacShane come from, nor where he went. Wisht I did."

"Why?" asked Gordon.

"Well, it's like this. I've knocked around quite a bit, take it first an' last, tradin, on my own hook, an' tradin' fer the Company, an' I kin most generally always tell from the gold in the blower where it come from. You've noticed the difference. Take the gold from the middle Yukon—Circle, an' Fortymile, an' around the Chandalar, it's light colored gold. The up-river gold is darker, an' the Koyukuk gold is light colored again. But, MacShane's gold—it was red—reddest I ever seen. It wasn't no Myrtle Creek gold, nor yet gold from anywheres that's ever be'n prospected before."

"But, he must of got it along the river, or some crick that runs into it," argued Gordon. "He couldn't pack no supplies off the river in summer."

The trader laughed: "MacShane can, an' he did. He's be'n in the country long enough to be onto all its curves. He was Siwashin' it. Said it was the first time he'd seen a camp fer a year an' a half. Didn't know there was a camp here even. He was hittin' fer Bettles. Yes, sir, MacShane comes nearer to livin' off the country than any white man I ever seen. Why the stuff he got wouldn't last an ordinary man three months, an' I bet he can make it do fer two years."

"But how did he get the stuff off the river?" persisted Gordon.

"Back-packin', him an' his dogs both. Yes, sir, he had fourteen dogs, an' he'd ripped up an old tent, or a tarp an' rigged pack sacks for 'em—that's Siwashin' for you!"

"Aye, he's a man!" agreed Gordon. "If he comes in again, tell him Old Man Gordon wants to see him."

"I'll tell him," answered the trader, "But I ain't lookin' for him back. Least-ways, not fer a year or two."

CHAPTER IX
ON THE KOYUKUK

ON MYRTLE CREEK, SIX miles above its mouth, the Gordons selected a cabin site, close against the shoulder of a mountain, where a thicket of spruce promised some protection against winter gales. And it was in the building of this cabin that they came first to realize the real comradery, the *esprit de corps* of the men of the Koyukuk. For the two or three hundred white men who live upon the Koyukuk and its tributaries, all but a half-dozen of whom are grouped far within the Arctic Circle, more than six hundred miles above the river's confluence with the Yukon, and isolated as few other camps in the North are isolated in the land of the strong cold and the long dark, count themselves more a family than a community. A man strikes it lucky, and the whole Koyukuk rejoices. Another meets misfortune, disease or accident, and down he goes for medical attention—Fairbanks—Vancouver—Seattle—and the Koyukuk pays the bills. And in no other gold camp in the world is it the common practice when a man "goes broke" for another more fortunate than he to invite him to "take yer pan an' go down on my claim an' git out what you need."

And so, in the building of the cabin. Hardly had Gordon felled the first tree when he was suddenly confronted by a bearded giant whose faded overalls were tucked into a pair of rubber boots: "Hello, neighbor!" greeted the man, "Goin' to locate? That's good. I'm Pete Enright, half a mile up the creek."

"Gordon's my name, Old Man Gordon, they call me down Dawson way. Yes, guess I'll try my luck here."

"She's spotted, Gordon, remember she's spotted. Lots of gold if you can only find it. Don't git down-hearted. She's here, but she lays in pockets."

Attracted by the sound of voices, Mrs. Gordon and Lou appeared from the little tent pitched close beside the creek.

"Well, for gosh sakes!" cried Enright, staring in surprise at the two. "Ladies! Real white ladies on Myrtle!"

"My wife an' daughter," introduced Gordon, "This is Pete Enright, our neighbor just above."

"You all's *skookum*, all right. First ladies on Myrtle, almost the first on the Koyukuk. No wonder you didn't stick around Dawson. They tell me the whole Yukon country is gummed up with shorthorns an' *chechakos*, till a man ain't got elbow room for to swing a pick. You all's moose chewers all right, an' you jist nach'ly had to come where the moose chewers is. Well, I got to go. So long, folks, see you agin. Don't cut 'em too long, Gordon. Little cabins is easier het than big uns. She gits away down there when the strong cold's on. Fifty below is common, sixty ain't nothin' to brag about, an' they claim she's hit way below seventy. My thermometer thicks up so's she ain't no good at sixty-seven, an' I know she gits colder, but I can't measure it. The cold's all right when yer fixed fer it. But she's God's own country—no shorthorns nor *chechakos*—plenty room to move around in. So long."

The man disappeared as abruptly as he had appeared. The three Gordons smiled. "Nice and hearty for a neighbor," said Mrs. Gordon. "Down below, the way it is now, if we'd have located within half a mile of one of those *chechakos*, he'd have been growling about our crowding in on him."

"Different breed of pups up here," replied her husband. "All malamutes an' huskies—no mongrels." The women returned to their duties about the tent, and Gordon resumed his chopping.

It was nearly noon the next day when eight men, headed by Pete Enright, threaded their way through the spruce timber, and came to a halt before Gordon. Each man carried an ax. "Hello, Gordon!" Enright greeted, and turned to his followers. "Boys, this here's Old Man Gordon, I was tellin' you about." He proceeded to introduce each man by name, and when he had finished, addressed them. "All right, boys, go to it!

"Wouldn't make it no bigger'n ten by twelve, Gordon. Mine's six by eight—warm as hell, but no room. There's only one of me, though."

At Enright's bidding, the men scattered about the timber and soon Myrtle Creek rang to the song of axes.

"Where'd they all come from?" asked Gordon, as Enright sank his ax to the helve into a standing tree.

"Come from? They're all Myrtle Creekers. I mushed on down the creek an' gathered 'em up. The Slate Creek boys all be growling 'cause I didn't let them in on it, but, shucks, there's enough of us here to roll up the cabin, an' chink it an' throw up a dog shelter, an' cut yer winter's wood in a couple days or so."

"I'm sure obliged," said Gordon, "I'll slip over to the tent an' tell ma to cook up an extra batch of grub."

"Not by a damn sight!" cried Enright. "We didn't come up here to eat off'n you all. We come to roll up a cabin. An' we packed our own grub."

"I'll not permit it!" cried Gordon. "Ye'll eat my grub, or ye'll not work on my cabin! Who d'ye think I am to—"

Enright laid a huge hand on Gordon's shoulder, "Hold on, Gordon," he said, "You listen to me. You ain't on the Yukon, now—you're on the Koyukuk. Our ways is a little different here, than some other places. But there's reasons for it. Take this grub business. It's a hell of a job to pack grub up from Coldfoot. You've figgered yer grub to run you till a certain time—everyone does. Of course if it was only one man, fer a few meals it wouldn't cut no figger. But there's eight of us fer may be three or four days, an' we ain't what you might say light eaters. Anyhow we'd make a hell of a hole in any man's grub pile. Now, we'd all be eatin' our own grub anyhow so it'll last as long as it was figgered to last. Hell, man! You might better roll up yer own cabin than be et out of grub. On the Koyukuk we like to do one another a good turn. An' when we do we don't want no half ways about it, neither. All we got up here is each other."

Four days later the eight men returned to their claims, leaving the Gordons in possession of the largest and most completely equipped cabin on Myrtle. Ten by twelve, it stood at a sharp bend of the creek surrounded by the thicket of spruce, all chinked, banked, and furnished, even to a rocking chair which one of the men had devised for the comfort of Mrs. Gordon. Nor did the cabin alone bespeak the handiwork of the miners, for conveniently grouped about it were an ample dog shelter, a pole meat cache, and a huge pile of dry wood, all chopped and ready for the stove, a reserve supply against the coming of the strong cold.

During the fall Gordon prospected the bars up and down the creek, staking several likely locations and panning, before the freeze-up, considerably better than wages.

When snow fell two men on Slate Creek "went pardners," and having no use for two dog outfits, Gordon bought a team of six good dogs and a sled. Then he and Lou took the outfit and struck into the hills for caribou, returning a few days later with six fine carcasses which were hoisted onto the meat cache.

The days rapidly shortened, and with the long nights came the cold. Gordon was burning in, now, on a bar close to the cabin. Each day at noon the sun hung lower and lower in the heavens, his rays weakened, and the shadows lengthened upon the snow. At last came the day when sunset followed sunrise with no interval of time between, and thereafter for many long days the only sunlight to be seen was the noontime gilding of distant mountain peaks. Daylight came to mean dim twilight, and a great deal of Gordon's work was done by the light of the moon and stars.

But he worked with a will, for his frequent test pans showed that he had struck pay. Lou helped, even with the cutting and carrying of cordwood to keep up the fire that thawed the gravel, and when she was not at her father's side she was off in the hills with the dogs and her little twenty-two rifle with which she added no small contribution to the family larder in the way of rabbits and ptarmigan. As Gordon chopped his wood, and laboriously man-hauled it on a rude travois to his workings, as he tended his fire, and as he shoveled out his layer of thawed gravel, his thoughts were always upon the time when he could afford a "b'iler" to loosen his gravel with steam. The boiler got to be an obsession. He talked boiler for hours on end to his wife and daughter, and he talked it to the men of Myrtle and Slate Creeks when chance threw them together. In vain the men argued that the cost of bringing a boiler into the Myrtle Creek country would be prohibitive, and that even if one were brought the spotted nature of the workings would necessitate its frequent removal to new locations. But Gordon remained obdurate. And amused, the men went their ways and among themselves dubbed him B'iler Gordon.

At Christmas time the Gordons made the trip to Coldfoot, as did most of the inhabitants of the creeks, for the midwinter trading. Beside the white people there was a goodly sprinkling of Indians and Kobuk Eskimos whose chief aim in life seemed to be to squat upon the floor of the trading room and listen with unconcealed delight to the scratchy music that wheezed from the horn of a cheap phonograph. The fact that they understood no word of the ragtime songs and talking records seemed to detract in no slightest particular from their delight, as over and over again the dozen or more badly worn records were proudly fed into the machine by one of their number who had been instructed in its manipulation.

Being the only white women with the exception of the dancing girls, Mrs. Gordon and Lou were the invited guests of the trader's wife. The men foregathered in the saloon which, with its dance hall, divided honors equally as to popular diversion, with the evening meeting conducted in the trading room by an itinerant missionary.

Two or three days would ordinarily have sufficed for the midwinter trading and its attendant social activities, but upon Christmas day the strong cold fastened upon the Koyukuk. The thermometer, which up to that time had hung between forty below, and ten above zero, on Christmas day dropped suddenly to sixty below. On the day following it was still sixty, and thereafter for ten days the warmest record was fifty-four below.

The men of the creeks waited for a let-up. There is a saying in the North that trailing at fifty below is all right as long as it's all right. Which means that if everything goes smoothly and without accident, no particular harm will result. But who can confidently expect to trail without accident? At fifty below the one absolute essential to life is constant motion. No clothing, however warm, that a man can possibly pile onto himself and pretend to leave any freedom of movement for walking, will protect him from the grip of the frost unless he keep moving. Any circumstance that necessitates a halt without shelter spells disaster. A broken dog harness, a damaged sled, or worst of all, encountering water on the ice, means a halt, and as nothing can be accomplished with the hand encased in heavy mittens, it also means baring the fingers to remedy the evil, and baring the fingers at fifty below for more than a minute or two at a time means that the fingers will freeze to the bone.

Water on the ice at fifty below? More chance of it than at any warmer temperature, for at fifty the creeks freeze solid to the bottom in the shallows, and the water thus dammed beneath the ice bursts through and comes rushing down in a torrent on top of the ice, but under the snow, so that before he knows it the unwary trail musher may find himself ankle deep in water, which at fifty below spells death unless he can immediately reach shelter and a fire. Nor can the danger be averted by forsaking the creeks, for in the land of the strong cold the level surface of the rivers and the creeks are the only practicable highways. And these things the men of the Koyukuk knew, and knowing them, waited for the let-up.

And as they waited the talk was of gold. Old Man Gordon discoursed at length upon the possibilities of a "b'iler." Someone spread the report of rich strikes further up the Koyukuk on Nolan Creek, and on Wiseman. Many signified their intention of hitting out for the new district in the spring. But Gordon was not one of these. He swore he would stay where he was, and would bring in a "b'iler" and show them all that the real bonanza of the Koyukuk was Myrtle. A stand in which he was upheld by Crim, the trader, and some few of the miners.

The morning of the fourth of January, with the thermometer at 30 below, saw a general exodus from Coldfoot. And as the sourdoughs mushed back to their claims, the Gordon sled was weighted with more than its freighting of grub, for when Lou had casually mentioned within hearing of some of the men in the trading store that she had read every scrap of paper in the cabin, there had been a general ferreting among the cabins of Coldfoot with the result that fifty pounds or more of well-thumbed books, and magazines were added to Gordon's load.

The coming of spring brought confirmation of the rumor of a strike on Nolan Creek. Coldfoot stampeded. The miners, all but a straggling few, hit the trail for the new diggings. The saloon followed the miners and the trading post followed the saloon. Coldfoot was dead. And Nolan became the metropolis of the Koyukuk.

Among the few who remained were the Gordons. Disregarding the advice of friends, the stubborn Scot stayed on Myrtle, insisting that when he should bring his "b'iler" in and begin thawing the gravel with steam, they would all stampede back to Coldfoot.

When he had finished sluicing his dump he weighed up dust enough to pay Crim, outfit himself for another year, and put aside a considerable sum toward the purchase and transportation of his beloved "b'iler."

Late in the fall Mrs. Gordon succumbed to an acute attack of appendicitis, and was buried by the grief-stricken husband and daughter upon a wooded knoll just behind the cabin. After the death of his wife, Gordon drew more and more within himself, and more and more he became obsessed with his one idea—his "b'iler." And so for three years he washed the bars in summer, and burned into the gravel in winter, the while his "b'iler" fund grew slowly.

In the meantime, quite without the old man's notice, Lou had developed from awkward girlhood into full rounded womanhood. And a very beautiful woman she was, the soft curves of her figure giving no hint of the splendid muscles that rippled and played beneath the velvet softness of her skin—muscles that rendered her absolutely tireless on the trail, and allowed her to swing an ax like a man. Perfect health steeled her nerves to an almost uncanny accuracy with the rifle. She did all the hunting, now, and no ptarmigan was brought into the Gordon cabin that had not been shot clean through the head with the twenty-two, or was any caribou hoisted to the meat cache that had not been instantly killed by a well-placed shot from the thirty-forty.

Left to her own resources, the girl divided the time not occupied with her simple household duties between hunting, and reading, and the breeding of dogs.

In the magazines which she devoured from cover to cover, she had occasionally run across an article upon the selective breeding of animals. One such article dealt with race horses, another with dairy cattle, and the information contained therein she eagerly digested, and proceeded to apply to the breeding of dogs.

Gordon took scant interest in her "putterin' wi' the dogs" and gladly turned over their entire management to her, allowing her to keep the profits of the venture for her own. By the end of the third year these profits had mounted to a tidy sum, notwithstanding the fact that she used of it largely in the purchase of books and magazines whenever and wherever she found opportunity, and also in the purchase of materials for the underclothing which she fashioned by her own handiwork into garments that copied those in the fashion plates of the magazines to the utmost nicety. Her outer garments, of fur in the winter and squaw cloth in summer, were the strictly utilitarian garments of the land of the strong cold.

Quick to realize their superiority, the girl concentrated on the two native breeds of dogs, the malamutes and the huskies. And the pride of her stud was a great upstanding brute of a dog called Skookum, whose mother a pure strain husky, she had mated with an old, but magnificently muscled husky she had bought cheap in Nolan, because his temper had soured with age until his owner feared to handle him. Later she shot him when in a fume of wolfish ferocity he ran amuck and killed two of his own pups. Upon Skookum, the sole survivor of the litter, the girl lavished a world of affection, and a wealth of patient training. For, from the first she had seen in the tawny, amber eyed puppy the making of a great dog, inheriting as he had the superb physical build of his father, and it is true, his father's wolfish temper, but blended with it the staunch loyalty and sagacity of his mother who was a famous trail dog on the Koyukuk.

The fame of Lou Gordon as a breeder of dogs had traveled the length of the river. She drove a ten dog team now, five malamutes and five huskies, and each dog in the team had been carefully selected from the pick of her kennels. Of this team Skookum was the leader, and few indeed were the trail tricks his mistress had not taught him. On the narrow trails of the Koyukuk the tandem rig was used almost exclusively, and following the leader came the other four huskies, and behind them the five malamutes. Thus, the longer geared huskies broke trail for the shorter legged malamutes which in turn compensated by bearing the brunt of the pull. As, among all her dogs, Skookum was the girl's favorite, so was he her constant companion, he alone being allowed to run at large.

Although not an inherent fighter like the malamute, the husky breed develops now and then a wonderful fighter. Skookum was such a dog, his longer legs and heavier body giving him a decided advantage over any malamute, and added to this physical advantage was the sagacious cunning of his generalship. Before he was two years old he had fought his way to the leadership of the team, displacing old Kamik, a crafty and incorrigible fighter, and an equally incorrigible thief.

Lou Gordon knew dogs. She had picked Skookum for a leader from tiniest puppyhood, and to that end she bent all her energy upon his training. She talked to him as she would have talked to a human companion, and it was her fancy that he understood every word she spoke. While in no sense a demonstrative dog, Skookum had nothing of the supreme indifference of the malamute. His smouldering yellow eyes followed her every movement, and by little signs and quirks of expression, he gave evidence of understanding. A raised eyebrow, a single wag of the tail, a pricking of the mobile ears, and on rare occasions, a lick of the long red tongue upon her face or hand, told the girl as plainly as words what was passing in the great brute's mind.

There was nothing of the brutal in Lou Gordon's training of her dogs. When occasion demanded she used the whip, and used it unsparingly, but always in the correction of an acquired fault, that if persisted in would detract from the value of the dog, or of the team as a unit. She never punished a dog for fighting, nor did she ever punish a hungry dog for stealing. Many hungry dogs came her way—dogs that she was able to buy cheap because through abuse and inadequate feeding they had become of little value to their owners. These dogs she took home, and by judicious handling and feeding developed them into able-bodied trail dogs that commanded top prices.

The care and management of from fifteen to thirty dogs was no small task. She owned and operated with the help of an Indian boy her own fish nets, and dried her own fish. She hunted caribou, and tried out her own tallow. For she early learned that on the trail her dogs could not be kept in condition on a straight fish or meat diet. She bought corn meal and rice by the hundred-weight, and when working, her dogs always got one feed a day of cooked ration, boiled rice or cornmeal, mixed with tallow.

The result was that her own team was by all odds the best team on the Koyukuk, and the dogs she offered for sale on her semi-annual trip to Nolan and Wiseman, were eagerly snapped up at top prices.

And so it was, at the approach of Christmas, on the fourth year of their residence on the Koyukuk, father and daughter were living alone on Myrtle, for the last of the others had long since gravitated to the new camps, the old man burning, digging, and dreaming of his "b'iler," and the girl busy with her dogs and her books.

CHAPTER X
ENRIGHT PAYS A VISIT

SKOOKUM RAISED HIS HEAD, pricked his ears, and pointing his muzzle up the creek, gave voice to a low throaty growl. Lou Gordon glanced down at the dog, and continued to throw dried fish over the fence of the pole-and-stake dog corral. When she had tossed the last fish, she smiled: "Who is it, Skookum? We don't have many visitors nowadays, do we?"

The dog stood silent, immovable save for a scarcely perceptible quiver of the nostrils, staring into the twilight.

The girl laughed: "Only one man, eh? And no dogs. And he's someone you know, and approve of. Oh, you see I can understand you as well as you can understand me! See, here he comes! Why, it's Pete Enright!"

The girl stepped forward, a smile of welcome upon her face: "*Klahowya six!*" she greeted.

"*Kahta mika?*" He smilingly returned her greeting in the jargon, and switched into English. "Well, well, Miss Lou, an' how's yer Pa? Still figgerin' on his b'iler, I s'pose. Lord, what a passel of dogs! How many you goin' to have to sell this trip?"

"I'll have six dogs, and dad's well. He'll be home in a few minutes. It's nearly time for supper. Swing off your pack. Yes, dad's still figuring on his boiler." Her face clouded for a moment. "And I'm afraid he's got almost dust enough saved up to get it."

Enright laughed: "Afraid? Why, you talk like you ain't got no faith in the b'iler to put Myrtle on the map agin."

She made a gesture of impatience. "And neither have you, nor anyone else but dad. He's thought and thought about that old boiler until he can't think or talk about anything else." She was silent for a moment, and a smile parted her lips as she continued: "I don't mean what I said. That is, of course I want him to have the boiler because I know he will never be happy until he gets it. But—it seems like an awful lot of money just thrown away."

Enright nodded: "Yup, Miss Lou, that's jist what it is—throw'd away. An' no chanct of gittin' it back. It's too bad, but he's that set on havin' it they ain't no mortal use tryin' to auger him out of it, I s'pose."

The girl shook her head: "Not the slightest. Anyway it's his money." She smiled and drew a step closer. "Do you know that I am making almost as much as he is. He don't know it. He never thinks of me as grown up, and really doing anything that's of any use. 'Putterin' wi' the dogs,' he calls it, and he never pays any attention to them. I've got quite a lot of money saved up, and maybe it's mean, when he's so set on getting his boiler, but I have never let him know I have it. You see, if he does put everything he's got into the boiler, an' then finds it won't make him rich right away, it's going to almost kill him. He's not as young as he was, and I don't think he'd have the heart to start all over again. So, when it comes to that, I'll have the dog money for us to live on."

Pete Enright's mittened hand patted the girl's shoulder and his big voice rumbled with approbation: "Don't you never figger fer a minute that it's mean. It's good common sense, that's what it is. You've got the head fer the two of you. You're the only one on the Koyukuk that seen they was any money in raisin' an' breakin' good dogs, an' the result is you get twict as much fer your dogs as anyone else does, an' they're worth it. Most everyone thinks a dog is just a chunk of the devil wropped up in fur an' put into the world to be kicked an' pounded, and swore at, an' starved, an' worked till he can't stand up no longer, an' then to be cut out of the traces an' left to die, an' his place filled in with another chunk of the devil. You seen how dogs was mighty near human, an' you treat 'em human, an' results is, your dogs is *dogs*! An' that's what I come down to see about, in a way—is dogs."

"Do you want to buy a team?"

"No, but you won't have no trouble sellin' the six yer goin' to fetch up to Nolan. They're sold already. An' a couple of more, too, if you had 'em. Joe McCorkill, he's in need of four to fill out his team, an' the mail carrier needs two, an' so does Johnny Atline. They's plenty dogs fer sale around the camp, but they won't none of 'em have no dogs but yourn. An', say, let me give you a tip, hold out fer a hundred apiece fer 'em. You'll git it. They all kin afford to pay it, an' they'd ruther pay it fer the kind of dogs they'll be gittin', than to pay twenty or twenty-five fer mongrels or Siwash dogs."

"And, did you mush all the way down here to tell me that?" smiled the girl.

"No, that ain't the p'int—not altogether. The facts is, Nolan's figgerin' to pull off a reg'lar celebration this Chris'mus. A sort of winter carnival, they call it, an' they'll be contests of every kind we kin think up, an' prizes fer the winner of each one. Everyone has kicked in an' doneated what he could afford to, an' we've got quite a sight of dust fer prize money. They'll be wrastlin', an' boxin', which owin' to the facts that there ain't no boxin' gloves on the Koyukuk, is looked fer to produce a bloody pastime. Then, they'll be snowshoe an' ski races, a football game between the Kobuk Eskimos an' the Injuns, whirlin' down contests, an' a dog race—mebbe."

"A dog race!" cried the girl, her eyes lighting with sudden interest. "Oh, I wonder if I could enter my team?"

Enright smiled: "That's what I come to see about—that, an' the trimmin's."

"The trimmings?" asked the girl, with a puzzled frown.

"Yeh, you see, Miss Lou, they's a little bit more to this here race than jist runnin' the dogs. Sort of a little—what you might call politics."

The girl's face darkened: "You mean—you don't mean that there's going to be anything crooked about it? That a certain team will be *allowed* to win?"

"No, no! Nothin' like that! Why, Miss Lou, you ort to know we wouldn't stand for nothin' like that on the Koyukuk."

"Of course I do! But, what in the world do you mean?"

"Hello! Here comes yer pa. We kin talk it over after supper an' then I'll mush on to my old cabin up the crick."

"Indeed you'll do nothing of the kind!" laughed the girl. "We've got plenty of room right here. You bunk with dad. I've got a room of my own all curtained off."

Gordon gained the top of the low bank, and came toward them in the gloom. "Dad," called the girl. "Here's Pete Enright come to make us a visit!"

The old man quickened his step and extended his hand: "Aye, Pete, lad, ye're welcome back on Myrtle. How's thing's up river? An' have ye seen Burr MacShane?"

"No, Burr MacShane ain't be'n saw nor heard tell of on the Koyukuk, fer it's goin' on four year or better. Nolan's all right. They's talk of a strike on Hammond River, further up the Koyukuk."

"They're fools an' daft, wi' their runnin' hither an' yon after new strikes. Continually runnin' after strange gods, as the Gude Book says. But, wait till I get my b'iler, an' start steam thawin'! Next summer—next summer if the dump sluices out big, Pete Enright, ye'll see Nolan, an' Wiseman, an' this new Hammond River, stampedin' back to Myrtle, an' every one of 'em that can afford it, wi' a b'iler on his claim."

"Well, mebbe—mebbe, Gordon. I ain't sayin' they won't, an' I ain't sayin' they will. Personal, I ain't got no faith in no b'iler fer gold diggin'."

"It's because ye don't know no better! Why, man, look here! Don't it stand to reason—" and Gordon launched into his favorite theme with enthusiasm that a thousand repetitions had not dampened, and while Enright listened in tolerant silence, Lou slipped into the cabin and began the preparation of supper.

The meal over, Gordon showed signs of renewing his discussion of "b'ilers," but was forestalled by Enright: "About this here dog race, Miss Lou, that I was speakin' of—"

"Dog race? Dog race?" queried the old man, "What foolishness is this about a dog race?"

"It won't be foolishness none whatever fer the winner," replied Enright. "We figgered on puttin' up a prize of about twenty-five ounces. That's four hundred dollars, an' not so bad fer a day's work, neither. That is, that's what we figger to put up if Miss Lou will enter her team. If she won't they won't be no dog race whatever."

"Why, how ridiculous!" cried the girl. "What possible difference can it make whether or not I enter? Surely, with a prize of twenty-five ounces, you can get plenty of teams in the race."

"Yeh, quite a considerable of 'em—if it wasn't fer Jake Dalzene. But, that ain't the p'int. I'll kind of give you a line on how things is, an' the way the boys thinks up the river, an' you kin jedge fer yerself.

"They's a low down skunk of a hooch-runnin' squaw man, name of Jake Dalzene that lives down to Rampart on the Yukon. You know they ain't no Rampart no more, she's plumb abandoned all but the native village, an' this here party lives there with the Injuns, you know the kind. That is, he lives there when he ain't off somewheres else peddlin' hooch to the Injuns off the river. He's plum *kultus*—has him a new squaw 'bout every full moon, an' kicks 'em an' beats 'em like he handles his dogs. Well, this here party is up to Nolan, him an' his pardner. Worked along up the river with a couple sled loads of hooch, an' got red of it tradin' with the Injuns fer fur. When he heard the talk about pullin' a big hurrah around Chris'mus, he begun to talk dog race, an' dog fight. He's claimed to be one of the hardest men on dogs in Alaska, but he's always got a good team. Either he figgers he kin haul more hooch with good dogs, or else he needs 'em to git away from the marshals, I don't know which, but anyway, he's got good dogs.

"First off, his dog race talk wasn't looked on none favorable. The boys figgerin' that their teams wouldn't stand no show again his'n. Then he pulls out a roll of cash money, in big bills, an' starts in wantin' to bet. He's got the money all right, rolls of bills big enough to choke a moose in every pocket an' plenty of dust besides. You see, bein' in the business he's in he don't dare to trust no one with his money, never knowin' when he'll have to light out, nor how far he will have to go, so he packs it with him. Well, as I said, he flashes his roll an' brags on his team an' offers to bet the hull or any part of it on his dogs on any race from a mile to a hundred mile. 'Course he don't git no takers, an' so he heaves in some more hooch, an' every time he takes a drink his dogs looks better to him, an' every one else's looks poorer. So he gits to offerin' odds—two-to-one at first, an then three to one, an' when I left camp it had got up to five-to-one that he could beat anything on the Koyukuk.

"Well we'd got kind of tired of hearin' him shootin' off his mouth an' so some of us got to kind of figgerin' if we couldn't bunch our dogs an' pick us out a winnin' team from the lot, seein' how the odds was gittin' pretty promisin'. But when we come to try 'em out we seen it wasn't no go. The dogs wouldn't work good together, the best ones bein' mostly leaders that wouldn't work nowheres but in the lead.

"Then I thinks of you all. When I mentions your team they was a whoop from the boys, an' every one of 'em agrees that if you'll enter your team we could make a cleanin' an' at the same time learn that skunk a lesson not to come hornin' in on the Koyukuk where folks like him ain't wanted."

Old Man Gordon snorted contemptuously and knocked the ashes from his pipe against the stove: "If ye're expectin' me to risk gude gold on the outcome of a dog race, Pete Enright, ye've had ye're trip fer nothin'. 'Twas better than eight year agone that Burr MacShane taught me the folly of riskin' gude money on a thing that ain't sure certain, an' I'm savin' my dust fer my b'iler."

"Sure, I know, Gordon. An' we ain't askin' you to put up a cent. It's like this, some of the boys says how Old B'iler Gordon wouldn't allow no dogs of his'n to be run agin money, not even fer a prize, bein' he's plum religious, that way. But, I know'd better. I says to 'em, I says, 'You all don't know B'iler Gordon like I know him. Religious he is,' I says, 'an' it's a credit to him. If we all had more religion onto us than what we've got it wouldn't hurt us none whatever. But, along with his religion B'iler has got a lot of common sense. If we put up a prize enough to make it worth while I bet he'll not have no 'bjection to runnin' his dogs, on account it ain't gamblin' when he don't put up nothin' agin the prize. It's jist simply earnin' the money by honest work.' Ain't I right, Gordon?"

The old man nodded affirmation: "Ye're right. A prize in any contest is fair earnt as long as the outcome ain't decided by luck alone. 'Tis what I told Burr MacShane."

"That's the idee," agreed Enright, emphatically, "I know'd you well enough to be sure you'd take the sensible way of seein' it. So I says to the boys, 'I'll jist slip down to Gordon's an' find out fer sure if they'll be up fer Chris'mus, and if he'll let his dogs enter the race.' You see, this here Dalzene party, he don't know nothin' about Miss Lou's team, an' he thinks he's saw the general run of Koyukuk dogs, an' he knows it's too late fer us to run in any reg'lar racin' team from over Nome way, an' that's why he's bettin' so high."

Enright paused, filled his pipe, and blowing a cloud of blue smoke ceiling-ward, continued: "Now, here's where the politics comes in. We all know that big ten team of Miss Lou's ain't never be'n raced, but we've got the hunch that they kin clean up anything this side of Nome. Us not bein' religious, an' not havin' no scruples about bettin' a little now an' then, jist by way of amusement, you might say, we'll jist cover Dalzene's pile, an' if we kin clean him out—bust him, it'll be a plumb religious move, 'cause he won't be able to get holt of so much hooch to peddle to the pore Injuns. Ain't that right, Gordon?"

"Aye, ye're right," affirmed the old man, judicially, "Don't it tell in the Gude Book how the Lord overturned the tables of the money changers, an' scourged them wi' scourges? He done it because they was ungodly men, an' a generation of vipers, so any act that will be as a scourge to the ungodly will be counted as righteousness. Ye've more religion between ye than I thought, Pete Enright."

"Sure we have, B'iler—a damn sight more than we thought, ourselves. But, it's like the itch, if you've got it, it'll show up, sometime. But, as I was sayin', the way to work it is like this: I'll take the six dogs that Miss Lou's goin' to fetch up to sell, an' pull out fer Nolan in the mornin'."

"Oh, not those dogs!" cried the girl, "They're good dogs, but they haven't worked together long enough. They couldn't win a race against a team that knew how to work together."

"Jist so," agreed Enright, "That's what I figgered. However, it ain't no harm in me takin' 'em along up fer you, is they, to save you the trouble? I'll see they're well took care of. Without sayin' nothin' I'll hit town with these here six dogs an' begin runnin' 'em up an' down on the ice. The boys'll crowd down there to watch 'em run an' then they'll begin to take bets offen Dalzene. Of course it might be such a thing that Dalzene will come down along with the rest an' he might somehow git the idee that this here was the team we was hangin' our dust onto. An' he might figger, him knowin' dogs a little, that his'n could beat 'em without half tryin'. It's ten days yet, till Chris'mus, an' every day I'll work them dogs out on the ice, an' every day we kin kind of cover more an' more of Dalzene's money, till we've got it all covered. Then the day before Chris'mus you come along an' hearin' how they's a race you enter your team. Meanwhile all these here bets has be'n made, the money is up, an' Dalzene has bet agin' the whole field fer his team to win. That's what he's offerin', his team agin the field, an' accordin' to his way of seein' it, it's as good a bet as any, 'cause he says he don't care if they's a dozen teams or one, he's only got to beat the best of 'em anyhow, an' he ain't worryin' none but what he kin do it.

"Now, the boys thinks that if we all make a clean-up on this here ungodless party from Rampart, on account of your team winnin' this here race, it wouldn't be no more than fair to add ten percent of our winnin's to the prize. What do you say to that?"

Gordon's eyes rested upon the face of his daughter. "What do ye say, lass? The dogs are yours, you've raised 'em an' fooled wi' 'em an' broke 'em, an' if we win the money's yours."

"Oh, I'd love to do it!" cried the girl, her eyes shining. "And I believe we can win, too. But what if he backs down when he sees my team? What if he won't race?"

"We aim to fix that. We all will lay our bets with the understandin' that if he backs out he loses. He's got to race an' win to take the money."

"How many miles shall we race?" she asked eagerly.

Enright considered: "Dalzene he's made his crack that he'll run anywheres from one mile to a hundred. The boys kind of left it to you fer to name the distance. As I said, them dogs of Dalzene's looks good an' fit. But they's only seven of 'em, agin' your ten. An' besides, his sled is a heavy, rough ice proposition, built more fer freightin' than speed."

"But, so is mine," interrupted the girl.

"Sure, I know. But the mail carrier's ain't. An' bein' as he'll have all the dust he kin scrape together invested in this here scheme for Christianizin' Jake Dalzene, it ain't goin' to be none hard whatever, fer to borrow that sled off him. So, takin' it all in all, as the feller says, I guess we better make it a middlin' long drag. Say, anyways forty or fifty mile. The longer it is, the heavier the pull is goin' to be on Dalzene's dogs."

"Why not go the whole hundred?" cried the girl.

Enright laughed: "I wondered if you'd say that. It'll sure tickle the boys when I tell 'em. It shows yer heart's right, an' yer game, an' you got belief in yer dogs—not that we didn't know you was game all right, Miss Lou," he hastened to add, "'Cause there ain't a man on the Koyukuk that wouldn't go plumb to hell for you." He paused, floundering awkwardly, "I mean, in a way of speakin', as the feller says," and encountering the twinkle of amusement in the eyes of the girl, proceeded: "But, they's two or three reasons why a fifty mile race would be better. First an' foremost of which is that they's a hard-packed trail from Nolan to Johnny Atline's cabin, twenty-five mile up the river. Beyond Johnny's the trail peters out an' they'd be a lot of trail breakin' ahead of the dogs. If you run to Johnny's an' back it's fifty mile, an' a ridin' trail all the way. That'll be to your advantage, 'cause Dalzene he weighs goin' on two hundred an' a quarter, an' it'll be so much more drag on his dogs. Then, agin, we don't want it so long that folks'll lose interest. You see, it ain't like the Alaska Sweepstakes over to Nome. They run better than four hundred mile, but it's the biggest race in the world, an' folks jist nach'ly can't lose interest. You'd ort to make it to Johnny's an' back in ten or twelve hours—"

"Ten or twelve hours!" exclaimed the girl, "With a good riding trail, and a light sled if I can't make it in less than nine hours I ought to lose!"

Enright whistled: "D'ye really think you kin beat ten hours? You got to remember yer team ain't broke to race."

Lou Gordon smiled: "Not now, they aren't—but *you* must remember it's ten days till Christmas."

CHAPTER XI
DISAPPOINTMENT

EARLY IN THE MORNING of the day before Christmas, Lou Gordon divided the bacon and flapjacks between two plates, and crossed to where her father lay snoring loudly beneath his blankets. The two had camped for the night in an abandoned cabin only five miles below Nolan.

"Wake up, dad!" she called, "Breakfast's all ready, and it's time to mush."

The old man stirred sleepily and opened his eyes. "What's the hurry, lass? We've got all day before us, an' only five miles to go. What's the sense in hittin' the trail this time of night?"

The girl smiled: "I want to be in and out of Nolan before it gets light."

"In and out! What d'ye mean, in an' out?"

"Why, tomorrow's the day of the dog race, and I want to take the dogs over the course today. I want to know the trail, and I want them to know it."

Old Man Gordon threw back his blankets and drew on his moccasins, "What are ye so particular about the trail for? Didn't Pete Enright say it was plain an' hard-packed—a ridin' trail all the way?"

"Yes, but it isn't going to do any harm to know it. I have never driven a race before, and I want to know everything there is to know about the trail. I'm going to win! And besides, I want to give the dogs a final workout."

The cabin was bare of furniture, and without rising from the floor Gordon drew one of the plates toward him. Lou took the other, and seated herself at his side.

"What's this talk about drivin' the race, an' knowin' the trail?" asked the old man, as he partook largely of a flapjack.

The girl glanced up in surprise. "Why, I said I want to know all about the trail so I can win the race tomorrow."

"Ye win it! Losh, lass, ye don't suppose I'd be lettin' ye drive the race—wi' twenty-five ounces at stake?"

"What do you mean?" cried Lou, in sudden alarm.

"I mean, I'll drive the race myself, of course! A slip of a lass like ye drivin' a fifty mile race! An' expectin' me to let ye do it! 'Tis never to be thought of. How could ye hold the dogs to the work? No, no, lass, the money'll be ye're own if ye're dogs win it. But it's a job fer a man, an' not a wee lass."

For a moment the girl remained speechless—stunned. She wondered if she had heard aright. Surely her father could not mean that he would try to handle the dogs—her dogs, that she had raised from puppyhood, and trained, and worked over. Why, she knew those dogs! They were hers. Nobody but herself had ever driven them. Nobody could drive them as she could drive them. They understood her as she understood them. And, what did her father know of dogs?

When at length she spoke her voice sounded strange and far off: "Do you mean that you are going to try to drive the dogs—my dogs?"

"Of course I'm goin' to drive 'em. Not that I think ye ain't a good hand wi' dogs, mind ye. 'Cause ye are. Ye handle 'em as gude as a man on the trail. But, not against a stake of four hundred dollars. Ye must remember that for all the pluck of ye, ye're but a lass. Ye lack experience—"

"Experience!" cried the girl, her face flushed with the mighty anger that surged up within her, "Experience! When did you ever have any experience racing dogs?"

"I never raced any dogs in my life, but all my life I've handled dogs—"

"And you don't know any more about dogs than I know about your old boiler! Why, dad, can't you see? Those are my dogs! I know every one of them, and they know me. I can get a hundred times more out of them than you can. Why, I *raised* them! And besides, you think I'm just a baby! You've been so full of that old boiler that you haven't noticed that I've grown up! But, I'm not a baby! I'm nineteen! And I can out-drive you, and out-mush you, any day!"

"Tush! Tush, lass! Ye're fergettin' yourself. Ye're lettin' ye're angry passions rise against ye're own father. Honor thy father an' thy mother, the Gude Book says, an' 'tis scant honor to face down yer own father wi' foolish prattle! I never thought ye'd be expectin' to drive the race yerself, or I'd told ye long ago. I can see how ye're maybe upset wi' disappointment, an' I'm not holdin' ye're hasty words against ye."

The girl's anger subsided as swiftly as it had arisen, and there were tears in her eyes as she answered in a voice that was not quite steady: "Forgive me, dad! Really I hardly knew what I was saying. We can't be angry with each other. Why, you're the only person I have in the world. And I do love you."

"Of course ye do, lass. Say no more about it. I've forgot it already."

"Oh, but, dad—can't you see that the dogs will work better for me than for anyone? I'm the one who has handled them, I feed them and care for them. To me they are just like so many people. I know each one—his faults, and his virtues. Please, dad, please let me drive the race. I'm not just a little girl. Look at me, I'm as tall as you are!"

"Aye, but for all that, ye're but a wee lass, an' 'tis foolishness to be pratin' of drivin' a dog race—to be tryin' to compete wi' grown men on their own terms. This Dalzene, I've heard of him down on the Yukon—an' no gude of him, an' I'm knowin' 'twill take a man to beat him."

"But the men of Nolan! Think of the men who have backed my dogs with their gold! They, too, thought I was going to drive. Pete Enright thought of course I'd drive. Surely you wouldn't do anything that would cause them to lose. All of them are your friends, and how would you feel if this horrible Dalzene went back to the Yukon with their dust?"

"Aye, an' it's to prevent just that I'm goin' to drive this race. It ain't in reason that their gude gold should be at the mercy of a striplin' of a lass."

"Let's leave it to them!" cried the girl, "Surely, you will agree that they have much more at stake than we have. Let them decide who will drive the race. It's their dust that's at stake, and they should be allowed to name the driver."

The old man shook his head stubbornly: "No, no, lass. 'Twould not be fair to put it up to them. There ain't a man them but would vote for ye to drive when they seen how you'd set yer heart on it. They're real men—the men of the Koyukuk. An' if they thought 'twould please ye, they'd vote the gold out of their own pockets wi'out battin' an eye. Don't fear, lass. I'm not forgettin' the boys."

Lou Gordon knew her father. She realized the absolute futility of further argument. Without another word she drew on her parka and, leaving the old man to pack up the camp outfit, stepped out into the keen air. At the shrill creak of the sagging door which she closed behind her, heads appeared above the dark furry mounds that dotted the surface of the snow, and below the pricked ears, ten pairs of eyes glowed in the reflected starlight like live coals. Here and there a dog got up, stretched with a prodigious yawn and settled back upon his haunches to eye the girl in eager expectancy. Of all the dogs only Skookum presumed to approach her. Stepping close he raised his pointed muzzle and the smouldering yellow eyes searched the face of his mistress. Dropping to one knee, Lou threw her arms about the great neck, and a dry convulsive sob shook her as she buried her face in the thick hair. Only for a moment she remained thus, and as she released the dog, his long red tongue shot out and caressed her cheek. And as he stalked slowly to his place at the head of the row of waiting dogs, Lou noted that the great white plume of his tail that generally flaunted high above his neck was carried at half mast. "He knows," she whispered to the brilliantly glittering stars, "Skookum knows that there is something wrong, and by tomorrow, they'll all know it. Oh, why can't he listen to reason!"

From a canvas bag she drew a ball composed of tallow and boiled rice which Skookum deftly caught in mid-air. One after another the dogs caught and wolfed down their portions, and righting the sled, the girl proceeded to harness them, each dog, as his name was called, eagerly taking his accustomed place in the team, as she deftly adjusted the harness.

When a few minutes later Old Man Gordon opened the door, the great ten team stood ready for the trail. The camp outfit lashed to the sled, the girl held out her whip to her father: "You better drive them on in," she said, "It will give you a chance to get acquainted with them a little, and it won't be quite so much of a surprise to them, tomorrow."

"Losh, lass, a dog team is a dog team. I've drove hundreds of 'em in my time." Nevertheless he took the whip, and gave the command to mush. The dogs remained stationary, and cracking the whip loudly, the old man repeated the command: "Hi, mush! Mush-u!"

At the sound of the whip, Skookum looked around in surprise, hesitated uncertainly for a moment, and seeing that the girl stood at the old man's side, decided it was all right, and started. The other dogs, not hearing the sound of the familiar voice, did not move with the leader, and the result was a jerky, awkward start. A hundred yards down the trail, Skookum deliberately stopped stalk still and looked backwards. Again it was all right. The girl was mushing along beside the sled, and the leader started on as Gordon shouted his command to mush. On and on they plodded, and as Lou's eyes rested upon her dogs she noted the listless, mechanical manner of their going—noted also that the tails showed an unwonted droop.

"Can't you see the difference, dad?" she asked at length, "They don't know what to make of it. They haven't got their hearts in their work." Before the old man could reply, a sharp bend in the trail brought them face to face with a dog team. "Gee! Gee! Gee!" cried Gordon excitedly, cracking his whip close to Skookum's ears. But instead of turning out for the oncoming team, the great leader lunged forward and snapped viciously at the lead dog of the other team. In an instant the two teams were at each other tooth and nail. Gordon and the other driver, sprang into the mêlée, striking right and left with the whips, and vainly trying to make themselves heard above the pandemonium of growls and snarls. An instant later a shrill whistle cut the air. The girl rushed to Skookum's side, and grasping his collar repeated the whistle. Instantly the great dog drew away from his opponent and stood quivering, every hair a-bristle. The other driver managed to collar his own leader, and repeating the shrill whistle the girl snatched the whip from her

father's hand, and brought the lash down with stinging force upon the back
of Kog, the fourth malamute from the sled. The blow had the desired effect.
The four other huskies had stopped fighting when Skookum stopped, and the
malamutes followed as Kog dropped upon his belly in the snow. Fortunately
there had been little or no tangling of harness, as the dogs had been separated
almost as soon as the fight began and a few moments later both outfits were
once more strung out upon the trail.

"Oh, dad, can't you see, now?" cried the girl. "They're not used to you. They
don't understand."

"They're ill broke!" growled the old man, stubbornly.

"They're not!" exclaimed the girl, "They are the best broken dogs on the
Koyukuk! Ask anybody."

"There's no one on the river, that would hurt ye're feelin's by sayin' aught
against ye're dogs, lass. But, 'tis no way for a leader to do, to fly at the throat
of a passin' lead dog."

"If he had been handled right Skookum would never have done it. Why
did you think you had to yell 'Gee' three times and crack your whip right at
Skookum's ears?"

"'Tis a trail of ample wideness to pass wi' plenty room."

"And they would have passed without even hesitating if you hadn't con-
fused Skookum by yelling at him as if he were deaf. Why, you can't even start
them without nearly jerking the outfit to pieces."

"It's because of they're trainin'. They ain't half broke, I'm tellin' ye. I know
what dogs should do."

"And I'll show you what these dogs can do, if they're properly handled. Give
me the whip!" The old man complied.

"Whoah!" At the sound of the girl's voice the team froze in its tracks.
"Mush!" Instantly, the team started as a single dog. The sled slipped smoothly into motion and the dogs broke into a brisk trot, their plumes a-wave.
"Steady!" The trot slowed to a walk. In the distance sounded the tiny tinkle
of bells.

"Here comes another team!" cried the old man, "Git to ye're leader an hold
him till they've passed! Next time, they'll tangle an' maybe we'll have a hurt
dog. They'd of tangled before if I hadn't got there just as I did."

"Get on the sled!" commanded the girl. "I'm driving, now, and I'll show you
something!"

Reluctantly the old man seated himself upon the sled. The tinkle of bells
sounded nearer. Grasping the tail rope the girl spoke to her father: "You
couldn't pass that other team at a walk. Watch me!"

"Mush! Mush!" the command cut clear, and the dogs sprang into a run. "Mush-u! Hi! Hi!" Faster and faster they flew over the hard-packed trail. Directly ahead, seemingly almost upon them in the gloom, a dog team topped a rise. "Mush!" The dogs increased their speed. "Gee!" The single spoken word cut clear, and swerving without a perceptible jerk, Skookum, threw his team to the side of the trail, and the next instant, they flashed past the oncoming team.

"That's drivin'!" called a voice from the darkness behind them, and Lou slowed her dogs to a walk with a word.

"Now, what do you say?" asked the girl.

"'Twas a foolhardy thing to do," announced Gordon. "I'd say ye were lucky. But it proves ye're not fit to drive a race."

The remainder of the trip was made in silence.

Enright himself greeted the outfit as it drew up to the roadhouse door, and while her father exchanged greetings with a half-dozen former residents of Slate Creek and Myrtle, the girl managed to call Enright aside.

"What's ailin' you, Miss Lou? You look like you expected to lose that dog race instead of winnin' it."

"That's just it. I'm afraid we will lose it. At least we won't stand near as good a chance of winning as I thought we would."

"What's the matter? Dogs gone sick on you?"

"No, they're in tiptop condition. It isn't that, but just this morning dad informed me that he is going to drive the race! Said it was a man's job. He just can't realize that I have grown up. And he don't know any more about handling those dogs than the man in the moon."

Enright whistled: "Plumb set on it, is he? Did you try to reason with him?"

"Reason with him! I've tried every possible argument I could think of. Even showed him how I could handle them on the trail, after he'd mixed up with an outfit we met. But it's no use. You know dad."

"Yup, he's the settest man when he gits an idee in his head I ever seen or heard tell of. Well, if that's how it is, it's got to be that way, I s'pose. Mebbe the dogs is so good that anyone could win with 'em. That's our only chance. Unless—"

"Unless what?"

"I was thinkin', mebbe, we might sort of kidnap him till after the race."

"No, no! Don't do that. He would never forgive you—or me either. No, we've got to let him go."

"All right, Miss Lou. You're the doctor."

"At least, I'll try to persuade him to take them over the course today, so they'll know the trail."

A few moments later she approached her father: "Dad, don't you think it would be wise to take the dogs over the course today, so they will be familiar with the trail. You ought to know it yourself."

"Losh, lass! I've be'n to Johnny Atline's, an' as for the dogs they can't get off the trail, it's a ridin' trail all the way."

"I know, but the dogs will travel any trail they know better than they will a strange trail."

"No, no. Now don't you go botherin' your head about that race. You leave it all to me. Even wi' the dogs broke bad as they are, I'll win. Go on now an' enjoy ye'reself. I'm goin' over there wi' the boys." And turning away, he followed the men who had already started for the saloon.

"He won't even take them over the course," she reported to Pete Enright, when her father had passed out of hearing.

"Dalzene's had his up an' back three or four times."

The girl who had been regarding the toes of her moccasins, suddenly looked up. "Where is Dalzene?"

"Oh, he ain't up yet. He got pretty well loaded up on hooch last night, an' he'll lay abed till noon."

"I'm going to take the dogs over the trail myself! Tell me, how will I know Johnny Atline's cabin."

"Can't miss it. Keep on up the river fer twenty-five mile. There's an island right opposite Johnny's claim with two big rocks standin' on the lower end of it. The boys was up the other day an' cleared a wide place in the snow for a turnin' place. You can't go wrong, they ain't no trail beyond, to speak of."

"Come on down to the river and see me off," smiled the girl, "and I want you to time me."

"Eight o'clock right on the dot!" cried Enright.

The girl waved her hand, and started her dogs, "Look for me about four!" she cried over her shoulder, as the great brutes bounded away.

Enright grinned: "'Bout six will hit her closter," he opined, and turned toward the saloon.

CHAPTER XII
"TWENTY MINUTES TO FOUR"

"WHAT'S THE MATTER WITH you all Koyukuk malamutes? Broke? Cold feet? Or, what? I've still got twenty-five hundred dollars here that's tryin' to talk! Five-to-one that my team'll come in first tomorrow! Who's got five hundred dollars that ain't workin'? Or, don't yer six mangy curs you be'n floggin' up an' down the river look as good as they did yiste'day?" Jake Dalzene stood at the end of the bar in the Aurora Borealis, Nolan's single saloon, a whisky glass in one hand and a roll of bills in the other, and blustered forth his challenge.

No one accepted the bet. Old Man Gordon, knowing his limitations, and realizing that he must keep a clear head for the morrow, after three or four drinks, had retired to the roadhouse where he was passing the afternoon close beside the big stove, alternately dozing and reading from a dilapidated copy of *Lorna Doone* that comprised the entire fictional section of the roadhouse library.

The Aurora Borealis swarmed with the men from the creeks. The roulette wheel, and the faro layout were crowded to capacity, games of stud were in progress at the poker tables, from above stairs came the incessant din of the dance hall piano, and the ceiling boards creaked to the thumping and scraping of moccasined feet.

At the bar, a group of sourdoughs heard the loud-bawled challenge of Dalzene, but heeded it not. Among them was Pete Enright, who had whispered the ill tidings that Old Man Gordon, and not his daughter, was to drive the dog race. Thereupon deep gloom had settled upon the camp, for not a man among them but knew the futility of argument with Old Man Gordon when his mind was made up, nor did a man among them have any faith in Gordon's ability to drive the ten team to victory.

"We all was sure hell-bent on makin' it plain that there wasn't to be no backin' out," dolefully reflected Angel Crabb. "I've got a thousan' in good dust locked up in Clem's safe there that yesterday sure looked like six thousand. An' now it looks like a busted flush that had be'n draw'd to an' missed."

"My five hundred don't look that good," opined Rim Rock Keets. "Busted flushes that wasn't helped on the draw has be'n made to drag down the pot—but they ain't no way to bluff through on a dog race."

"It ain't so much the dust that's botherin' me," confided Enright, "I got quite a heft of it put up, too. But, it's the idee of this here low down scum comin' up here an' makin' a killin' off'n us Koyukukers. That—an' knowin' how bad Miss Lou feels about it. They ain't none of us that feels as plum disapp'inted as what she does. Damn Old Man Gordon!"

"We might git him stewed so bad he wouldn't be fitten to drive no dogs tomorrow," suggested a man from Sheep Creek.

Enright shook his head: "No we mightn't, neither. First off, it would be playin' it low down on the girl. An' anyone that tries that game, him an' I is goin' to put in some spare time blackin' one another's eyes, an' otherwise roughin' things up. I've know'd that girl, a little better'n four year, an' so has quite a lot of us—ever since she come into the country. She don't like fer the Old Man to drink much—an' that settles that. Onct an' a while he gits stewed, but that's his business, an' not ourn. But even if anyone was to try I don't think he could git another drink down Gordon this day. He's the settest man there is, an' he don't aim to git drunk—leastwise till after the race."

"He might win it, at that," said the mail carrier, hopefully.

"'Tain't hardly likely," replied Enright. "Gordon he ain't no hell of a dog musher, that anyone ever heard tell of, an' the dogs would have to be jist nach'ly so damn good that they couldn't lose before he could win. No, I guess we all kin kiss our dust good bye, er try to git it back bettin' on some other race er fight, er wrastle."

"Can't win it back off'n Dalzene," growled Rim Rock, "He wouldn't bet less'n he thought he had a sure thing."

A slow grin overspread Enright's face as he eyed the speaker: "Yeh, but you know, on this here race we was kind of workin' a little, what you might call, politics, ourself."

The outside door opened and the men turned casually to see the newcomer, when with a startled exclamation, Enright pushed hurriedly through the group, and passing the man without a word, disappeared through the door.

"What in hell ails him?" asked Angel Crabb.

"Busted out like he'd be'n sent fer, an' had to go!"

Johnny Atline joined the group, pinching icicles from his mustache.

"Who's outside, Johnny?" asked Rim Rock, "I ketched sight of a dog outfit when you shoved open the door. Must be someone Enright is plumb mindful to meet up with."

Before Atline could answer, Enright himself reentered the room. At the rear of the bar, Dalzene was still roaring his challenge between drinks. Enright drew his watch from his pocket and meticulously compared it with the bar-room clock. "Twenty minutes to four," he muttered, incredulously, and then he repeated, still staring at the face of his watch, "*Twenty minutes to four!*"

"Well, what's so damn curious about twenty minutes to four?" asked the mail carrier, "It's be'n twenty minutes to four, twict a day ever sence I kin remember, but I never heer'd no one ravin' about it before."

"Oh, nothin' much," replied Enright, "Only, it's jist exactly the time I aim to lay a bet."

Carelessly, he sauntered toward the rear of the room. Dalzene saw him coming, and a sneering grin twisted his lips. "Here's the man with the team of six world beatin' fish hounds!" he cried. "What's the matter today, Enright, can't you rake up five hundred more dollars, or has yer guts gone back on you?"

"Still got some money left to bet?" drawled Enright.

"Here it is!" the man shook his roll of bills before the other's face. "Twenty-five hundred agin five hundred that my dogs wins! I be'n bawlin' it out here fer a couple hours, an' I hain't had no takers. You Koyukuk sports is sure plumb timid when it comes to puttin' up real money."

"Is that all you got?"

"Every damn cent, except some chicken feed that'll run me till tomorrow evenin'. I'll have all kinds of money then—dust an' bills—Koyukuk dust."

"I'll take it," remarked Enright, and turning to the proprietor of the saloon, he tossed a sack of dust onto the bar. "Weigh her out Clem, five hundred dollars, an' lock it up along with Dalzene's twenty-five hundred. I'll be callin' around tomorrow evenin' fer both batches."

"Haw, haw haw!" laughed Dalzene, as he counted out his bills upon the bar, and shoved them over to the proprietor, "So you'll be callin' around fer it will you? Lemme tell you somethin', Enright. I'll tell you now, seein' how I got all my money up, an' no objeck in holdin' out on you. I made the run up an' back yeste'day in nine hours an' ten minutes! The best you've did it is around 'leven hours. Why them six old pelters of yourn couldn't win a race agin a string of mud turtles! I'll jest walk off tomorrow an' stop fer lunch at Atline's, an' then trot in ahead of the bunch an' collect my wages—three thousan' in dust fer part of a day's work hain't so pore! I've got jest fifteen thousan' bet, at five-to-one. Nine hours an' ten minutes, Enright, think of that!"

"Yeh," drawled Enright, turning away, "That had ort to git you in fer supper, Dalzene, but the bets'll all be cashed, an' a lot of the money spent 'fore you even see the smoke of Nolan."

"What d'ye mean?"

"No use sp'ilin' yer fun," grinned Enright, tauntingly, "You'll find out to-morrow." And, deliberately he walked away and joined the group at the forward end of the bar.

Instantly, he was besieged by a chorus of questions: "What in hell did you lay that bet fer?"

"You must be plumb crazy, sendin' good money after bad! What ails you?"

"What's twenty minutes to four got to do with it?" persisted the mail carrier.

"Jist this," answered Enright, speaking slowly. "Miss Lou took them dogs of hern over the race trail today. *She started at eight o'clock!*"

"Eight o'clock! An' back a'ready!"

"Yer crazy as hell!"

"She never went the hull ways!"

"It's plumb onpossible!"

"It means," said Enright, ignoring the exclamations, "that any team that can burn up the snow like that is good enough to carry my money no matter who drives 'em."

"But, I tell ye, she couldn't of gone the hull distance!" insisted the man from Sheep Creek.

"The hell she *didn't!*" exclaimed Johnny Atline, whose presence had been entirely forgotten in the interest that had centered upon Enright's last bet. "I know, 'cause I was up to my cabin, an' I rid down with her. She rested 'em ten minutes at the turn, an' they carried double comin' down—her an' me, both. I've saw dogs I thought could run before—but *Gawd!*"

CHAPTER XIII
THE START

THE CAMP OF NOLAN was early astir the following morning. The entertainment committee, consisting of Crim, the trader; Clem Wilcox, proprietor of the Aurora Borealis Saloon; and Henshaw, keeper of the roadhouse; had decreed that the dog race was to start at eight o'clock, in order that the other events should be out of the way before the finish of the race late in the afternoon.

At six o'clock Old Man Gordon accompanied his daughter to the dog kennels which, in the land of the strong cold, is a necessary adjunct to every roadhouse. Lou handed her father the canvas bag containing the balls of tallow and rice: "You had better feed them this morning, dad," she advised, "Begin with Skookum and toss one to each. Then, we'll harness them and take a turn or two on the river. It won't do any harm for them to understand that it's all right for you to be driving. They'll work for you, I'm sure—if you will keep the whip off of them and don't confuse them with too much yelling at critical moments."

Strangely enough, Old Man Gordon meekly acquiesced in everything the girl suggested. He had read disapproval of his decision to drive the race in the faces of the men of Nolan—a disapproval that, while it merely served to strengthen the decision, nevertheless burdened him with a sense of responsibility.

"I took them over the whole course, myself, yesterday," Lou informed him when they were upon the river. "And I made it in seven hours and forty minutes."

"Ye did!" exclaimed the man in astonishment. "Why, lass, it don't seem possible."

"I did it, though. And I rested them for ten minutes at the turn. You must rest them there, too, if you run them all the way up. The trail is good and fast, and plenty of room to pass except in a few stretches. But remember this: Don't use the whip or crack it close to Skookum's ears! Oh, why won't you let me drive?"

"I've told ye 'tis a man's job, an' that's an' end to it," he replied, and the girl accepted the ultimatum as she noticed that the lines hardened at the corners of the old man's mouth.

"You take them down and back for a mile or so, and get all you can out of them. I want to be sure they understand that they've got to run for you."

"*Down* an' back!" exclaimed Gordon, "Why not *up* an' back? There's a gude wide trail all cleared for the finish."

Lou smiled: "We don't want to take a chance that they'll stop, or even hesitate at that same place when the race is on. They might think that is what's expected of them."

Ten minutes later Gordon halted the team at his daughter's side: "They done fine!" he cried, "They'll win! Never I seen such runnin' as they done."

"They ran, all right," admitted the girl, "But I think we can get a little more out of them at the start and the finish. We'll see. Try again, now. Only, this time let me start them. And when you come in on the return, I'll stand here and see if I can't get an extra spurt out of them at the finish."

Once more the team was headed down river, and the girl gave the command to start. The get away was smoother and faster than before, and on the return, as soon as the dogs were within earshot, she advanced a little distance, and giving a shrill whistle, turned and ran.

At the familiar sound the dogs redoubled their efforts, and a few moments later the great ten team was at her side.

"Better yet?" cried the old man, "'Tis the way we'll work it in the race."

"Why don't you leave the whip behind?" asked the girl, "I think you will do much better without it because, really, you don't need it to get speed out of them, and a little whipping, at the wrong time, may lose the race."

"Losh, lass! Who ever heard of drivin' dogs wi'out a whip? I'll take the whip, but I'll mind what ye've said, an' I'll be sparin' of it. But, there's times when the sting of the lash is gude meat for any dog."

The dogs settled their bellies onto the snow, and father and daughter seated themselves upon the sled. Overhead the stars glittered, their brilliance not yet paled by any hint of dawn. Voices came from the direction of the camp, and presently the forms of men could be seen making their way through the Arctic gloom. More forms appeared. Nolan was assembling for the start.

Enright drew near with Lou's six dogs harnessed to a clumsy sled. He greeted the two with a grin, and seating himself on his sled, made a great show of limbering up his dogs.

The Gordons soon found themselves the centre of a close standing group of men, who eyed the dogs appraisingly, and conversed among themselves in undertones. From beyond the encircling crowd a gruff voice called loudly.

"Hello, Enright! Takin' the kinks out of them freight hounds? What's the excitement over yender?" A moment later Dalzene forced his way through the crowd, and stared open-mouthed astonishment at the great ten team that lay strung out on the snow at his feet. One by one he scrutinized the dogs, his eyes resting for what seemed a full minute upon Skookum. In the crowd someone snickered: "What's the matter, Dalzene? Froze yer tongue?"

The taunting words goaded the man to sudden fury: "What the hell's comin' off here?" he roared, facing the men of Nolan with blazing eyes, "Whose dogs is them? Where'd they come from? They don't git in on this race! My money's up agin Koyukuk dogs! You don't run in no ringers on me! Who the hell do you think I am? I wasn't made in a minute!"

Clem Wilcox stepped close and faced the infuriated man: "Maybe you wasn't," he said, in a voice that cut cold, "But you'll be gittin' made *over* in about a minute if you don't quit yer cussin' where ladies is. Up here on the Koyukuk we respects women. An' what's more you don't happen to be runnin' things up here, neither. Them dogs is entered fer this here race, all proper an' regular an' they're goin' to run. They're Koyukuk dogs, belongin' to the Gordons down on Myrtle—"

"Myrtle! You can't work that on me! Coldfoot's dead, an' Myrtle's dead an' forgot about!"

"Mebbe you've fergot about it," grinned Wilcox, "But, you wont never fergit it no more, Dalzene."

"I tell you I won't run agin them dogs. I ain't supposed to run no seven dog team agin' a ten dog team! All bets is off! I won't run!"

"Jest as you say, Dalzene. It won't make no particular difference to the boys whether you run or not. But the bets rides. I happen to be stakeholder, an' it was made plain that if anyone hauled out, his bets loses."

"Besides which," added Enright, who had joined the group, "We didn't hear no partic'lar kickin' on your part when you figgered on runnin' seven dogs agin my six."

The enraged man whirled on the speaker: "You know'd damn well them dogs of yourn couldn't run!" he roared, "I've be'n hornswaggled! It's a frame-up!"

"Ain't it hell!" taunted Enright. "But, cheer up, Dalzene, it sure grieves us to see you onhappy. An' say, if it'll ease yer mind any, I don't mind lettin' you in on a secret—seein' all yer money's up, an' we can't git no more bets off'n you. That there team rambled over the trail to Johnny Atline's an' back yesterday, in seven hours an' forty minutes, an' carried double half ways. That's jist an hour an' a half better than that there pack of muscle-bound flea pastures of yourn done it."

Dalzene turned to Wilcox, "Jerk out three of them dogs, an' I'll run!" he demanded. "I ain't goin' to run no seven dogs agin' a ten dog team."

Wilcox laughed: "Suit yerself. If you don't toe the mark at eight o'clock, which is in ten minutes from now, I'll begin payin' off bets, an' we'll go on with the show." With a muttered oath, Dalzene turned and elbowed his way through the grinning crowd.

"Might's well draw fer place, an' get that settled," remarked Crim. "They's only three entries, so here goes." Tearing a paper into three small squares, he numbered them with a stubby pencil, placed them in his cap, and after shaking it a bit, offered Gordon the first draw.

"Number Two!" announced the old man, holding the scrap of paper to catch the light of the paling stars.

Enright drew Number One, and chose center place, leaving Gordon free to chose the space to his left which was the better position.

"Git set!" cried Wilcox, "an' take yer instructions."

The teams moved into position, Dalzene's sullen rage manifesting itself in blows of his whip upon his cringing dogs.

Wilcox stepped before them: "The race is to Johnny Atline's an' return," he announced. "Bill Britton's up there to see that all teams goes the hull route. The driver an' sled, an' every dog that starts has got to cross the line at the finish, an' the outfit that crosses first wins. The committee, consistin' of I, an' Crim, an' Henshaw is the judges, an' Johnny Atline is the starter." Wilcox paused and allowed his eyes to rest on the sullen face of Dalzene. "All passin' on the trail must be done on the haw side. Any interferin' whatever with another team will be a foul, the driver or team doin' the interferin' is throw'd out. Onnecessary crowdin' hittin', or hittin' at, another team with the whip, throwin' anything, or any other ways interferin' with the runnin' of a team is a foul. The trail's plenty wide fer passin' except in one or two stretches, an' if any team piles up on one of them places, he's got to haul out, an' let the other teams pass."

"Who's goin' to prove this here interferin'?" growled Dalzene. "S'pose this here Gordon says I interfered, an' claims a foul, it'll be his word agin mine."

"In such case," replied Wilcox, looking his questioner squarely in the eye. "It will be up to the judges which one to believe. We know you both, an' in decidin' we'll naturally take the one's word that's got the best reputation. Git set, now. Atline, he'll count three, an' then fire his revolver, an' at the crack of the gun you're off!"

Lou Gordon took her place beside the sled upon which her father was seated. "Be careful of the whip, dad," she whispered, nervously. "I'll start them, and I'll be here at the finish."

Dalzene caught the last words. "Hold on, there!" he roared, "What business has that woman got startin' them dogs? Git her out of there! If she's goin' to drive that team, she's got to go the hull distance."

"Shut up, Dalzene!" called Wilcox. "Her givin' the word to the dogs on the start ain't drivin' 'em. You got a right to have a dozen yellin' at yourn on the start if you want to."

Dalzene subsided, and Atline took his position: "Ready! One. Two. Three." Bang! At the report of the gun Lou Gordon's voice rang clear. "Mush! Skookum, Mush-u! Mush!" Instantly the ten big dogs started, and before the words had fairly left the girl's lips, they shot away over the ice, gaining speed at every jump, so that as the teams blurred and were swallowed up in the gloom of the Arctic day, the big ten team was well in the lead.

"First distance race I ever seen that took a ridin' start," opined Crim, "The trail's awful fast. They ort to make good time."

"They will make good time," declared Lou Gordon, "If dad will only sit tight and forget his whip."

"That's some dog—that leader, Miss Lou," ventured Atline. "I don't suppose you'd sell him?"

"What, sell Skookum! No sir! There isn't dust enough on the Koyukuk to buy Skookum. No dog in that team is for sale. But, that reminds me, Pete Enright said you wanted to buy a couple of dogs. The six that he is driving are for sale."

"No, mom, they ain't," grinned Atline. "Enright he said how you was holdin' 'em at a hundred apiece. It's a pretty stiff price fer dogs when they ain't no stampede on, but we know your dogs is worth more'n the common run, so I bought two, an' Joe McCorkill, took two, an' the mail carrier took two. The dust's waitin' fer you in Crim's safe. Here comes Enright, now."

"Come on, Enright!" yelled a man in the crowd, which having witnessed the start, was already dispersing and straggling back into the camp. Others took up the cry, and standing upon his sled whirling his whip high above his head, Enright dashed cross the finish line amid a chorus of good-natured banter:

"Hooray fer Enright!"

"Five minutes an' two seconds! That's the world's record fer fifty miles!"

"Enright wins a can of corn!"

"Wait till I thrash my bananas, an' I'll hang a wreath of 'em around yer neck!"

"Watermelons would look better!"

"Much obliged, gents!" laughed Enright, "But, what's more to the p'int, while these here decorations is bein' got ready, let's go up to the Aurora Borealis an' I'll buy a drink!"

"That sounds reasonable!" agreed Rim Rock, "an' then we kin go ahead with the wrastlin' match an' the fist fight."

"Boxin' exhibition, you rough neck!" corrected Wilcox.

"Why sure," seconded Enright, "The idee of callin' it a fist fight! Rim Rock, you bloodthirsty devil, you ain't fit to be heard talk in p'lite society! This here is goin' to be a strictly scientific sparrin' match—bare fisted, with gougin', bitin', an kickin' not barred, an' pulled off all in one round of an hour and ten minutes, unless a knockout is secured in the meantime. Come on you malamutes! The dance hall for us till time fer the finish of this race!"

Hailing the three men who had bought the six dogs, Enright turned them over. "Here you all, divide up yer dogs. We sure had Dalzene fooled good an' proper with 'em. They're good dogs, too, but they wasn't no use runnin' 'em over the trail agin them other teams, so when they got out of sight, I hauled out."

On the walk back to camp, Enright fell in beside Lou Gordon: "Well, Miss Lou, the last I seen of 'em yer pa was leadin' by about a good pistol shot, an' goin' strong. I believe he's a-goin' to win this race."

"If he can keep well ahead so he won't think he has to use his whip he will probably make it almost as fast as I could. The dogs are a little bit used to having him drive them. But, if Dalzene should overtake him and try to pass, I'm afraid something will happen. Dad will get excited and the first thing he will do will be to use the whip, and then the whole team will go to pieces."

"Yes, but if that dirty hound of a Dalzene fouls him, we win anyhow."

"I almost wish I hadn't told dad to rest them at the turn. That may give Dalzene a chance to pass, and I'm afraid dad never could regain the lead without mixing up."

"He'll be so fer ahead at the turn that he kin rest 'em fer an hour an' still keep the lead," opined Enright. "Anyways, I'm satisfied my money's on the right team. An' now about these here wrastlin' an' boxin' stunts. Do you want to see 'em? If you do, I'll see that you git a good seat."

"No, thank you. I'll visit with Mrs. Crim until the ski and snowshoe races, and the tug of war come off."

"All right, Miss Lou, an' don't worry about that race. I really believe we're a-goin' to win. An' if we do, she's worth about nineteen hundred dollars to you."

"Nineteen hundred dollars!" cried the girl, stopping and peering into the man's face in wide-eyed surprise. "Nineteen hundred dollars! What do you mean?"

"Why, don't you remember I told you that in case we win the boys thought that it wouldn't be more than fair to add ten percent of their winnin's to the prize? Well, Dalzene's got fifteen thousan' bet on this race. An' ten percent of that is fifteen hundred, an' the race stakes is four hundred, an' that makes nineteen hundred."

"Nineteen hundred dollars," breathed the girl, as they walked on through the gloom, "That's a lot of money."

"Yes, Miss Lou, it's quite a heft of dust fer a girl to clean up. But it ain't nothin' to what you could make if your dogs win this race—an' I ain't so sure I wouldn't try it if I was you, even if you don't win."

"Try what? What do you mean?"

"I mean the Alaska Sweepstakes. Take them dogs over to Nome in the spring an' run 'em agin' some real dogs. An' if they win today they'll be plenty of Koyukuk dust over there to back 'em. They don't know nothin' about your dogs over there, so the odds ort to be right promisin'."

"Oh, do you think I could—really? I—win the Alaska Sweepstakes!"

They had reached the door of the Aurora Borealis through which the men were already crowding. "Well, Miss Lou, I ain't sayin', of course, that you could win. But, I will guarantee that them dogs of yourn will give anything they've got over there a run fer their money." And, as Enright turned to enter the door, Lou Gordon proceeded on toward the trading store, with her brain in a whirl.

CHAPTER XIV
THE FINISH

AT THREE-THIRTY IN THE afternoon, with the other events of the celebration out of the way, all Nolan once more collected upon the river. Great bonfires of spruce tops and loppings were built upon the ice behind the finish line. For a half-mile or more up river, the first and the last half-mile of the race trail, the ice was bare of snow, or rather, the snow had become incorporated into the ice by reason of a great overflow which had taken place several days before. It was an ideal stretch for the finish, broad as the river itself, and with a surface smooth, but not the glassy smoothness of glare ice.

It was a scene not soon to be forgotten. The Arctic darkness of the middle of the afternoon dispersed by the yellow-red glare of the flames that crackled and roared as they leaped high above the heaps of dry spruce, which sent showers of red sparks skyward with each addition of fuel. The tense, excited faces of the men and women grouped about the fires. The quick, nervous laughter. The curious blending of hoarse voices. The continuous short journeyings to the outer rim of the firelight, and the intent peering up river toward a spot a mile and a half away where the stream narrowed between two cut-banks. For it was from that point that the first tidings of the race would be flashed. A man had been stationed on top of each cut bank, each with a heap of dry wood waiting for a touch of the match to make it spring into flame. Should Gordon be first to sweep through the cut only one fire would be lighted. If Dalzene was leading two fires would blaze out simultaneously.

Lou Gordon did not mingle with the crowd about the fires. Out in front of the finish line, well without the circle of the firelight, she stood straining her eyes up river. Now and then, to overcome the chill, for the thermometer registered thirty below zero, she paced back and forth upon the ice, but always her eyes stabbed the outer darkness for the first glimmer of light that would tell of the race. Beside her, Enright, scarcely less vigilant, sought to relieve the tense strain that gripped the girl to the very soul. Inside those heavy mittens, the man knew that the girl's nails were biting into the flesh of her palms.

"Four o'clock, Miss Lou," he announced. "I didn't figger he'd make it as quick as you did. But he don't need to. Dalzene's best time was nine hours an' ten minutes. That's what he bragged on. It might be an hour or more yet, before they show up. You run along back to the fires an' mix with the folks a little. It'll do you good, I'll wait here an' beller out the news jist the second I git the first flash."

But the girl would have none of it, as with tight-pressed lips she answered with a shake of her head. Back and forth, back and forth she paced with quick, nervous strides, or standing motionless as a carved statue, sought vainly to pierce the outer dark.

"Half past four," announced Enright, "They'll be showin' up soon, now. Another half-hour an' we'll know."

But, in another half-hour they did not know. It was quarter past five, and still no flash from up river. The girl's tense excitement had communicated itself to the others. There was no murmur of hoarse voices now—and no laughter. The outer rim of firelight was crowded, and the deserted fires, flared feebly with now and then a flash of brilliance as a spruce top fell into the embers. The sound of breathing could be heard, and the soft rasp of moccasins and mukluks upon the ice.

Suddenly there was a sound, a quick swishing sound that was a sharp in-gasping of breath.

"*Look!*" The voice of a dance hall girl cut shrill and thin with excitement. Men and women stood frozen in their tracks, as far away in the depths of the blackness a tiny flare of light appeared. Seconds passed—tense fraught seconds—seconds of silence, absolute, profound, as hundreds of eyes focused upon that single ever increasing flare of flame.

"*One fire! It's Gordon!*" With a bellow the voice of Enright shattered the unnatural silence. Instantly, a pandemonium of sound blared forth. Men seemed to go crazy. Caps and mittens flew into the air. Men grabbed dancing girls and whirled them over the ice in a mad waltz. Others locked arms and jumped foolishly up and down, howling like beasts. In the pandemonium the voices of the judges were drowned as they charged frantically up and down trying to drive the crowd behind the line.

"Go back! Git back! Dammit, you're in front of the line!" Gradually other men helped, and within a few minutes the crowd was being forced slowly back, howling and dancing like demons.

Then, suddenly came a great calm. Once more every eye was staring into the dark. Where only a moment before a single fire had burned, two fires now flared.

"God!" cried a man hoarsely, close to Lou Gordon's side, "Two fires! Dalzene!"

A low murmur, sullen, growling, swept the crowd. The excitement was gone. Slowly, muttering, they receded toward the dying fires.

"What—what does it mean?" faltered Lou Gordon, who paused at the line to stare at the two distant fires.

"I'm 'fraid it means, Miss Lou, that Dalzene's leadin'. But the race ain't over yet."

"But—the signal!" cried the girl, in a voice that faltered and broke. "Surely—it—was—one—fire. And now—two."

"I s'pose one of 'em had trouble lightin' his fire, an' the other one got the start," explained Enright. "We'd ort to be seein' the dogs presently."

Together they stood and strained to catch the first dim blur of motion. Behind them the crowd hugging the fires, seemed suddenly to have lost all interest in the race.

Lou sprang forward: "Look! Look! I can see them! It's—it's Dalzene! But—Oh, look! Look! Dad's right behind! Here they come!" With a wild cry that broke into a sob, the girl leaped forward. Behind her the crowd came to life as from an electric shock. As a man, they crowded the finish line, peering into the gloom.

Lou Gordon was running toward the oncoming dogs.

Voices roared from the crowd: "Come on, Gordon!"

"Whip 'em! Whip 'em!"

"Gordon!"

"Gordon!"

A shrill whistle cut the air. Enright leaped to the line where the judges already waited expectantly. "*Shut up!*" his voice bellowed like thunder, causing a momentary silence, during which the voice of Lou Gordon out on the ice could be heard:

"Hi, Skookum!" Again the shrill, peculiar whistle, followed by words of encouragement.

"Skookum! Skookum! Mush-u, Skookum! Hi, mush! Mush!"

Suddenly the girl turned and ran for the finish line. Hardly more than a hundred yards away Dalzene's dogs were running straight for the line. His voice could be heard howling at the dogs, and his arm rose and fell like a flail as he whipped.

A wild yell broke from the crowd which watched with bulging eyes. Gordon's dogs seemed suddenly to have sprung into being side by side with Dalzene's. Fifty yards, now! Again that shrill whistle. Gordon's arm rose and fell. There was a sudden swerve of the great leader as he seemed to spring at Dalzene's lead dog. Shrill and loud the whistle from the lips of the girl once more cut the air. The leader swerved again—away from Dalzene's team. A loud cry forced itself from a hundred throats. Gordon's light sled was on its side. His dogs were plunging neck and neck with Dalzene's!

"He's draggin'! He's holdin' on!"

"Hold on, Gordon!"

"Fer God's sake! Git out of the way!"

"Here they come!"

"Give 'em room!"

"Hold on!"

"Hooray! Gordon! Gordon! Gordon!" Once again the crowd went wild. "Plumb clean crazy wild," as Enright later described it. "Fer, By God, them dogs with eyes a-shinin', and a-glarin', an' their muscles fair bulgin' their hides, *drug* Old Man Gordon acrost the finish half a length ahead of Dalzene! Yessir drug him holdin' on to the handle bars, face down—a-ridin' on his whiskers!"

CHAPTER XV
"MINER'S MEETIN'"

FOR A GOOD HALF-HOUR following the spectacular finish of the dog race pandemonium reigned on the Koyukuk. Fresh fuel was heaped upon the red embers of the fires and in the light of the leaping flames the men and women of Nolan gave themselves over to a wild orgy of noise. Lou Gordon and her father were lifted bodily onto the shoulders of strong men and a leaping, dancing, howling procession was formed that wound in and out between the fires. Like a mad man Dalzene pranced about in a vain effort to make himself heard. The furious bellow of his hoarse voice but added to the general din, and those who noticed him at all paused in their jubilation to thumb their noses with yells of derision.

It was not until the men of Nolan, crowding the bar of the Aurora Borealis, waited for Wilcox to open his safe that the man was able to make himself heard. His red face distorted with rage, he clawed his way to the bar upon which he pounded with mittened fist. His cap pushed back so that its ear flaps, their strings a-dangle, stuck straight out from the sides of his head, showed a forehead glistening with sweat, bisected by a thick blue vein that stood out in the acetylene glare with startling distinctness. As Wilcox swung wide the door of his safe and rose to his feet, Dalzene faced him with blazing eyes: "Pay them bets, an' pay 'em to me!" he roared, and disregarding the mighty chorus of jibes and jeers that rose on all sides, he continued, "Damn you, you can't frame me! I win that race, an' I drag down all bets!"

A slow irritating grin greeted the announcement. "Oh, you win it did you? Now, that's curious. My eyesight ain't so bad, an' it looked to me like it was Gordon's dogs that romped over the line first. But, mebbe I was wrong. The other two judges is here. We didn't take no formal vote on it yet, so we might as well do it now. Hey Crim, who win that race?"

"Gordon win it!" answered Crim.

"Henshaw, who win that race?"

"Gordon did."

"It's a damn lie!" roared Dalzene.

"We'll talk about that, later," answered Wilcox in a voice of ominous quiet, "But, in the mean time, the vote of the judges is unanimous that Gordon win the race, *an'* the bets will be paid accordin'."

"He fouled me, an' besides, he never brung in all he started with."

"Seems to me I seen ten dogs, an' a sled, an' him hangin' on to it like all hell couldn't jerk him loose, when the outfit crossed the line ahead of yourn."

"How about his whip that he lost when his sled tipped over?" there was an exultant gleam in the narrowed eyes.

"The whip don't cut no figger," informed Wilcox, "I stated it plain that sled, dogs, an' driver had to cross the finish line, an' they did. An' as fer the foul, when do you claim he fouled you?"

"Right there on the smooth ice! That damn big leader of his'n made a dive fer mine an' throwed him out of his stride!"

Wilcox laughed: "You'd ort to picked out a play that we didn't all see to claim a foul on, Dalzene. Gordon's leader wasn't within fifteen foot of yourn at no time, an' what's more your leader never went out of his stride, neither." Reaching into the safe Wilcox withdrew a packet.

"Pete Enright!" he called, loudly, "This belongs to you. It's the last bet you made. Here's yer five hundred in dust, an' yer twenty-five hundred in bills."

"Don't you pay that bet!" screamed Dalzene, furiously pounding the bar, "You can't rob me! Fifteen thousan' dollars of good money gone to hell! You can't rob me!"

Clem Wilcox was a small man, in physical estimate, but what he lacked in weight he more than made up in nerve and agility. Hardly were the words out of Dalzene's mouth before Wilcox had hurdled the bar and as his two feet struck the floor his fist landed with a vicious twist on the point of Dalzene's chin. Again Wilcox struck, and again, and clawing feebly at the bar, Dalzene sank slowly to the floor.

"You've called me a liar an' a robber," said Wilcox, quietly, to the man that lay on his back blinking foolishly into his face, "You've got my personal answer to that. But likewise you've insulted the whole Koyukuk—an' now you'll git yer answer to that." He faced the men who crowded about him. "I'd say, boys, the case calls fer a meetin'."

"A meetin's right!"

"A meetin'!"

"Miner's meetin'! I nominate Wilcox fer chairman!"

Wilcox shook his head, and held up his hand for silence: "Not me, boys. We don't want it said they was anything personal in it. I nominate Pete Enright. All in favor signify."

A chorus of affirmation greeted the words, and before it had subsided Dalzene scrambled groggily to his feet and leaned against the bar for support. "Hold on! Hold on, boys! Don't call no meetin'! You got me wrong! I—"

"Meetin's called!" announced Enright, "Shut up!" Seating himself legs a-dangle, upon the end of the bar, Enright motioned for Dalzene to be brought before him. The man's face was livid as he was ungently jerked into a position facing Enright. He groped for words: "You got me wrong—"

"Shut up," again commanded Enright, "You'll git a chanct to do yer lyin' later." He glanced over the faces crowded about him. "Boys," he began, "Is they anyone kin show cause why this here party name of Jake Dalzene ain't a low down, whifflin' skunk of a rot-gut peddler that ain't wanted on the Koyukuk?" Enright paused and let his glance travel slowly over the silent faces.

"All them in favor of turnin' him loose an' allowin' him to stay amongst us an' come an' go as he likes, is called on to signify." Again he paused, and no word being ventured in Dalzene's behalf, continued, "All right, boys, this bein' a lawful an' duly organized miner's meetin' for dispensin' with justice, we'll hear a few suggestions. Gents, what's yer pleasure?"

"Git a rope!"

"Send him on the Long Traverse!"

"Hang the son of a bitch!"

"If we had some tar we could tar an' feather him, if we had some feathers!"

"Send him back to Rampart where he come from—"

"—with his hands tied behind his back, like they done on the Chilcoot!"

"You tell us, Enright!"

"That's right! What you say goes!"

"Put it to a vote!"

Enright eyed in disgust the white faced man who cringed before him. "Dalzene," he said, "You've heard the suggestions, an' you've got to admit that to any right minded man they're all fit an' proper. The sense an' the will of this meetin' seems to be plain that here in Nolan we'd ruther have yer room than yer company. Facts is, Dalzene, yer about as pop'lar on the Koyukuk as a litter of fleas in a bedroll. Now, they's several ways of exterminatin' a man from where he ain't wanted. Some is more thorough than others. One of the most convincin' is a rope applied vertical from the man's neck to a rafter." Enright paused, Dalzene's eyes seemed about to pop from their sockets, and he continuously wet his lips with his tongue. "But, us Koyukukers ain't no ways a bloodthirsty race. They's some of us would ruther let a man live than kill him. We aim to do the right thing by you. We ain't hard men, but we're purposeful." He turned abruptly toward the crowd: "Boys, what I suggest is that we let this bird go back down to Rampart where he come from. He ain't no ways fittin' to live amongst white men, nohow—nor Siwashes neither, for that matter—but that's their hard luck. All them in favor of this, signify, an' I'll pass sentence."

A chorus of "Ayes" ratified the suggestion, with here and there a word of dissent by those who favored more drastic measures. But the dissenters were in the minority, and Enright silenced them.

"All right, boys, she's carried."

"And now, Dalzene, you listen to me, an' if yer judgment's good you'll act accordin'. Yer dogs bein' tired, you'll be give twelve hours to leave Nolan, an' leave it fer good. It's six-thirty now. By six-thirty tomorrow mornin' you'll be mushin' down the river. An' you'll keep on mushin' till yer plumb off the Koyukuk. An' you ain't never to show yer face on the river, nor no part of it, nor no river nor crick that runs into it, from now on. Yer outlawed on the Koyukuk. From six-thirty tomorrow mornin' it's open season fer you the year around. An' any man ketchin' you on the Koyukuk from then on, an' don't kill you on sight, is shirkin' his public duty, an' a traitor to the Territory of Alaska. You ain't the kind of man that's wanted on this river. News of the rulin' of this here meetin' will go down river clean to the Yukon with the mail carrier, an' they ain't a man on the Koyukuk but what will abide by it. If you've got anything to say, say it now."

Dalzene had recovered his nerve to a great extent as the course of Enright's remarks drew away from the idea of the rope. For he knew the temper of miner's meetings, and well he knew that had Enright seen fit to have put the suggestion of hanging to a vote it would have carried as easily as the order to stay off the river had carried. And he also knew that having passed sentence the men would abide by their decision, and that, for the present, he was in no danger of physical violence. So it was with an air of truculence that he addressed Enright: "Yer a hell of a bunch of sports, you be! Frame a man, an' bust him, an' then start him off on a six hundred mile trail without grub enough to git him half ways! You, Pete Enright, you've warned me off one of the best tradin' grounds I had, an' how do you expect me to make Rampart without grub nor dog feed?"

Enright grinned: "Well, Dalzene, it looks from here like you was the one to worry about that, not me. An' as fer knockin' you out of yer tradin' grounds, it's time us white men begun to give a little thought to the Siwashes. I was thinkin' mostly of them when I was passin' sentence."

"What damn business is it of yourn if I make an honest livin' off'n the Injuns?"

"Try it on the Koyukuk Injuns an' you'll have a long time in hell to figger that out fer yerself."

With a snarl, Dalzene turned to Crim, the trader: "Am I good fer a couple hundred pounds of grub an' dog feed?"

"If you got the dust to pay for it you are," answered Crim.

"I tell you I'm broke!" whined Dalzene.

Crim shrugged, and turned away.

"I suppose you'll stand me off fer a couple of drink's Wilcox, seein' we're in the same business."

"You kin guess agin, then, Dalzene," answered Wilcox, "An' don't make that mistake—about us bein' in the same business. I do mine legal, open an' above board with white men. I don't sneak through the brush tradin' rot-gut to Injuns fer ten times what it's worth, an' takin' the fur they need fer grub in pay fer it."

"I need a couple of drinks an' I'd buy 'em if I had more'n jest enough on me to pay Henshaw fer my tonight's lodgin'."

"Don't save it fer me," snapped Henshaw. "I ain't got no room. I'm full up."

"But, I got a room there, now. I've had it fer ten days. I paid you up this mornin', but I didn't give up the room!"

"It's give up all the same. A party from Noo Orleens reserved it. I'm expectin' him on the first train."

With an oath Dalzene drew a silver dollar from his pocket and slammed it onto the bar: "Give me a couple of drinks!" he growled.

Wilcox looked him squarely in the eye: "Yer money ain't no better here, Dalzene, than what yer credit is. They's party from Panama bought up all my stock. He'd ort to be waftin' in most any time, now."

In the room not a man laughed. For the space of seconds Dalzene stood staring straight in front of him. Then, slowly his eyes traveled over the faces of the men that crowded the room, but not one friendly glance met his. Nor did a single unfriendly one. Yet every eye in the room was upon him—hard, level stares that bored through, and beyond him, yet took no note of him. It was unnatural. Why didn't someone laugh at the preposterous excuses of Henshaw and Wilcox? It was suddenly as if he, Dalzene, had ceased to exist. He was alone. From the life of the camp—from the men of the camp, he was a thing apart. His credit was no good. Even his money was no good. A great wave of self-pity swept over him. His shoulders drooped, and clutching his dollar tightly in his hand he turned and slunk from the room.

The night air revived him somewhat, but even that could not stimulate his broken spirits to even a semblance of the mighty fury to which he was addicted. He was unutterably lonely, with the bitter loneliness of a man forsaken of his kind. In a sort of dull apathy he bent his steps toward the roadhouse, whose frosted panes showed a yellow square of light. Pushing through the door he stood blinking in the lamplight. A girl sat beside the stove reading. She glanced up, and with a start Dalzene recognized the woman who had that morning sat upon the sled with Gordon, and whose starting of the dog team he had protested. The morning of this same day—not quite twelve hours ago—and it seemed years. And twelve hours from now he would be alone upon the river, mushing southward—alone—alone. The man drew a deep breath. Maybe this girl would speak to him—would talk to him if only for a few minutes. She was reading again. After that first swift impersonal glance that held in it nothing of approval or of disapproval—even of recognition, her eyes had returned to the open page. Surely, this girl could know nothing of the miner's meeting, yet her glance had been the same impersonal glance of the men in the saloon after their vote had segregated him from his kind. Dalzene cleared his throat harshly, and endeavoring to inject an ingratiating note into his voice, spoke: "Good evenin', Miss, didn't I see you this mornin' down on the river?"

"You did," answered the girl, without raising her eyes from the book.

"Ain't you Old Man Gordon's darter?"

"I am."

"My name's Dalzene." The announcement apparently went unheard. "Where's yer pa? I didn't see him in the saloon."

"He's in bed. He hurt his knee at the finish of the race."

"Too bad. I hope it ain't hurt much."

"Not badly, I guess, just stiffened up."

"I don't bear yous no grudge fer winnin' the race." Dalzene paused, expecting a reply, but receiving none, he continued: "Do you know if he would sell that dog?"

"What dog?"

"That leader of his'n. Pretty fair lookin' dog. I might buy him."

"He's not for sale."

"I might go a hundred dollars."

"I get that for culls."

"*You* do! Be they your dogs?"

"Yes."

"Well, two hundred."

"He's not for sale."

"That's alright, but folks'll sell anything they got if the price is right. What do you hold him at?"

"I said he is not for sale. Do you understand? That dog is not for sale."

"How about one of them malamutes, then, er two of 'em."

"No dog in that team is for sale!" exclaimed the girl, for the first time raising her eyes to his. "And if I had a thousand dogs for sale and you were to offer me a thousand dollars apiece for them, I wouldn't sell you a single dog. Not after seeing the brutal way you handled your own dogs."

"Oh, come now, Miss. I know all about dogs. Anyone'll tell you that. It ain't no use gettin' sore at me." He stepped a little closer. "Mebbe—it might be such a thing, we could kind of work up a deal, an' go pardners. I make plenty money. Why, I lose fifteen thousan' on that dog race today, an' you don't hear me kickin', do you? What's fifteen thousan', when they's plenty more where that come from? What d'you say? What's on Myrtle? She's worked out an' dead. Throw in with me an' we'll go where we kin have some fun—down on the Yukon, or over to Nome, that's where the bright lights is." As the words poured from the man's lips he gained confidence. The ingratiating tone gave place to something of the gruff bluster that had become habitual with him. His eyes, quick to note the physical beauty of the girl, lighted as he talked, with a bestial gleam of lust. The girl's eyes had returned to her book. Dalzene waited for her to speak. She turned a page. "Well, what d'you say?" His voice had regained its accustomed rasp. "If yer a-goin' with me, we got to be mushin'. You think it over while I drag my pack out of my room. I'm hittin' the trail right now." The man disappeared abruptly through a door and a few moments later reappeared, dragging a bulging pack sack and a bed roll. Before the outer door he released his burden and straightened. "Goin'?" he rasped.

The girl's eyes were still upon the open page. It was as though she had not heard. Only for an instant the man stood silent, and in that instant a mighty rage surged up within him. He took one swift step forward and fixed her with blazing eyes: "Yer just like the others! Won't have nothin' to do with Jake Dalzene! Well, the time'll come when you will talk to him—an' talk pretty! Yer safe enough up here where yer friends is. But you ain't seen the last of me yet! You can't rob me out of no fifteen thousan' an' git away with it. Time'll come when you'll learn that Jake Dalzene don't never fergit!"

Without looking up, Lou Gordon turned another page, and muttering to himself, Dalzene jerked the outer door open and dragged his belongings onto the hard-packed snow.

Passing around to the rear of the roadhouse where his dogs were chained to their allotted kennels he paused suddenly. All about him the snow was lighted by the reflection of a brilliant wavering aurora, and as he looked the sacking over the door of one of the kennels was thrust aside, and Skookum stepped out onto the snow and walking to the end of his chain, eyed the motionless man in silence. Dalzene's eyes glittered as they took in the lines of the superb brute; the rangy legs, the long powerful body, and the mighty shoulders. Fascinated he stepped closer, staring into the yellow eyes that glowed like live coals. Cautiously his mittened hand reached out as if to caress the broad head, and instantly it was jerked back as the great silent brute crouched with bared teeth.

"Oh, that's it, is it? Damn you! You'd eat a man up if you onct got goin'. Well, I kin take that out of you!"

For a full minute the man stood eyeing the dog, while his brain worked rapidly. Then, swiftly he returned to the corner of the roadhouse and peered down the street. No one was in sight. From the direction of the saloon came the muffled tinkle of the dance hall piano. It would be late this night when the men of Nolan would seek their beds. They were celebrating his defeat—spending his money! Gordon was in bed with a stiffened knee. The girl was absorbed in her book. All Nolan was occupied in its own affairs. The dogs had long since been fed. No one would visit the kennels until morning—and by morning he could be far to the southward—even far off the Koyukuk—the Fort Hamlin short cut! He knew the trail, forgotten these several years. In the morning pursuit would be too late. The only team on the Koyukuk that would have any chance to overtake him would be demoralized for want of a leader—and, once on the Yukon—they would search for him at Rampart City—but, they wouldn't find him! To hell with Rampart! To hell with his squaw! He was going to haul out anyway pretty soon. That missionary from Fairbanks, damn him, was stirring up the authorities down to Fort Gibbon in regard to his hooch-running activities, but more especially in regard to the parentage of certain half-breed children who had been abandoned to the care of their mothers in the miserable cabins of the native village. The hooch-running they could hardly prove—he was wise enough for that—but the half-breed children, if the squaws who had received nothing but abuse at his hands, should talk, would be more awkward. He could hole up for a while in an abandoned cabin he knew on the head of Dall River, where he had a *cache* of grub and dog feed to last a month, and when the pursuit from Nolan had swept by down the Koyukuk and the Chandalar, he could cross the Koyukuk and hit straight for Nome.

Swiftly he harnessed his own dogs, and armed with a heavy blanket, the half of a dried fish, and a babiche line, he again approached Skookum who eyed his approach sullenly. Halting just beyond reach of the chain, Dalzene tossed the piece of fish onto the snow at Skookum's feet. And as the dog lowered his head to take it, Dalzene, the blanket outstretched in both hands leaped straight upon the dog, bearing him onto the snow by sheer weight. A low, muffled growl came from the folds of the tightly held blanket, as the great brute thrashed furiously to rid himself of the weight. But, Dalzene had handled bad dogs before, and using his body, his legs, and his arms, he was able to hold the struggling animal while his hands tightened the blanket about the mighty jaws. Then, deftly he released a hand and the next instant the slip knot in the end of the babiche line tightened about the dog's throat and three or four adroitly turned half hitches secured his blanket wrapped jaws. It was but the work of a few minutes to encompass the thrashing legs in the blanket, where coil after coil of the line held the great dog trussed like a roasted turkey, and the work of a few more minutes to lash him securely upon the loaded sled.

Fifteen minutes later Dalzene reached the river, pausing on the bank to shake his mittened fist toward the double square of light behind which he knew the men of the Koyukuk were making merry in the Aurora Borealis. A string of blasphemous curses that ceased only when the man's imagination had run the gamut of all things foul and vile, poured from his lips, and in his unreasoning fury, slashing at his dogs with his whip, he turned and headed down river alone under the aurora-shot Arctic sky.

CHAPTER XVI
OFF THE RIVER

BEFORE NOON THE FOLLOWING day all Nolan knew of the disappearance of Skookum. And all Nolan knew also, that the disappearance of the great lead dog had happened simultaneously with the disappearance of Dalzene. And Nolan was neither slow nor loath to establish the relationship between the two occurrences. With tears in her eyes, Lou Gordon told of her conversation with Dalzene, and of the man's angry threats before he departed. Whereupon another miner's meeting was hastily called in the Aurora Borealis, a substantial reward was posted for the return of the lead dog, and certain resolutions were adopted which had to do with a more permanent and conclusive disposition of Dalzene than warning him off the river.

Shortly after adjournment of the meeting two dog teams pulled out of Nolan and headed southward down the Koyukuk. The men camped that night in one of the deserted buildings of Coldfoot, and next morning Johnny Atline and Rim Rock swung off the river and headed eastward across the South Fork for the Chandalar in hope of overtaking the fugitive at Caro or Chandalar native village, while Pete Enright and the mail carrier kept on down the Koyukuk.

At the roadhouse, midway between Coldfoot and Bettles it was reported that Dalzene had stopped for breakfast the previous morning, but had pushed on down the river without resting. Inquiry revealed the fact that the man was driving seven dogs, and that, to the best of the roadhouse proprietor's knowledge, there had been no other dog riding on the sled. He was very sure that had there been another dog he would have noticed it. After informing the man of the pronouncements of the miner's meetings, the two pushed on.

"He's sure be'n makin' good time," opined the mail carrier, when they were once more upon the trail. "Them dogs of his'n'll know they be'n somewheres time he gits to where he's goin'."

Enright nodded, "An' if I was in his place," he answered "Twic't as fast as the best time I could make wouldn't be no more'n about half as fast as I'd want to be goin'. Mebbe he's figgerin' on restin' his dogs at Bettles."

"Kind of cur'us about him only havin' seven dogs. You don't s'pose that there Skookum dog could of got away hisself?"

"No," answered Enright, "He wouldn't never leave Miss Lou. Him an' her's like two pardners. He ain't never kep' on a chain or in a corral only except they're away from home. No, Dalzene's got him all right, but he ain't takin' no chances with him. He knows damn well that dog ain't a-goin' to let him handle him without a fight, an' he ain't in no shape to waste no time tryin' him out. He had him all right, prob'ly on his sled tied up an' covered with a tarp."

"Wisht they was some new snow so we could track him," ventured the mail carrier. "This trail's in better shape than I ever seen it, most."

"Yes, but we kin see if he leaves it. He's got to leave a trail if he branches off—an' where in hell would he branch to?" The mail carrier shook his head dubiously; "He's a pretty slick, an' he knows the country down this way better'n what we do. Git us off'n the river, an' we don't know nothin', but he's off'n it half the time tradin' hooch to the Siwashes."

"Slick don't give him no license to fly. He's got to leave a trail wherever he hits off the river."

Despite their anxiety to reach Bettles they camped that night on the trail, and it was nearly noon the following day when they drew up before the trading store to find that Dalzene had left the previous morning after having laid in some three hundred pounds of supplies on credit.

"You better figger on losin' that there bill of goods, then," grinned Enright, "But a sled load of grub ain't goin' to bust the Company, nohow."

"What do you mean, Pete? I don't like Dalzene no more'n you nor no one else does, but he makes big money, an' he's good."

"He may be good all right, but he's goin' to be a damn sight more good than what he is, soon as one of us up-river men runs acrost him."

"What do you mean?"

"I mean that we held miner's meetin' on him Chris'mus night an' warned him out of the Koyukuk country, an' next day we held another an' sort of widened the territory, you might say, to include the rest of the world."

"What's he be'n doin' up river?"

For answer Enright gave a brief, but comprehensive, survey of the situation to date, at the conclusion of which the trader picked up his book and opening it, drew a line around the list of Dalzene's supplies. Below the entry, and included within the line, he wrote "Lost in freightin'." Then, to Enright he said: "I'll pass the word to the boys, Peter. Chances is, you up-river fellows won't git no crack at him noways, 'count on him havin' to pass here to git there—if he ever comes back."

"Where you headin' now, Pete?"

"Rampart City."

"Alone?"

"Yeh, that is, I'll be alone after Fort Gibbon. Joe, here, he'll have to head north with the mail agin."

"You want to keep yer eyes open down to Rampart. Dalzene, he's the only white man livin' there now. 'Course them Yukon Injuns is plumb gentle an' cowardly, but keep an eye on 'em. Dalzene he's got too many wives amongst 'em fer to take no chances."

"Hell! They'd be glad to see him git what's comin' to him! I've heard tell how he abuses 'em. Treats 'em worse'n what he treats dogs, an' then kicks 'em out an' takes another one."

"Um-hum," grunted the trader, "But that don't give *you* no license to horn in on it. Wimmin is all alike—white er red."

Late that afternoon the mail carrier halted the dogs and he and Enright stooped to examine a trail that led off the river to the eastward following the snow-buried course of a small creek.

"Only five dogs an' a toboggan," said Enright, after an interval of careful scrutiny. "Some Siwash trapper, see his tracks. Dalzene had Yukon shoes. I seen 'em." The mail carrier agreed and the outfit moved on down the river, and as they swept out of sight around a bend, Dalzene arose from the snow behind his screen of scrub bushes on the rim of a high bluff and removing the cartridge from the chamber of his rifle returned to his camp in a spruce thicket, and prepared for a two days' rest.

And a much needed rest it was, for almost from the moment of pulling out of Nolan, the man had been forcing the trail. And it was owing solely to the splendid condition of his seven great malamutes, just in from the fifty mile race, that he had been able to keep ahead of, and even to gain on his pursuers.

Dalzene was no fool. Traveling in the night down the Koyukuk from Nolan, he had resisted the impulse to swing eastward at Coldfoot when by crossing the South Fork, and a high divide, he could have headed down through the wind-swept Chandalar Gap, and thus avoided being seen by any one for upwards of a hundred miles. He knew a better plan, and in the carrying out of this plan it was within his scheme of things to be seen at the roadhouse, and later at Bettles. For having ascertained that he had pulled southward from Bettles, his pursuers would take it for granted that he would follow the main trail to Fort Gibbon. And except for the remote possibility of their meeting someone on the trail, they would be unable to check up on his movements until the Yukon was reached, for the new mail trail to Fort Gibbon leaves the river and swings southward before the native village of Arctic City is reached.

At the roadhouse he had stopped to feed his dogs and eat breakfast, and had immediately pushed on, arriving at Bettles, forty miles down the river, late that night. In Bettles he hunted up one, Andrew, a worthless half-breed who had occasionally helped him to dispose of hooch among the Indians. Andrew's cabin was well on the edge of the camp, and there Dalzene spent the remainder of the night, and there he fed his dogs liberally, all except the unfortunate Skookum, who, still wound in the blanket, he carried into the cabin and deposited upon the floor without even so much as loosening a turn of the babiche line that had held him in his cramped position on the sled without food or water for nearly thirty hours.

It was Dalzene's intention to strike away from the river a few miles below Bettles, and hit for the cabin at the head of Dall River, but the thing that had been worrying him all the way was how to leave the river without leaving a trail for his pursuers to follow. This difficulty solved itself quite by accident, as he was devouring the meal Andrew prepared for him. Standing against the wall in a corner of the cabin was a toboggan. Now, the toboggan is rarely used on the Koyukuk, the river trails being without exception sled trails. Only those Indians whose hunting grounds lay in the soft snow country to the eastward of the river traveled with toboggans, and it was from one of these Indians that Andrew had got it in trade. The moment his eyes fell upon it, Dalzene knew that his problem was solved. He would pull out of Bettles in the morning with a sled, but he would leave the river with the toboggan, and instead of his own Yukon snowshoes, he would be wearing Andrew's Siwash shoes.

A trade was easily effected and early in the morning Andrew pulled out with Skookum on his toboggan, and with orders to wait some eight or ten miles down river until Dalzene came up with him. Dalzene lost no time in transferring his load to the toboggan, and when Andrew pulled back up river with the sled, the hooch-runner pulled two dogs out of his team and toggling them, threw them onto the sled for, although it was a serious tax on the strength of the remaining dogs, he would leave the sign of a five dog team, whereas his pursuers knew that he was driving seven. This accomplished he struck into the hills with the toboggan, after following the windings of the creek some three miles, swung into a spruce thicket and made camp.

That at least one dog outfit would start on his trail as soon as the men of Nolan discovered the loss of the girl's lead dog, Dalzene had no doubt, and he calculated with remarkable accuracy that the pursuers would not pass the point where his trail swung from the river before noon of the following day. Therefore he went about the preparation of his camp deliberately. He even pitched his small A tent, cut boughs for a bed, and set up his stove. Come what may, he knew that this camp must be of several days' duration. His dogs needed a thorough rest, for no man could afford to take chances in the wind-swept, almost treeless stretch of country between the South Fork of the Koyukuk and the head of Dall River, with played-out dogs.

Having fed his team, Dalzene turned his attention to Skookum, and after locating the dog's collar ring with his fingers, he carefully worked back the edge of the blanket and snapped on a strong chain. This done, he dragged the dog to a nearby tree to which he affixed the chain and unwound the babiche line. The moment the last turn of the line loosened, the great dog struggled to his feet, threw off the blanket and with a low growl of fury tried to leap at Dalzene's throat. But weak from hunger and thirst, and with the muscles of his legs cramped and stiffened and lamed by upwards of forty hours in the tightly bound blanket, his effort was but a pitiful lunge that landed him head foremost in the snow at the man's feet. For Dalzene had taken no chances, and stood just beyond reach of the chain.

The man laughed aloud as the dog staggered to his feet and with lowered tail, wolfed down great mouthfuls of snow. Walking to the tent, he picked up a dried fish and securing a stout club, again approached the dog which ceased eating snow to glare at him with his smouldering amber eyes, and emit low, menacing growls. Marking well the limit of the chain, Dalzene held out the fish. He noticed that the dog's nostrils quivered as the scent of the food reached him, but instead of taking it from the outstretched hand, Skookum leaped again, straight at the man's face. Dalzene's right arm swung and with a vicious crack, the inch-thick club of green wood met the dog's skull in mid-air. Skookum collapsed in the snow, lay still for a moment, and dizzily regaining his feet, stood swaying weakly.

"You will, will you?" sneered the man, "You damned devil, you! I'll tame you! When I git through with you you'll know who's boss! I'll tame you, or By God, I'll kill you!"

Once more he tendered the fish, but the dog made no move to take it, his half-closed, smouldering eyes glaring at his tormenter sullenly. After a few moments of fruitless trying, Dalzene gave it up for the time being. "If you wasn't so damn valuable I'd let you starve before I'd give you anything to eat without you took it out of my hand," he grumbled, "But I don't dast to take a chanst of losin' you; I need you in my business. It's me fer Nome, an' if I kin pick up a couple more good dogs, with you fer a leader, I'll git in on them Alaska Sweepstakes. Here's yer fish, but mind you it's the last one you git, without you take it out of my hand." He tossed the fish at the dog's feet, but the yellow eyes never lowered their gaze, and with an oath, Dalzene stuck the club into the snow, and returning to the tent wrapped himself in his blankets and slept.

So utterly body weary was he that it was nearly noon next day before he awoke and lighted the fire in his stove. Tossing a fish apiece to the dogs, he took another and advancing upon Skookum, pulled the club from the snow and approached to the end of the chain. Only for an instant did the yellow eyes rest upon the club, then their gaze centered on the face of the man. Dalzene stretched out his hand, and mincingly grudgingly, with back hair a-quiver with hate, the great dog came forward and took the proffered fish. Dalzene laughed: "Learn some sense did you? Oh, I've handled mean dogs before. You better not try any monkey business with me, or I'll cave in yer ribs." Returning to the tent, the man bolted a hasty meal, and picking up his rifle, threw a cartridge into the chamber, fastened on his snowshoes, and started for the river.

Now, the last thing in the world Dalzene wanted to do was to kill a man. Yet, he well knew that unless his dogs got a good rest they would never make Dall River through the deep snow. And he knew, also, that should the pursuers swing onto the toboggan trail that left the river, and come upon him in his camp, they would without the slightest hesitation make short shrift of him. "It's them 'er me if they take my trail, no matter which way you look at it," he muttered. "An' if they ain't more'n four or five of 'em it's goin' to be them."

A half-hour's tramp brought him to the rim of a high bluff which he followed to a point that gave an uninterrupted view of the Bettles trail, of the point of departure of his own toboggan trail, and of the narrow creek valley that the toboggan trail traversed. Concealing himself behind a screen of scrub bushes, the man noted with satisfaction that anyone traversing the valley must pass within easy range of his rifle, with absolutely no chance to seek cover, or to scale the bluff and come to close quarters. "An' they can't work no sled up through that deep snow, neither," he grinned. "If they tackle that trail it'll be back-packin'—an' they won't git far. The way things lays, I'm good fer a dozen of 'em. But—at that—I don't want to have to do it. Someone would git me—some time—an' when they did—" his voice trailed into silence, and he shuddered.

The sky was cloudless, and far to the southward, from his vantage point, he could see the red disk of the sun, visible for a few minutes above the horizon. He watched it till it disappeared. "Hell of a country, this here, north of the circle," he growled, "Daylight all summer, an' night all winter. Nome's better'n what this is, anyway. I'll lay up in the cabin fer a couple weeks, an' then I'll hit fer the Kobuk, an' on to Nome. I got plenty grub an' dog feed to last." For some minutes after the sun went down the man scrutinized the up-river trail. He shivered. "Gittin' colder," he muttered, "Damn 'em! They chased me off the river, an' now the strong cold's comin' on, an' me in the

God fersakenest strip of country they is anywheres. I bet she's fifty below down there on the river, right now." He rose to his feet and took a turn up and down the snow, taking care to keep well back from the rim of the bluff. This performance he repeated at intervals, pausing behind his screen to peer into the deepening twilight of the up-river trail. After a couple of hours his vigil was rewarded. A dark spot appeared on the snow, and concentrating his gaze the man saw that the spot was moving. It was a dog outfit coming down the trail. Grasping his rifle, Dalzene threw himself upon his belly and peered over the edge. He made out two men and a dog team. At the parting of the trails they stopped to examine the fresh toboggan track. After some moments they walked back to the sled. They were—yes—they were moving on down the river. Breathing an oath of relief as they passed out of sight around a bend, the man rose to his feet, threw the cartridge from the chamber of his rifle, and walked back to camp.

That evening he tossed Skookum a ball of rice and tallow, and next morning he proffered another fish which the great dog took from his hand in the sullen manner of the previous day with his eyes on the inch-thick club.

Despite the fact of the strong cold, Dalzene decided to attempt the twenty mile stretch of treeless waste that lay between him and the South Fork of the Koyukuk which must be crossed in order to reach the head of Dall River. "I'll rest easier when I'm a little further off the Koyukuk," he grumbled, "There's timber where the Jim River runs into the South Fork, an' I kin rest up fer the forty mile pull to the cabin."

What to do with Skookum was a problem. He hated to add the dog's weight to his load in the deep snow, and yet he knew that the great brute was not sufficiently cowed to allow him to harness him into the team. "Guess I've got to tackle it. Might's well git it over with now as any time. My own leader'll foller along." In the tent, he made a muzzle out of babiche. It was a cruel muzzle, known as a "persuader," or twitch, and used only by the more brutal of the dog-mushers of the North. It consisted of two loops about the jaws, one a fixed loop, held in place by lines running to the collar, and the other a running loop at the end of a long twitch line playing through a small fixed loop, or eyelet in one of the lines to the collar. Thus a jerk on the twitch line in the hand of the driver would cause the running loop to bite cruelly into the dog's jaws. The refined deviltry of the twitch consists in administering the jerk at a moment when the laboring animal's sweat-dripping tongue lolls from between his teeth. And Dalzene was a past master in the refinement of cruelty, as witness the devilish cunning with which he affixed the muzzle. Approaching close to the end of the chain he tossed a running noose about the dog's neck and by main force dragged the struggling, choking brute in a circle that narrowed as the chain wound about the tree. With the dog's body hard against the tree a few tightly drawn turns of the babiche line held the animal helpless until the muzzle was in place. Cutting the noose, he released the babiche line, and unwound the chain by dragging the dog around the tree by the twitch. After which he picked up his club and approached the muzzled Skookum, who when he saw the man was well within reach of the chain, launched himself at his face. The thick club descended with a muffled thud along the dog's ribs. A single whimper of pain escaped him as he fell into the snow to be viciously jerked to his feet by the twitch. Eyes glaring, Skookum crouched at the end of the twitch line and Dalzene laughed as a drop of blood from the dog's mouth reddened the snow. "Guess that'll learn you they ain't no pretty faced gal a-handlin' you now! I've got you an'—I'll git her, too! Some of these fine times I'll be slippin' back to Myrtle Crick. They's only her an' the old man left over there—an' with Coldfoot dead, it's a hell of a ways from the neighbors."

It took a good half-hour and much clubbing to get Skookum into the lead dog's harness, but at last it was accomplished, and with the outfit ready for the trail, Dalzene took his place beside the leader, club in one hand, twitch line in the other, and gave the command to mush. Skookum made no move to obey, and the club fell upon his back. Instantly he whirled and hurled himself upon the team, vainly trying to sink his fangs into their thick coats. But the muzzle rendered him harmless, and a moment later, with the harness in hopeless tangle, the dogs piled onto the new leader, ripping and tearing at their helpless victim. Dropping the twitch line, Dalzene sprang among them, raining blows and furious curses as he beat them to the ground. When some semblance of order was restored, he released the dogs and set himself to the task of untangling the harness. As he removed the lead harness he kicked the bleeding Skookum to his feet.

"You will, will you? I'd ort to let 'em et you up! But I didn't resk stealin' you fer nothin'. I need you, or I'd kill you, an' kill you slow, with a club. I ain't got time now to work you in the lead, but you wait till we git to Dall River! I'll tame you! An' you'll work till you git there, too! I won't haul you, an' I don't dast to turn you loose, so you'll work behind, an' Mick, kin run loose.

"Mush on, there!" cried the infuriated man, when he finally succeeded in stringing the team out. And with their own leader in his accustomed place, the dogs pulled. Sore and bleeding, Skookum moved along with the rest, his head hanging and his plume held low. And so the traverse of the desolate barren to the South Fork was accomplished, Dalzene breaking trail and urging on his dogs with whip and voice. It took thirteen hours for the twenty miles, but as he crawled between his blankets that night the man breathed easier.

The forty miles to the head of Dall River was made in two days, after one day of rest. Skookum traveled between the traces and gave very little of his strength to the pull, a fact that brought him much abuse by whip and twitch, whenever Dalzene could spare time from trail breaking.

On reaching the head waters of Dall River, the man ensconced himself in the cabin. Skookum, his muzzle removed, was left on the end of his chain, tethered to a tree, where each day for a week, Dalzene took fiendish delight in provoking an attack and then knocking the great dog down with his club. The procedure never varied. Each morning Skookum took a fish from the hand that Dalzene extended to the extreme limit of the chain, and always his yellow eyes were fixed on the club the man held in his right hand. Later in the day Dalzene would approach with the hated muzzle in his left hand instead of the fish, and then it was that the yellow eyes would blaze, the hair bristle along the dog's back, and the low growl rumble continuously from the mighty throat. "I'll tame you, damn you! One of these days yer goin' to stand while I muzzle you without windin' you up, an' I'll keep on knockin' you down till I do!" The man would approach to just within the limit of the chain, the dog, lips drawn back to expose the gleaming white fangs, would crouch in the snow, his yellow eyes blazing hate, and with muscles taut, would launch his eighty-five pounds straight at the man's face. A quick backward spring, and the heavy club would crash against the great body in mid-air, and Skookum would fall in the snow to stagger to his feet and glare his abysmal hate.

At length came a day when the strong cold gave way before heavy clouds. The temperature rose to near zero, and early in the morning snow began to fall. Skookum took his fish as usual, and withdrew to the tree to eat it, and Dalzene stood for a moment and watched him.

"We'll be pullin' fer Nome, soon, you hellion! An' we might's well finish this thing one way er another, today. Yer goin' to work fer me—an' yer goin' to work in the lead! An' yer goin' to begin now!" For some moments the man studied the superb lines of the great dog. He had been wiser had he studied the chain, and still wiser had he noted that upon several occasions during the week of torture, before the body of the huge brute had fallen into the snow, it had described a half turn which had caused the chain to kink close against the collar. But of this Dalzene knew nothing and an hour later he approached through the driving snow storm, muzzle in one hand, club in the other. Instantly the great dog crouched. The yellow eyes glared, the throaty growl rumbled savagely and beneath his body the mighty muscles of his legs tensed. With outstretched hand the man drew just within the limit of the chain, his fingers tightening upon the club. It was the first warm day, and he had thrown off his heavy mittens. Like a flash the great dog hurtled out of the snow straight for his face. He leaped backward, club arm raised to strike at the instant the chain checked the dog in mid-air. A shriek of mortal terror froze on Dalzene's lips as the chain parted. Instinctively the hand that held the muzzle was thrown up to guard his face, and in that instant the hand was seized in a grip of iron, as he was hurled backward into the snow. A single agonizing flash of pain shot to the man's shoulder as the gleaming fangs ripped through the flesh to the bone. The next moment he realized that the hand was free, and that the great dog had disappeared in the storm.

Struggling to his feet, Dalzene rushed for his rifle, but by the time he reached the cabin, Skookum had vanished, and staring into the void of whirling snow, the man burst into an insane tirade of shrill curses. The dripping of warm blood from his finger tips gave him pause, and he gazed in horror at his mangled hand. Then stepping into the cabin, he proceeded to bandage it as best he could with strips torn from an extra shirt.

That night he could not sleep for pain, and next morning, with much difficulty, he harnessed his dogs, and headed southward down Dall River. "Might's well hit fer the Yukon," he muttered savagely. "They won't have nothin' on me down there, now that I ain't got the dog. An' there's an army doctor at Fort Gibbon."

CHAPTER XVII
SKOOKUM!

BACK AT NOLAN THE men of the Koyukuk had a hard time to dissuade Lou Gordon from accompanying the men who took Dalzene's trail. Beside herself with grief and rage, the girl vowed she would trail the thief to the ends of the earth, and would shoot him if necessary to recover the great dog that was the pride of her heart. Better council prevailed, however, and she consented to let the men take the trail, with the proviso that in case they should return without the dog, or evidence that he was dead, she herself would strike straight for the Yukon and would never return until she had found Skookum.

It was with a heavy heart that two days later, she and her father, whose knee had recovered sufficiently to stand the trail, loaded their sled with provisions, and with the malamute, Kog, in the lead traces, headed back for Myrtle.

"Ye're a fine lass, my daughter, to be givin' the old man the half of ye're winnin's," said Gordon, when they were once more back in their own cabin on Myrtle, as he added the contents of a gold sack to his precious "b'iler" fund, "The way it is now, the dump won't have to show nothin' big to have enough to set that b'iler on the claim. An' then, lass, ye'll see! I'll show 'em! I'll begin takin' out the dust so fast I'll have 'em all back on Myrtle! Why, lass, it stands to reason now, don't it, that wi' cuttin' wood takin' more'n half the time fer wood thawin', if ye'd use a b'iler an' do ye're thawin' wi' steam—"

"Yes, yes, dad. I know. We've been all over the whole thing thousands of times before. But, oh, if Skookum were only here! I hope they catch that horrible Dalzene! I hope they kill him!"

"Tush, tush! Lass, who be ye to be pratin' of killin'! 'Vengeance is mine, saith the Lord.' 'Tis the word of the Gude Book, itself. Have patience, lass, an' I make no doubt, Enright an' Rim Rock, an' Johnny Atline will find ye're dog for ye. But, if they don't, ye can break in another leader."

"Another leader!" cried the girl, "Just as if leaders like Skookum grew on trees. I tell you there never was a leader like Skookum, and there never will be! Why, do you know what I was going to do? I was going to Nome and enter my team in the Alaska Sweepstakes this spring!"

"Nome! Ye were thinkin' of goin' to Nome! An' run the Alaska Sweepstakes! What talk is this? Why, lass, the teams that run the Sweepstakes is worth thousands of dollars. Some of them is owned by millionaires, an' what chance would ye're dogs have against the likes of them?"

"Just the same, I was going to try. My team is worth thousands of dollars, too. I could have won their Sweepstakes! But it's no use to think of it, now. With Skookum gone, they're no better than a lot of outfits. Skookum was the dog that made the whole team. With Skookum in the lead every dog in the team was worth three times as much as he is with any other leader. Why, dad, those dogs could just fly! I never let them do their best—even when I made the fifty miles in seven hours and forty minutes, I let them take their time. They were the best team in the world!"

Old Man Gordon smiled: "There, there, lass. Ye've worked wi' them dogs so much ye've got the one idea in ye're head. Ye should not let ye're thoughts run to one idea. Ye should take a broad view of things—"

"One idea!" cried the girl, "Why, dad, can't you see that you are the one who has let one idea creep in and absorb your whole life? You can't think or talk about anything but your old boiler."

"But that's different. It's a money makin' scheme—a business proposition."

"And, so is the Alaska Sweepstakes a business proposition! Don't you know that the prize for that race runs anywhere from three to ten thousand dollars? And not only that, but think of the money it would mean to me in the price of the puppies I could sell! Why, dad, if I could win that race, you could order your boiler without waiting to clean up your dump—could have it delivered at Bettles on the first steamboat this summer."

"Ye don't tell me! Are ye sure there's so much money put up on a dog race? An' if we'd win it, would ye let me have the thousand dollars I'm still lackin' fer the b'iler?"

"Why, of course I would, dad! But, it's no use to think about it, now. Skookum's gone. And without Skookum, we couldn't possibly win."

"Take heart, lass," encouraged the old man, "The boys'll find him. An' when is this big race comin' off?"

"In April, about the tenth or twelfth. But it's about six hundred miles to Nome. They've got to find Skookum and get back here by the middle of February. Because if we go I want to start by the eighteenth. I've figured it all out. If we start the eighteenth of February we can make Nome by the first of April, and that will give me time to take the dogs over the course and rest them up for the big race."

"But, lass, forty days for six hundred miles is allowin' a lot of time. We could make it in a month."

"Yes, we could make it. But I want to take it easy. If we allow forty days, we only have to average fifteen miles a day. That won't crowd the dogs nor wear them out. It will just keep them in fine condition."

"Do ye know the way? Is there any trail?"

"Yes, I know the way. Rim Rock came across last winter, and he drew me a map. You go down the river to Alakaket Mission, then up the Alatna to the Kobuk portage, then down the Kobuk to its mouth, then swing south across Hotham Inlet, down the Choris Peninsula, and across Eschscholtz Bay to Candle, then on down to Council, and then to Nome."

"But surely, there ain't enough travel that way to give us a trail!"

"Well, not exactly a trail, all the way," admitted the girl "but we can make it all right. Some of the Kobuks that were up at Nolan for the celebration came and went by way of the Alatna, so their trail will help even if it is snowed under. Then there is always some travel up and down the Kobuk. And after we reach Candle there is a good trail to Council and Nome."

The old man shook his head slowly: "I'm feared 'tis a hare-brained scheme, ye've got. But, the stakes are worth tryin' for, if ye believe ye've got a chance to win. What do the boys say? Have ye told 'em?"

"Yes indeed! It was Pete Enright that first suggested it, and I talked with several of the others, and they all say that my dogs have a chance, and a good chance to win. And if we go they want to send a lot of dust down to back my dogs. They say that the odds ought to be big against them because nobody off the Koyukuk has ever heard of them." She paused, the light faded from her eyes, and as she turned away, her voice trembled: "But—it's no use—without Skookum."

The old man comforted her as best he could with prophecies of the dog's early return, but long after she had gone to bed he heard her sobbing softly to herself.

As day after day passed with no word from the men who had taken Dalzene's trail, Lou Gordon's spirits sank lower and lower. Her hope of recovering Skookum diminished with each passing day and with it came the one big disappointment of her life. Ever since Pete Enright had suggested that she enter her dogs in the Alaska Sweepstakes, anticipation of the trip to Nome had filled her mind to the exclusion of everything else. Nome! The very name breathed enchantment. And, she herself, Lou Gordon, should actually see Nome! Nome, with its great stores, with its windows glittering with diamonds and wonderfully wrought jewelry. With its hotel that had running water and wonderful white bath tubs that would be filled with hot water by the simple turning of a faucet. With its big church and its wonderful organ. With its mines whose great dumps were piled higher than the top of the tallest tree, veritable mountains of pay dirt. And all these things that Rim Rock had seen and described to her, she should see for herself. Of course, she had always known that such things existed. In books and magazines they were depicted in the advertisements, and were mentioned casually in the stories as common appurtenances to the everyday life of that wonder land that was the "outside." But her world, far within the Arctic Circle—the world she lived and knew, was so far removed in her imagination from the world of the great "outside" that it had always seemed to her that the "outside" was a fanciful world of enchantment. True, most of the men she knew had seen these things at some time in their lives, had even accepted them as a part of their normal existence, had ridden in railway trains, and great steamboats, and even in automobiles, but that was before they had come into the Arctic.

Often she had wondered as she talked with these men why they had deliberately left all these things behind them and of their own choice had come into the land of the strong cold, the winter darkness, and the midnight summer sun. She knew that the answer was "gold." But what was there about gold that made it worth the sacrifice. The money of the "outside"—the money made of paper was just as good as gold—was much better than gold, for could not one carry many thousands of dollars' worth of it in a very small flat wallet? Why then did they want gold? And why was there no gold in the land that had everything else? For years she had pondered these things, had read, and had studied the books and the magazines, but the answer had never seemed quite clear. And, at last, she was to see Nome! Rim Rock had told her there was a railroad at Nome—not a very long railroad, he had admitted, but it was as wide as any railroad, and maybe she could ride on a train! She, who had never seen any camp bigger than Dawson! And had never expected to see any. That was the rosy dream she had dreamed—and now—it was gone! She would never see Nome. Not for her was the luxury of the smooth white bath tub with the warm water that poured in at the touch of her hand, not for her to ride on a railroad train, not for her eyes were the glitter of the diamonds and the jewelry in the windows. Oh, well—ice glittered, as brilliantly as diamonds, Rim Rock had said. And one could ride on a dog sled, and one could bathe in the empty petrol tins, and could warm the water on the stove. It did not really matter—only— At this point, despite herself, the tears would start from her eyes, and she would hurriedly brush them away and call herself a fool.

On the morning of the fifteenth day after the disappearance of Skookum, the girl stepped from the cabin with her bag of rice and tallow balls and walking to the dog corrals, began to toss the balls over the fence to the waiting dogs. Suddenly she heard a sound behind her, and the next instant two great paws reared high, she pitched forward into the snow, and the next moment was aware that a great tawny shape stood over her, and that a soft red tongue was gently caressing her cheek.

"Skookum! *Skookum!*" she cried, the word ending in an hysterical scream that brought Old Man Gordon wide-eyed from the creek bed with his ax gripped in his two hands. The next moment the girl was sobbing with her arms about the great dog's neck and her face buried in the thick hair of his shoulder.

"Is Enright here? Who brought him, lass?"

For answer the girl held up the four-inch length of chain that dangled from the collar: "He broke away!" she cried, "He couldn't hold him—couldn't keep him from me! And look! Look at the scars on his nose, and that split in his ear! He's had him muzzled, and then the other dogs fought him when he was helpless!"

"He's yanked him around wi' a twitch!" exclaimed the old man, indignantly, "I've seen Injuns do it."

"And he's starved him, too. See how thin he is. But he's all right! He's the same old Skookum, and it won't take long to get him into shape again. And, oh, dad, now we can go to Nome!"

Early in February, Lou Gordon made a flying trip to Nolan. There she found Rim Rock and Johnny Atline who were waiting for Enright to return, and break the news to the girl that the search had been fruitless. All Nolan crowded about her as she halted her dogs before the roadhouse, and all Nolan listened to the story of Skookum's return, and rejoiced in the girl's good fortune.

"And, now, we are going to Nome," she concluded, "and try for the Alaska Sweepstakes. We'll start on the eighteenth, and that will give us plenty of time to get there by the first of April."

"An' I want five hundred dollars' worth of the best odds you kin git me, that you'll win!" cried Atline, "I'll give you the dust soon as Clem weighs it out."

"Me, too," said Rim Rock, "But, say, Miss Lou, ain't they no way you kin figger to drive them dogs yerself?"

The girl laughed: "Yes, Rim Rock," she answered, "I will drive them myself. I don't know how I'll work it, but I'll manage it, somehow. Poor dad! He nearly lost us the other race, and I don't intend to take any chances with this one."

"Do you know how come Dalzene to pass him, Chris'mus?" asked Bill Britton.

"No, dad never said much about the race. I've asked him, and all he would say was that Dalzene passed him at the turn, and that he couldn't get Skookum to take the lead again."

"Well, you know, I was up to the turn to see that all teams went the hull route, an' yer dad came in and pulled up to rest his dogs. Said you made him promise to rest 'em fer ten minutes. Well, the ten minutes was up, an' the old man, he jumps onto the sled and yells at the dogs, an' cracks his whip right between the lead dog's ears, an' the next minute the team was all fightin' an' in the doggondest mixup you ever seen. It tuk us an hour to git 'em strung out and started agin, an' meanwhile Dalzene had passed an' gone."

"I knew it!" laughed the girl, "I knew that whip would get him into trouble. I tried to make him leave it behind, but he wouldn't listen to me. I broke those dogs, and I rarely use the whip."

"If you're goin' to drive the dogs, I'll take a thousand dollars' worth of what ever you kin git," broke in Wilcox. Other sacks were produced, and until nearly every man in the camp had expressed his eagerness to bet anywhere from three hundred to a thousand dollars on Lou Gordon's dogs.

"Guess they'll know us Koyukukers is willin' to back Koyukuk dogs!" exclaimed Wilcox, as he accompanied the men to the saloon to weigh out the dust.

"Too bad Enright ain't here," opined Atline, "He'd sure like to be in on this."

"I'm puttin' him in fer a thousand," said Wilcox, "He'd go that much, an' it ain't right he should git left out. But, say, this here ain't never goin' to do!" he cried, eyeing the sacks of dust that littered the bar, "Them folks has got a long trail ahead, an' if they've got to pack all this dust, they won't have no room fer grub an' dog feed." Producin' pencil and paper, he listed the bets and added the total. "Thirteen thousand, five hundred dollars! Let's see, that's more'n fifty pound of dust!"

"Use Dalzene's bills," suggested Atline, "He sure left enough of 'em around here. You must have a bunch of 'em, Clem, an' Crim's got some, an' we'll hit out an' locate the rest. They're jest as good an' a heap easier to pack."

"Now, you've got it!" cried Wilcox, "I paid off them bets an' I recollect that about nine or ten thousand of his money was paper. You all skittle around an' collect it together, an' we won't have to send down much dust."

"Lord!" grinned Atline, "If she wins that race, with the odds say at five- or ten-to-one agin her, she'll have to hire a elephant to pack the dust back."

"Elephants is sacred at Nome," reminded Rim Rock, "But they's banks there. She kin bring it back in paper."

"An' they'll be paper on the Koyukuk," grinned Atline, "For the next fifty years, where they never was no paper saw till Dalzene sprinkled his'n around. First thing we know we'll be plumb civilized!"

CHAPTER XVIII

ON THE LONG SNOW TRAIL

Immediately upon returning to the cabin on Myrtle, Lou Gordon began to put the finishing touches on the training of two handsome young huskies which she intended to add to her team for the big race. Great strong dogs they were, half brothers to Skookum, and they threw themselves into the work with a will. Each day found the girl upon the trail with her dogs, now urging them through loose snow, now on the hard-packed surface of the creek, lying flat on the sled fairly "burning the snow" as she timed off the passing miles, and again, accustoming them to eat rice balls and handfuls of meal in the harness, with only a few minutes of rest.

The day of departure arrived. She had a race team of twelve dogs now, and her father expressed surprise as she proceeded to harness six of these dogs, with six others of only ordinary ability.

"What ye doin' wi' them dogs?" he asked. "Ye surely ain't figurin' on racin' them!"

"No, but I'm taking them with me just the same," answered the girl. "It's their business to work every day till we hit Nome, and that will let the race dogs have every other day off. I'll only use half the race dogs each day and let the other half run free."

"Losh, lass! Wi' a twelve dog outfit, an' forty days fer six hundred miles, you wouldn't be wearin' out ye're dogs none. An' how about feedin' eighteen dogs on the trail? Ye can't load grub an' outfit, besides feed fer eighteen days fer six hundred miles on any sled."

"I don't have to, there won't be any trouble getting dog feed on the trail. There are Eskimos all along the Alatna and the Kobuk, and some white men."

"Too many dogs, far too many dogs, lass. Ye better leave them trail dogs here wi' the Siwash boy that's goin' to look after the bitches an' puppies. An' ye better let me do most of the drivin' an' the handlin' of 'em on the trail, so they'll be more used to me. I'll take holt of Skookum an' learn him that a crack of the whip don't mean the signal to fight. Because when I drive that big race I don't want any foolishness about it. The stakes are too high."

"I think, dad, that I'll drive this race myself," answered the girl, as they made fast the lashings of the sled.

"Tush, tush!" exclaimed the man, "What are ye sayin'? Why, if I wouldn't let yer drive a fifty mile race, how come ye to be thinkin' I'd let ye drive a four hundred mile race, that takes several days of the hardest kind of trailin'. If a fifty mile race is a man's job, a four hundred mile race is a man's job—an' a gude man! Think no more about it, lass. I won the other race—an' a mighty close one it was, as ye'll admit. An' I'll win this one."

It was upon the girl's tongue to retort that had she been driving the race would not have been close, but she answered nothing. Nevertheless, she had no intention of allowing the old man to drive. She knew that by no possibility could he be argued out of his determination. But she, herself, would drive that race, and she had nearly two months in which to lay her plans. In Lou Gordon's philosophy there was no use in crossing a bridge till you got to it, and two months is a long time in which to plan. So she smiled when the old man repeated his offer to handle the dogs.

"Oh, I love to drive them," she said, "They're used to you, now. It was only at first—before the other race that there was any danger of their not working for you. Come on, let's go!" And, with a few words of parting instruction to the Indian boy, she swung the team down the creek, and with the old man at the handle bars, they struck out on the long snow-trail.

The first leg of the journey down the Koyukuk was uneventful enough with stops at the roadhouse, at Bettles, and at Alakaket Mission. Upon the Alatna the trail of the returning Kobuks was not deeply snowed under and afforded a good footing.

They were in the Eskimo country now, for the Koyukuk River forms the dividing line between Indian and Eskimo hunting grounds. The Alatna and Upper Kobuk Eskimos, while as typically Eskimos as their brothers of the sea coast, have many of them never seen salt water. Nevertheless, they are as truly maritime in their habits as though they dwelt upon the treeless tundras of the coast. Living in a country that is replete with caribou, ptarmigan, and rabbits, they rarely eat game, contenting themselves with fish which they take in vast quantities from the rivers and inland lakes, and with seal oil that is carried up river and traded by the coastal Eskimos. It is the same with their housing. Living as they do where timber for cabins is plentiful, they build no cabins, but live in igloos built half underground and their clothing consists of sealskin, also an article of trade, instead of caribou skin which abounds within their own territory.

For two days the trail held to the river. Each night they pitched their tent close beside an igloo, Lou after one glance into the reeking interior of the first of these huts, declining as gracefully as possible, the urgent invitations of the occupants to share their hospitality. On the high plateau of the Alatna-Kobuk portage they experienced the first difficulty in following the trail. Rim Rock's map showed that it held straight west for nearly fifty miles, but a new fall of snow had obliterated every vestige of trail. The timber on the plateau was exceeding sparse and consisted of straggling patches of stunted spruce widely separated by level stretches of snow. One not versed in Arctic winter trailing would think that the exact location of the trail under such circumstances would be a matter of small moment, but the sourdough who does the winter traveling knows differently. Once off the trail, he must fight the deep snows of all the winter which means intolerably slow travel with no footing for the dogs. No matter how deeply buried under new snow, where the old trail is there will be found a hard bottom which furnishes the footing that is necessary for the dogs to exert any traction. And no amount of trail breaking without the old trail underneath will afford anything like a bottom.

The first few miles of the long portage were reasonably easy, for the trail was blazed on the trunks of a straggling stand of spruce. When the spruce gave place to open country the girl cut a slender sapling, sharpened it, and walking ahead of the dogs, prodded the point down through the foot and a half of new snow, locating the trail by the increased resistance of the packed snow. They took turns trail breaking, which of itself is no light job in loose snow. The broad snowshoe is useless for this work so one must resort to the narrow trail shoe that packs down the snow rather than overrides it. The trail breaker must walk ahead locating the trail as he goes, then return to the team, and walk ahead, again, thus traversing every foot of the distance three times, while his companion follows at the handle bars. Ten to fifteen miles of this is a big day's work, and it took the two four days to make the fifty miles, including one-half day spent resting on the head waters of Hog River.

The evening of the fourth day found them at the cabin on Lake Noyutak that Rim Rock had marked on his map. All Alaska even to the remotest outland, is dotted with these decaying cabins, mute monuments to dashed hopes. Some lone prospector forces his way far beyond the outposts, builds his cabin, works like a slave in the muck for a year—two years, swallows his disappointment and moves on to build another cabin until at last the North claims him—drains him dry of everything but his vision of gold—starves him, freezes him, and when at last he falls a mottled, marbled thing into the snow, she feeds her wolves with his bones. Years later some traveler of the wastes, fighting the strong cold and the shrieking wind, stumbles upon the cabin, and in the blessed life-giving warmth of its shelter, gives fulsome thanks to its builder—but the builder never knows.

Another day's trail breaking took them well onto the Kobuk, and early the following morning a small party of Eskimos mushing up river gave them the benefit of a trail. The trail shoes were returned to the sled, and that day they made thirty miles. The third night on the Kobuk brought them to another cabin which they shared with two Eskimo boys who were journeying up river with sealskins to trade. The sun, so long in seclusion, shone every day, and travel on the good trail of the river ice became a pleasure rather than a hardship. At Shungnak they replenished their supplies and a week later rested for two days at Squirrel River native village.

They were now well into the coastal country, and the trail ceased to be a matter of supreme importance for the reason that the hard, wind-packed snow was crusted to a degree that gave good footing anywhere upon its surface.

At the delta of the Kobuk they bore southward, crossed Hotham Inlet, and following the Choris Peninsula to its southmost extremity, crossed the wind-swept ice of Eschscholtz Bay and camped that night at Kiwalik. The next day they made Candle, and it was there that Old Man Gordon found the vindication of his much scoffed theory. At Candle, they were thawing with steam! "I told 'em! I told 'em it would come!" cried the old man excitedly, as he fairly dragged the girl to the Candle Creek workings. "I told 'em in Dawson before the big rush, an' I be'n tellin' 'em on the Koyukuk ever since! An' they wouldn't believe me! An' now ye can see fer yerself!"

"But, they burn coal here, dad," objected the girl.

"Aye, they burn coal because they ain't got the wood! An' if it's coal ye need, which it ain't, there's plenty coal on the Koyukuk, an' better coal than this ice-clogged stuff they're shovelin' under their b'ilers, here." For two whole days the girl was forced to remain in Candle while the old man haunted the workings, asking innumerable questions, and boasting to anyone who would listen that he, himself, was the father of "b'iler thawin'."

When at last Lou succeeded in persuading him to resume the journey, it was to find that the dog race had been entirely supplanted in his mind by the astounding fact that he had actually seen frozen gravel thawed with steam. "An' they tell me they're usin' b'ilers at Nome, an' pilin' up dumps as big as mountains!" he burst forth as he paused on top of a great mountainous ridge, that overlooked Candle, "I'll find out all about it, an' when we go back I'll fill the valley of Myrtle from rim to rim, an' I'll reckon' my gold by the pound!"

Lou answered nothing as the outfit fairly flew over the hard trail but as she ran beside the dogs, she smiled. Here, possibly was the solution of her difficulty. She would encourage the old man to devote all his time to the study of boilers on the chance that he would entirely forget the dog race. Foolish hope, as she was soon to realize. Because, for weeks before the great event Nome talks nothing but dogs, and the Alaska Sweepstakes.

The going on the wind-packed snow of the Seward Peninsula was the fastest of the entire trip. The fastest, and by far the most trying and disagreeable, for the wind never for a moment ceased to harness and to buffet them. Nowhere in the known world does the wind persist with such malevolent, devilish force as upon the treeless waste of ridges and flats that lie between Nome and Candle. Forty, sixty, eighty, a hundred miles an hour it roars down upon the struggling traveler, seemingly endowed with intelligence and a certain devilish ingenuity for the annihilation of his outfit. To pitch a tent, or indeed to erect a shelter of any kind is an absolute impossibility. And there are times when the whole outfit is pushed, skidding and sliding off the trail to bring up with a crash against the first natural obstruction. Luckily, during the three days' traverse of the one hundred and thirty miles to Council, the Gordons had the wind at their backs, so that on numerous stretches both father and daughter rode the sled with the dogs tearing along at full speed to keep from being run down. At Council Lou again had hard work to persuade her father to push on, for here, as at Candle, they were thawing with steam. After one day's rest, which was no rest at all for Old Man Gordon, who visited every steam boiler within five miles of town, they pulled out early in the morning on the last lap of their long journey. "Only ninety miles to Nome!" cried the girl, as they flew over the crusted snow. "Soloman tonight, and tomorrow night—Nome!"

"Aye," answered the old man, "But 'twill be too late to see the big dumps. They tell me they're several miles out. I'll have to wait till next day to go out there."

At Topkok the two got their first view of the vast Pacific, its deep blue waves tossing their white manes high in the everlasting wind. The dogs were halted, and for a long time both stared in awed silence upon the mighty vastness of the scene. The dazzling whiteness of the snow in the bright sunshine, the cold green glitter of the great ice crags that reared their heads along the coast, and the warm blue of the ocean beyond held them in rapt admiration until the stinging wind tugging at parka hoods, and forcing its cold breath beneath their clothing, caused them to push on.

The wind was at their side now, and the difficulties of the trail were innumerable, the heavily loaded sled turning over every few miles, or crashing sidewise into the telephone poles that lined the trail.

The following day the wind blew even harder and it was not until long after dark that the weary travelers pulled into Nome, where too tired to even attempt the exploration of her brilliantly lighted wonder city, Lou Gordon gave her dogs into charge of the hotel dog keeper, and retired to her room where a few moments later she crept between the first white sheets she had ever seen, and sank into a deep and dreamless sleep.

CHAPTER XIX
ON DEATH VALLEY HILL

THE JOURNEY TO NOME had consumed but thirty-three of the allotted forty days, and during the week following her arrival, Lou Gordon rested from the long snow-trail. For a while each morning she worked with her dogs, getting them into condition, putting the finishing touches on them for the big race that was scheduled to start at nine o'clock on the morning of the thirteenth of April. The heavy trail-sled had been replaced by a strong, light affair, built for speed, yet braced throughout against possibility of damage upon the hard, wind-swept trail.

During this first week in Nome, the girl was left very much to herself, her father spending the entire day, and sometimes half the night, among the dumps and the boilers of the beach line diggings.

One morning, as she paused on the trail to make some slight adjustment of harness, a team of eighteen superb dogs halted beside her and a cheery voice greeted her from the depths of a close-drawn parka hood. "Need any help?"

"No, thank you," answered the girl, her eyes drinking in every detail of the eighteen great animals, "What wonderful dogs!"

The man laughed; "They sure are. But that's no scrub team you're drivin'. Goin' to enter 'em?"

"Yes," the girl smiled, "And I'm going to win, too!"

"That's the talk! Johnson's my name—John Johnson."

"Oh, I've heard of you!" exclaimed Lou, "And I've heard of your team. Lots of people have picked you to win the Sweepstakes—you or Scotty Allen, or Fred Ayer." Again she smiled: "But, that's because they don't know my dogs."

"I guess they don't, all right. I don't know 'em, an' I thought I knew every race team in this part of the country. Where you from?"

"From the Koyukuk. I am Lou Gordon."

"The Koyukuk!" exclaimed Johnson. "I didn't know they bred good dogs over there. Did you come across from the Yukon?"

"No, we came by the Kobuk."

"You're some sourdough!" exclaimed Johnson, "To come that way. But all the Koyukukers are, as far as that goes. It must be a God-forsaken country up there."

"It's the best country there is!" interrupted the girl, quickly.

"That's right! Say, I don't mind tellin' you that if I don't win the big race myself I'd rather lose it to you than any one else. I like the way you talk. Are you goin' to drive 'em yourself?"

A slight frown puckered the girl's forehead: "I want to drive them," she confided, "But my dad thinks it is no job for a girl. He can't see that I've actually grown up. And, really, I do handle them lots better than he does."

"I'll bet you do! But, say—he's dead right—about it not bein' a girl's job! Believe me, Miss Gordon, I know! She's some trail! Especially if there's a blizzard on."

"Do you know the trail?"

"I sure do."

"Will you draw a map for me. I want to take them over the whole course before the race."

"Sure, I'll map it for you. Where you stoppin'?"

The girl gave him the name of her hotel, and he continued: "If you say so I'll come over there this afternoon an' then you can see me make the map, an' it will give me a chance to tell you about the trail. There's some mean places an' it helps a whole lot to know about 'em."

"Oh, will you? Are you sure you are willing to do that—when it might be the means of my winning the race?"

Johnson laughed: "If them dogs of mine can't win because they can out-run, an' out-trail yours, you're welcome to win. I don't want no advantage. An' let me tell you that you're doin' a good thing by takin' 'em over the trail. There's more to that than some folks savvies. There'll be a lot of 'em entered this year. An' outside of three or four of us, they ain't none of 'em be'n over the trail. Here comes Scotty Allen now!" he exclaimed, as they watched the approach of a big team of pure malamutes. "Him an' a woman down in California is pardners in that team—an' they're good dogs, too."

As the driver drew up and halted Johnson hailed him. "Come here, Scotty, an' meet Miss Lou Gordon from over on the Koyukuk, an' at the same time take a squint at some good dogs. Look at that lead dog! Some animal! I was just tellin' Miss Gordon that if I don't win I'd rather she would than you, or Ayer, or Sapala, or Eskimo John. The rest ain't got no show, anyhow."

Allen acknowledged the introduction. "I'm sure glad to meet you, Miss Gordon. So you've come over to give us a run for our money, eh? That's the stuff! But don't you believe for a minute that John here, an' that pack of wolves he's drivin' is goin' to cut any real figure in the big race. Here's the team you've got to figure on, right here. If you beat out these malamutes, you've won the race!"

"Hear him rave!" laughed Johnson, "Why, Miss Gordon, them malamutes will be lucky if they don't set down an' freeze in before they hit Gold Run. I figure on packin' extra grub for Scotty, so he can make it in a-foot." And so it went, the two great dog-mushers exchanging good-natured banter, and the girl enjoying it hugely.

"Anyway, I hope the best team will win!" she exclaimed, when they had exhausted their stock of ready repartee.

"You said it!" seconded Allen.

"You bet!" exclaimed Johnson. "I hope we don't have to run in the snow. It's a hard grind in clear weather, but with a blizzard on, it's fierce."

"You don't figure on drivin' the race, yourself!" exclaimed Allen.

"If I don't drive it, one of you will win," laughed the girl. "My dad wants to drive, but he can't win."

"Just the same, I hope he don't let you tackle it," said Allen, seriously, "It ain't no woman's race—the Sweepstakes ain't."

"It will be a woman's race this year!" smiled the girl. "You'll see!" and with the good-natured laughter of the men ringing in her ears, she headed the dogs for town.

Two days later she took the trail for Candle with Johnson's map stowed safely in her pocket. Old Man Gordon had grudgingly given his consent to the trip, although insisting that it was all foolishness, and again warning her that she most emphatically was not going to drive the race. Careful to take no issue with him on that point, she reiterated her contention that the dogs, especially Skookum, would be able to clip hours from the time if they knew the trail, and so won the old man's grudging consent.

It was with growing apprehension that the girl swung the dogs onto the trail. For she realized that with all Nome talking dog race, her father could not forget the big event even though there had been ten times as many boilers to inspect. With the race still more than two weeks off, everyone was thinking dogs, and talking dogs—and nothing else. And as the time approached the girl racked her brains for some maneuver that would allow her to drive the great race.

In vain she racked her brain for a solution of her problem as her sled slipped smoothly over the hard trail. "I'll just have to hire someone to kidnap him," she muttered, "And then he'll never forgive me. I don't see why he can't listen to reason!"

Just before she drew into Soloman, an event happened that drove all thought of her father out of her head and gave her fresh cause for worry. A dog team came into view and as it approached, the actions of Skookum caused the girl to stare at him in amazement. The great leader had stopped dead in his tracks, and stood, half crouched, with muscles tensed, and the hair of his back standing bristlingly erect. From his throat issued a low, menacing growl, and stepping quickly to his side the girl saw that his amber eyes were fixed upon the driver of the approaching team. Suddenly the team halted and the girl found herself staring into the face of Jake Dalzene!

Only for a moment the man stood facing her in the trail. But in that moment his face registered intense surprise, followed instantly by an abysmal fear, as his glance centered on the menacing figure of Skookum. Then, swiftly he swung his dogs clear of the trail, and urging them on gave wide margin on the frozen crust. As he passed his eyes met the girl's in a gleam of sullen hate. The next moment he was gone, and Lou started her own dogs and continued on to Soloman.

"What in the world is he doing here?" she wondered, "Surely he is not going to enter his dogs in the Sweepstakes! Oh, why couldn't he have stayed on the Yukon? Why did he come to Nome? He'll never try to steal Skookum again. He's deathly afraid of him, and he has a right to be. I never saw Skookum act that way before! Why, he would have eaten him up! But, he might try to kill Skookum! I wish Pete Enright were here. He would keep an eye on Dalzene for me. As long as Dalzene is in Nome I'll worry every minute that my dogs are out of my sight. I know he's up to some deviltry. I could see it in his eyes. Maybe it's just hooch-running," she reasoned, when the first shock of the meeting had worn off. "Because he evidently didn't expect to see me here. His face showed surprise until he saw Skookum. Then fear. Oh, why didn't you chew him up, Skookum?" she cried aloud, but for answer the big dog increased his pace, and ran on.

The girl spent the night at Topkok, fifty miles from Nome, and got away early the following morning with Telephone Creek, seventy-two miles further on, as her destination. It was on this stretch of wind-beaten trail that for the first time she really let the dogs go. Riding the sled for long stretches she urged them to their utmost, and her heart thrilled as the great brutes responded with all that was in them and the sled fairly flew over the snow. Twice that day she stopped and fed a handful of meal to each dog—an extra trail ration to balance the extra exertion, and to hearten them for the long pull. She passed Boston Roadhouse shortly after noon, and arrived at Telephone Creek at four o'clock, an hour and a half ahead of her schedule. In the morning she headed for Candle, eighty-four miles away, which is the turning point of the race. It was particularly of this stretch that Johnson had warned her. Here one must cross the wind-swept reach of Death Valley, and while in clear weather the only serious danger is a wind-smashed sled, it is a real menace should the unfortunate musher lose the trail in a thick snow-fog or a driving blizzard, for Death Valley Hill is cut by sheer bluffs and cut-banks over which an outfit might easily plunge to destruction.

On the summit of Death Valley Hill she halted and fed the dogs the while she took careful note of the lay of the land. So engrossed was she that a dog outfit from the north was almost upon her before she noticed it. A moment later it drew up beside hers. The driver's bared hand fumbled for a moment with his snow goggles, and in that moment the girl noted that the goggles were of the Eskimo type, consisting merely of two bits of hollowed wood provided with slits. The goggles came off, and she found herself looking into a pair of grey-blue eyes set deeply in a face that was wind-tanned to the color of a native. Then she was aware that the eyes were smiling, and that a fan-shaped spread of tiny wrinkles radiated from their corners. The lips were smiling, too, as they greeted her in jargon:

"*Klahowyam!*"

"*Klahowya six!*" smiled the girl, gazing frankly into the blue-grey eyes. Somehow those eyes seemed to fascinate her. They looked young, and yet—no, not young. There was a hint of deep wisdom in their depths, but the face was not the face of an old man. White even teeth showed between the smiling lips, and every movement of the well poised body bespoke health, and strength, and vigor. He was speaking:

"Great dogs you've got there!" Before she could warn him, he had stepped swiftly to Skookum's side, and his bared hand was laid upon the big leader's head.

"Oh, look out! Please!" he glanced up at the cry, and again his lips smiled, as he noted the look of utter amazement that showed in the girl's face as she stared at her great lead dog whose amber eyes were gazing mildly into the man's face. "Be careful! Skookum don't like strangers. No one has ever touched his head before—not even dad!"

"Well, then, I'm not a stranger—and I'm glad. Skookum and I understand each other, don't we Skookum?" The hand pulled playfully at the great dog's ear.

"But—I don't understand!" cried the girl, "He couldn't have known you! I raised him, myself, and he's never been away from me, except—"

"Except when?" asked the man, so quickly that the girl wondered.

She was about to reply, when he forestalled her: "Except about two months or so ago," he said, "And then, he wasn't away from you for very long."

"Why—how do you know? Do you know about Dalzene?"

The man laughed: "Never heard of him," he answered.

"Then, how do you know?"

The stranger's fingers were caressing the scars of the twitch that still showed on the great dog's jaws. "I know because these scars are only about two or three months old. And I know that you never jerked him around with a twitch."

"Dalzene stole him. He's a horrible old hooch-runner, and I won a race from him, or rather dad did, over on the Koyukuk, and then he stole him when he found I wouldn't sell him. But Skookum broke his chain and came home."

"And probably ate the hooch-runner, before he did it," mused the man, staring into the amber eyes. "I know a little bit about dogs and I wouldn't care to have this particular specimen for an enemy."

"No, he didn't," answered the girl quickly. "I—I almost wish he had!"

The man laughed: "I don't blame you," he answered. "If Skookum was my dog, and somebody stole him, I think I would wish the same thing—only I think I would be inclined to save the dog the trouble."

"Of eating him?" exclaimed the girl, and they both laughed aloud.

"You live on the Koyukuk?"

"Yes, on Myrtle Creek."

"Out of Coldfoot?"

"Yes, only there is no Coldfoot, now. They've all pulled out for Nolan—except dad and me."

"So, Coldfoot's dead, eh? I kind of thought the gravel was too spotted to last."

"You have been there?"

"Quite a while ago. I pulled out before there was any Coldfoot, I was back there once since and bought an outfit of grub from Crim. I pulled north from there."

"North!" exclaimed the girl, "To Nolan, or Wiseman?"

"North of everywhere," smiled the man. "Way north. North of the Endicott Range. This is my first trip out in four years. And my second trip out in eight."

"Four years!" exclaimed the girl, "And no camps up there?"

"No camps. I've sent Eskimos to Shungnak sometimes for supplies. This spring I thought I'd come out myself. I'm going to Nome to take in the sights, and the big race. What's the old world been doing in the last four years?" he asked.

The girl smiled: "The Koyukuk has been flowing into the Yukon and Coldfoot has stampeded to Nolan," she answered, "That is about all I know of the world. But, I have been to Nome."

"And not staying for the big race!" exclaimed the man.

"Yes, I'm staying for the big race. I'm going to win it!"

"You! You're going to drive the Sweepstakes!"

"Yes. I'm going to drive—and I'm going to win, too."

The man's eyes studied the dogs, one by one. After several minutes he looked up. "You might do it," he said. "There isn't a scrub in the outfit. They've got the chests, and the backs, and the legs, and they're in condition."

"I've got to win!" exclaimed the girl. "If I don't win we'll be broke. This trip will take all we've got. Hotels are expensive, and I've just got to win. It will break dad's heart if he can't get his boiler."

"Boiler—on the Koyukuk? What does he want of a boiler up there?"

"Oh, he thinks that if he can thaw out the muck with steam, his everlasting fortune will be made. It's the only thing he can talk about, or think about. 'B'iler Gordon,' they call him on the Koyukuk."

"Gordon," repeated the man, in an even voice, "There was a Gordon down Dawson way, before the big stampede."

"That was dad. His claim petered out, and we went up on the Koyukuk."

The man glanced at his watch. "We may as well eat," he said. "It's nearly time anyway, and it would be foolish for us both to pull on for an hour and then eat alone, wouldn't it?"

"Of course it would!" agreed the girl, and as they ate she found herself telling this kindly stranger all about herself, her hopes and ambitions, and her fears. And she listened while he told of the unexplored country along the Colville and its tributaries, and of how he believed himself upon the verge of a big strike.

"But is it worth it?" she asked, "Is the gold worth it all? Is it worth enough when you get it to pay for all the years of cold, and darkness, and hard, hard work? Don't you realize that up here we are missing it all?"

"Missing it all?" asked the man, softly, "Missing all what?"

"Why, missing everything—missing *life*!"

It seemed a long time before he answered: "Maybe we are," he said, "Maybe we are missing—life. I'll think about that—and if I find the answer, I'll tell you. You are coming back to Nome, of course?"

"Oh, yes. I'm just taking the dogs over the trail, so it won't be all new to them when the race starts. I'll reach Candle tonight, and rest all day tomorrow. The return trip I will make in two days. I'm going to really drive coming back."

The man nodded: "That's right. Make them do it. Force them and crowd them as if you were driving the race. They told me at Shungnak that the race starts the thirteenth, that will give them plenty of time to rest up in Nome, and it will show them what's expected of them."

"You know dogs," said the girl.

"Yes," he answered, "I know dogs. But, that is only half of it. Dogs know me. And that is the real secret of handling dogs. You wouldn't believe me if I told you that I could take those dogs of yours and handle them as well as you can yourself. Dogs know all about a man the moment they scent him. It's a sense we don't know anything about, but it's there. They know a lot more about us than we know about them. A dog knows a vicious man the instant he scents him, he knows the good-natured, easy going man, that he can take advantage of, and he knows the man he can trust and respect. He will work his toe nails off for the right man—because he trusts him. For the others, he will do just as little as he can get by with. He will do just enough to keep from under the club of the vicious man, and he will shamelessly loaf for the good-natured man who pampers him."

The girl nodded: "I believe that. I believe every word of it. I have been handling dogs for several years, and I know it's true. I should like to talk more about dogs," she added, "but, really, I must go. I want to make Candle tonight."

"You'll make it all right," he answered. "Can I look you up in Nome?"

"Oh, do!" cried the girl, "I'd love to have someone to talk to—someone who knows dogs, and who knows the real North—the country beyond the Yukon. Dad is so busy finding out about boilers that I hardly ever see him."

"I'll be waiting for you day after tomorrow evening," he promised. "You will be too tired to talk dogs or anything else, but I'll be looking for you. I want to see how your team stands the trip."

CHAPTER XX
MAN OF THE FAR NORTH

History, local in character, unrecorded for the most part, but epic in virile intensity, makes with startling rapidity where men answer the call of raw gold. And it is history, not delicately graven by master hands of diplomacy; but rough hewn and slashed broad by self-centered men who let the chips fall where they may. The past is forgotten. The future is yet to come. But, there is gold in the gravel today! Raw gold! Yellow gold! Coarse gold! And dust! With no thought of future men will starve for it, will freeze for it, and for the chance to gouge it from the earth will undergo all hardship and privation known and unknown. With their eyes fixed on the golden sands of California, men gave no heed to the rich and fertile loam lands of the middle west as the wheels of their wagons rutted, and their feet trampled that golden storehouse of the future. For there is gold in the gravel *today*!

The grazing lands of Australia, with their golden future in cattle and sheep were worn bare by the trails of the stampeders. There is gold in the gravel *today*!

And the forest lands and the tillable lands of Oregon, and Washington, and British Columbia were passed with hardly a glance by the nondescript army that surged Northward to answer the call of gold. Timber and grain are of the future—but there is gold in the gravel *today*!

And never did history make more rapidly than when that horde of *chechakos* swarmed over the Chilcoot and poured into the valley of the Yukon. Good men, and bad men, poor men, and rich—clean-lived, clean-muscled farmer boys aglow with the ruddy health of the outdoors, rubbing elbows with the pasty-skinned degenerates of the city's slums—all dumped together into a land of ice, and of snow, and of rugged mountains! Into a land that by no possibility of development could be made to supply the one tenth part of their sustenance!

Rough hewn is the history of the Yukon. Its makers drowned in its waters, froze on its hillsides, and starved on its creeks; or miserably back-trailed to the place they came from! They paid with their lives for their ignorance; or crept cravenly back in defeat. Those were the incompetents. But, a few of the fit survived. Supermen, who lived on and thrived where human life was the only cheap thing in the whole lean land—beat the North, and gutted her creeks of their riches!

So history made fast on the Yukon. Camps sprang up in a day, flourished for a month—and were forgotten. The hero of today supersedes the hero of yesterday, and tomorrow will be unremembered. The heroes were the men who found gold. Camps grew into towns, and towns into cities, and banks superseded the safes of the saloon keepers and the traders as repositories for the miner's gold.

And so it was that eight years after Burr MacShane bid Camillo Bill good bye and headed North in the darkness, his name had been long forgotten, where once it had been the big name of all names. A dozen or more of the old timers would occasionally shake their heads in reminiscent regret that he had gone. Always they spoke of him in the past tense—all but Camillo Bill, who regularly deposited large sums in the bank to his credit. To the bank Burr MacShane was only a name—the name of its heaviest depositor. In answer to inquiry Camillo Bill had vouchsafed the information that Burr MacShane was his partner. That he was on a prospecting expedition somewhere in the North. And, that when he got ready he would return. And with the passing of the years MacShane's dust piled up its interest.

But, of all this, MacShane himself, knew nothing. Far to the northward, in that land of winter darkness where the Colville River winds its unmapped way to the frozen sea, Burr MacShane played a lone hand. There was something on the Colville—something big. Somewhere upon its upper reaches was a huge storehouse of gold—red gold. Gold that gripped him as no other gold had ever gripped him. It was like no other gold he had ever seen. Gold that stirred his imagination to its profoundest depths—wonderful—mysterious—red!

Slowly and methodically he worked the bars of the lower river, panning the precious red particles from the muck. It did not run rich, a couple of dollars to the pan, hardly more. But what would it show deep down? There was no timber. He could not burn in. The second winter he laboriously hauled wood from the foothills of the Endicotts a hundred and fifty miles, pulling the sled with his dogs! Six round trips he made—and burned to bed rock in a week! So he worked up river, southward. One by one he explored the tributaries. For four years he worked—living like an Eskimo—delving like a gnome. Then he made a hurried trip to Coldfoot for supplies, and for another four years he buried himself in the North.

During the long daylight of the short summers he explored the lower river, pan-washing the bars. And in the perpetual darkness of the long winters he would mush back to the foot hills and work the tributaries where some scraggy spruce timber furnished the necessary wood.

And in the course of time he had learned a strange thing. The red gold of the lower river was top gold—new gold. It had not been washing long enough to have worked down even to the shallow bed rock. The gold of the upper river and its tributaries was old gold, paler, and deeper down.

Therefore, he reasoned that somewhere between the two places he would one day find the source of the red gold. Some convulsion of nature—an earthquake, the fall of a cutbank, or an overhung spur of a mountain, had within a comparatively recent time, opened up this storehouse of red gold and the waters of the river were washing it down with the surface sand.

On the trail of red gold MacShane forgot civilization. What was it he had told Camillo Bill—maybe a year from now I will be taking out a thousand dollars to the pan? More than a year had passed—many years. But the storehouse was there. What difference did it make? He would find it—sometime. And so with the utmost patience he rode his hunch—the hunch that had driven him into the North. Wandering Eskimos knew him and brought his supplies from Shungnak on the Kobuk, two hundred miles to the southward.

Early in March of his eighth year on the Colville, he located a spot on a tributary that flowed in from the westward, where indications showed that the course of the river had been changed by an enormous slide of rock. Powder! Powder, he must have to blast his way into the towering mass of stone. And, as he studied the mass, he knew that all the powder in the camps of the Koyukuk, and the Kobuk would not even scratch the mighty pile. Nome was his only hope—Nome, the city that had sprung up near the mouth of the Salmon River; where years before, he, himself, had struck color in the beach sands, but decided it wasn't pay. He had heard of Nome at Coldfoot, and of the fabulous wealth that those same beach sands were yielding—and he had grinned. For that was in the past. But, on the Colville, there is gold in the gravel *today*!

"Guess I'll just hit down there an' have a look at this city that's got rich off what I couldn't find," he said to himself that night in his igloo-like hut. "It's a hunch. I feel it workin'. I'm right now knockin' at the door of a big strike. 'Go to Nome,' it says. That means get powder an' blow this hill to hell." For a long time he sat and stared at the red squares that glowed at the draft of his stove. "Maybe it means that I'm just naturally plumb homesick to talk to someone. It's—why, hell! It's four years since I've seen a white man, or spoke a white man's word to anyone but myself an' the dogs. An' I ain't seen a white woman in God knows when! I wonder if they've got regular saloons, with mahogany bars, an' foot-rails, an' dance halls. I wonder if they've got anyone there that can make the old piano talk like Horse Face Joe could? There's one way to find out for sure," he grinned, and put a huge batch of dog feed to cook.

Morning found him on the trail. Four days later he pulled into Shungnak to find everyone in the isolated little mining camp talking dog race.

"Where is this race? An' when is it comin' off?" asked MacShane.

"Over to Nome. An' she starts the thirteenth of April," informed the saloon keeper, "How you bettin'? Me—I'm bettin' even money John Johnson's team wins agin the field. Or, I'm bettin' two-to-one on him to beat out any team you kin name."

"How many teams are racin'?" asked MacShane, indifferently.

"I don't know. Four or five—mebbe more. It don't make no difference. They can't none of 'em beat Johnson's wolves."

"I'll take a thousand that this Johnson's team don't win," said MacShane, tossing a sack onto the bar. "I don't know anything about Johnson or his team, either. But I'm headin' for Nome, an' I guess I'll just hang around and see the race. It'll be more interestin' if I've got somethin' up on it."

"Take another thousan' if you want it," invited the saloon keeper.

"No, a thousand will be enough. How's the trail down river?"

"You'll have a trail. An outfit pulled through the other day from the Koyukuk. Old Man Gordon an' his gal. Purtiest gal I ever seen, too. They've got a string of dogs they think kin run, an' they're goin' to enter 'em in the Sweepstakes." The man laughed harshly, "They ain't got no more show than a rabbit, runnin' agin them Nome race dogs."

"Gordon? Old Man Gordon, you say?"

"Yes. Know him?"

"Knew a man named Old Man Gordon once down to Dawson—before the big stampede. Maybe it's the same one."

"Might be, at that," agreed the saloon keeper. "But that gal of his'n! You'd ort to see her. Didn't know they grow'd peaches on the Koyukuk. Baudette, here, he's French, an' nach'ly runs to wimmin more'n what us others does—she makes such a hit with him that he offered to bet her dogs would win. I give him odds of ten-to-one agin 'em. They can't win."

"Got any more dust at ten-to-one that says they can't win?" asked Mac-Shane.

"Why, do you know them dogs?" queried the man suspiciously.

MacShane laughed: "Never saw 'em or heard of 'em," he replied. "It's just a hunch—an' when I get a hunch, I ride it. Ten-to-one's a good bet if I lose."

"How much do you want of it?"

"Oh, couple hundred."

"All right, you're on fer two hundred. If them Koyukuk dogs wins, you stop in on your way back an' collect three thousan'."

"I'll stop," grinned MacShane, and headed his dogs down river.

At Candle he bought an entire new outfit of clothing, and after a night's rest, pulled for Nome. On the crest of Death Valley Hill he met the girl. Mac-Shane had never, in any sense of the word, been a lady's man. The dance hall girls, with their association of liquor and music amused him for an evening, and were promptly forgotten. Of other women he knew nothing whatever. With MacShane the trail was the thing—the trail, and what lay just beyond. He had been in the van of a dozen stampedes. He had owned scores of good claims. But always the onrush of the stampeders had driven him on. He had plenty of gold—how much he had no idea. Much of it he had taken from the gravel with his own hands, and much of it was the proceeds of the sale of claims. He did not care for gold, only for the finding of gold. He loved the game, and he played it—not for the gold, but for the game. It was this spirit that had held him for eight years far in the North beyond the haunts of men. To find the source of the strange red gold became his fetish. The red gold appealed to him as no other gold had ever appealed. And its quest kept him sane and keen, though living apart from his kind through the long drear nights of eight Arctic winters, and the unceasing daylight of eight short summers.

And now, at last, he stood upon the threshold of his golden storehouse! During all the hours of the snow-trail he had pictured to himself what he would find when he had blasted his way into that mountain of fallen rock. A pocket? A crumbling lode? He would soon know. Trailing down the Kobuk, from Shungnak he had been almost sorry he had decided to stay at Nome for the dog race. Oh, well, what did it matter. A week, a month, a year? A couple of weeks in the big camp would do him good. And then he would hit the trail, and when he again struck a camp a stampede would follow his back trail—a stampede for red gold! Then—he would move on. Would harness his dogs and hit the long trail. Where? What did it matter, just so he got away from the crowd? There were other strikes to come. Dawson had not been the last strike, nor the Koyukuk. And the Colville would not be the last strike. There always would be another strike, and he, Burr MacShane would head some other stampede, on some other far-off river. And again his name would be a by-word throughout all the North.

He smiled whimsically: "They've all forgot me by this time. I've be'n too long gone. There won't anyone know me in Nome. There wasn't any Nome when I come through this part of the country. It's—let's see—it's twenty years ago. Twenty years—an' in a little over a year I'll be forty! Old Man Mac-Shane, they'll be callin' me, then. Yup, Old Man MacShane!" and he laughed.

When the girl disappeared on the trail to Candle MacShane mushed on. For an hour he mushed steadily, and with a start of surprise, he realized that during that hour he had been thinking entirely of the girl he had met on the trail. He remembered that Christmas in Dawson, when he had lifted her onto the piano. He remembered that he had picked out the prettiest doll on the Christmas tree, and given it to her. "Funny I never noticed her, then," he mused. "Must be because she's grow'd up. But, eyes like that—I sure ought to have noticed. Kind of soft, an' dark, like you could look way down into 'em—an' all the time you know she's lookin' into your own—sort of sizin' you up. If a man had anything on his mind that he had to hide, he couldn't look into those eyes.... Wonder how much powder it's goin' to take to move enough of that rock to find out what's under it.... Swung out behind those dogs like a man ... I'll bet she can trail all day.... Ton of powder ought to do.... She broke 'em herself, an' she's set on drivin' that race.... I can start in on the lower end an' work up through.... God! where'd she be if a blizzard hit, an' she got caught here without shelter?... Main trouble's goin' to be handlin' the damn rock after it's blow'd out.... Old Man Gordon won't know me.... I wore a beard those days.... Anyhow, I ain't goin' to be bothered with water, I'll work into it before the thaw ... I won't let on who I am.... Wonder what he thought when he found his dust salted back in the shaft? Wonder if he told *her*? Hell—I hope not! Won't make any difference, though, if they don't know me." And so it went, the man struggling to concentrate upon his red gold, and the girl obtruding his thoughts—muddling his problem. Half-angrily, he decided to banish thought of both the girl and the red gold from his mind. And so he continued his journey to Nome, thinking continuously of the girl with the soft dark eyes.

MacShane drove a fast trail and arrived in Nome early in the evening of the second day after his meeting with Lou Gordon. He had heard that Nome was a big camp, and a live one. But he was totally unprepared to find a modern, electrically lighted city on the bleak coast of Norton Sound. "Camp—hell!" he exclaimed, as he passed along the brilliantly illuminated street, "She's a town! I sure passed up a big thing when I quit this country an' headed for the Yukon. But, I was only a kid, then."

Putting up his dogs, he strolled about the streets for a while, the displays in the shop windows holding his attention. Men passed him on the sidewalks, singly and in groups, and men accompanied by women muffled to the ears in rich furs. But they paid him no heed. Now and then he saw a man clad in parka and moccasins but for the most part they were dressed as they would have dressed in Seattle or Vancouver. "Dude camp," muttered MacShane, and for the first time in his life he knew that he was lonely. He grinned at the realization of it. He—Burr MacShane, who had mushed more lone trails than any man in the North, was lonely in the biggest camp in the North. One hour of Nome had accomplished what eight long years in the Arctic solitudes had failed to accomplish—it had made him long for his kind.

A door opened, and from a glittering palace of fun two men stepped, and passed on down the street. Attracted by the sound of music, MacShane entered the place and found himself in a spacious room the floor of which was dotted with small tables at which men and women were seated, eating and drinking. Upon a raised platform at the rear an orchestra was rendering music. To the right, a long bar ran the full length of the room. Men stood at this bar, each with his foot resting upon a polished brass rail, and poured their liquor from cut glass decanters that glittered in the blaze of light. Here was something he understood. While not in any sense a drinking man, MacShane's visits to civilization had always been celebrated with more or less whiskey. He enjoyed the exhilaration of it. It was part of the game.

"All this camp needs is wakin' up," he decided, and crossing to the bar, smote it loudly with his fist. "Surge up, you trail-hounds an' have a drink!" he roared, in a voice that carried to the far corners of the room. But, there was no crowding to the bar. The orchestra played on, and the men and women at the tables stared. One or two snickered. The men at the bar turned on him in frank astonishment. Some of these also laughed. The linen-clad bartender opposite him stared at the gold sack that lay upon the bar before MacShane, and from the rear a man, also linen-clad, hurried toward him.

"Cut that out!" he ordered, curtly.

MacShane was bewildered. He felt as though he had been plunged suddenly into cold water. "What do you mean?" he managed to ask.

"I mean you lay off the rough stuff, or out you go—see? We don't stand for that, here!"

Before MacShane could reply, a large man detached himself from a group at the bar and stepped to his side. The man's eyes were twinkling, and his lips smiled. The linen-clad one accorded him deference. MacShane noted that the steel-grey eyes of the big man hardened momentarily as he addressed the other.

"You go back, Strake, before you start something. Leave him to me."

"Certainly, Mr. Smith. It's all right, Mr. Smith," the man rubbed his palms together, and slipped away.

"Let's liquor," invited the man, "Here, shove this in your pocket." He lifted MacShane's sack from the bar, upon which the bartender had already placed decanter and glasses. Still in bewilderment, MacShane poured his drink, and the big man followed.

"Trouble is with us—not you, sourdough," he smiled. "We think we ain't a camp any more—we're a city. We're dudes! There ain't a man in the house that could make twenty-five miles on the trail to save his life. We're civilized plumb helpless. An' it wasn't so long ago that I struck this camp with a pair of greasy overalls an' a ragged parka, an' drunk whiskey out of a tin can. An' Strake run the lowest lived dump in the camp. But times have changed. There's more raw gold here than anywhere else in the world—yet Strake ain't even got a pair of scales. We don't pan-wash an' hand-sluice any more—an' we pay our bills with checks."

The man paused and uplifted his glass. "Well, here's how." MacShane drank and returned the empty glass to the bar: "I see," he said, slowly. "An' I'm sure obliged to you for tellin' me. I'd buy a drink, but I ain't got a check."

The big man laughed. "Down the street," he said, "and around the first corner to your right, you'll see a sign that says MALAMUTE SALOON. *Saloon*—not café. If I was you, I'd kind of loaf down there. It's—our kind of a dump. The boys will be glad to see you. An' there's scales sittin' on the bar."

"Thanks," said MacShane, "I'll go there. So long." As he passed close beside a table on his way to the door, he heard a man whisper to his companion, "That's H. P. Smith. He's cleaned up ten million, dredging."

In the Malamute Saloon, MacShane ordered a round of drinks, but he did it unostentatiously, half-expecting another rebuff. But the men in moccasins and woolens crowded the bar and drank his health heartily, and he was immediately swamped with invitations to drink with them. One more drink he took, and retiring to a table toward the rear, ordered supper. All about him, as he ate he could hear men discussing the great dog race. Argument waxed hot. Bets were made, and the stakes put with the proprietor. Life here was as it should be. Nome hadn't all turned dude.

But despite the familiar surroundings, MacShane realized that there was something lacking. The three drinks should have produced a mild exhilaration. A pleasant glow in his belly, and a faster coursing of the blood through his veins. At this very moment he should be feeling in a mood for comprehensive goodfellowship. He, too, should be placing his bets on the dog race. But, the liquor was taking an opposite effect. He felt depressed. His thought kept recurring to the girl on the trail. Why should he keep thinking of her? She was nothing to him. But, those eyes—those dark eyes that seemed to look deep into a man's very soul. Suppose something should go wrong out there? It is a bleak country, the wind-swept trail to Candle. Why hadn't he waited on the trail. A waiter dumped an array of thick dishes before him, and mechanically, MacShane ate. "She'll be here tomorrow night," he muttered, "If nothin' happens." For a long time after the finish of his meal he sat and watched the men at the bar, and at the card tables that lined one side of the room. Slow anger rose within him. Anger at the girl with the haunting eyes. Here was he, Burr MacShane, for the first time in years in a live camp, his pockets bulging with dust, good liquor for the ordering, dance halls, every ingredient of a good time, and yet, here he sat lugubriously watching others disport themselves, as he longed to be disporting himself. Yet the sport had lost its appeal. He could not understand it, and unconsciously his mind took an introspective turn. What did he want to do? There was no answer. Try as he would he could arouse no spark of enthusiasm for anything. He thought of the mass of loose rock at the end of his long trail. But, even the red gold had lost its appeal. In disgust, he rose from the table, paid for his meal, and walking straight to his hotel, went to bed.

CHAPTER XXI
THE PLOTTING OF JAKE DALZENE

WHEN LOU GORDON DROVE her dogs straight for the bright lights of Nome at the finish of their long run from Candle, she recognized the dark figure that waited beside the trail on the outskirts of the town, and halted the dogs with a word. A moment later she found herself pouring the story of the great run into the eager ears of this tall stranger, who listened with little nods of approval. When she had finished, the man went to the dogs and examined them one by one. "There ain't a played-out dog in the bunch," he announced, "Not one. They'll do, all right. But how about you? You must be about all in."

The girl smiled into the face that peered so solicitously into her own. "Oh, I'm all right. I could do it over again, if I had to! I'm tired, of course. But I'm good for a whole lot yet."

"You're game, all right, Miss Gordon, but I wish you wouldn't drive that race. It ain't a woman's job. Tell you what—let me drive for you!"

"No, indeed! No one can handle those dogs like I can. No, if I win, I've got to drive them myself—and I've got to win!"

Together they made their way into town, and after bidding her good night, MacShane took a long, long walk and then went to bed.

In the morning they met at breakfast, and MacShane asked after her father.

"I hardly ever see him," laughed the girl, "His room is always empty by the time I get up, and he's had his breakfast and is off to watch those boilers work."

"And, what do you find to do here all alone?" he asked.

"Oh, I take the dogs out for a run in the morning, and manage to fill in the rest of the day just looking around, or reading, or sewing. Would you like to go with me, out on the trail with the dogs?" she asked.

"I sure would!" exclaimed the man, so quickly that for some reason they both blushed furiously, and laughed.

From that time on the two were together every day, and for the greater part of every day.

"Do you know," said the girl, one day when they were out on the trail with the dogs, "That you have never told me your name!"

MacShane laughed: "You never asked me," he said. "But, I don't think I'd tell you if you did—not yet, anyway."

"But, why not?" she asked, searching his smiling eyes.

"Oh, we'll just pretend it's a kind of a game we're playing. I know you, but you don't know me. You'll just have to take my word for it that I ain't a hooch-runner, or a criminal of some sort. I ain't really. I'm somethin' of a minin' man—in a small way—like your father, an' thousands of others up here in the big country."

"But," objected the girl, "I've got to call you something!"

"Call me—*Huloimee Tilakum*."

"*Huloimee Tilakum*," repeated the girl, "Stranger. I don't know whether I like that, or not."

"It's the name you, yourself gave me—back there on the trail the first time we met," he smiled, "Don't you remember you warned me that Skookum didn't like strangers."

"But, sometime you will tell me your name?"

The man was silent for a space of seconds. "Yes," he answered as he raised his eyes to hers, "yes, sometime, I think I shall tell you my name."

It was through MacShane that Lou Gordon was enabled to place the money that the men of Nolan had sent down to bet on her dogs. At first he readily got odds of ten-to-one, but as more and more money appeared to back the unknown Koyukuk dogs, the odds shrank to eight, to seven, to six, and on the last day before the race, MacShane found difficulty in placing the last thousand at five-to-one.

During all this time he had only seen Old Man Gordon once. The old man did not recognize him, and with Lou sitting by and endeavoring to turn the conversation into other channels, MacShane listened patiently to a two-hour discourse on the absolute supremacy of "b'ilers" over wood-thawing. Later, when Lou apologized for her father's harangue, MacShane laughed. "Oh don't bother about that," he assured her, "I believe he's right."

Jake Dalzene's surprise at meeting Lou Gordon on the trail between Nome and Soloman swiftly gave place to an outburst of rage that found vent in an outpouring of meaningless curses and a senseless abuse of his dogs during the remaining journey to Nome.

Dalzene's presence on the Seward Peninsula had but indirectly to do with the Alaska Sweepstakes. With the escape of Skookum on Dall River, had vanished all thought of entering the great race. An infection in his mangled hand held him at Fort Gibbon in care of the Army surgeon who had saved the member only to have it heal into a twisted, and all but worthless, claw.

It was while at the fort that Dalzene learned of the appearance on the Yukon of a United States marshal who was as proficient as he was persistent in the extermination of hooch-runners. And so it was that when the hand had healed sufficiently for travel, he quietly slipped up to Rampart City, loaded his remaining stock of liquor onto his sled and hit the trail for Nome. It was a long trail. Dalzene would have much preferred a trip up the Koyukuk. But, far rather would he have taken chances with the marshal and the Yukon, than to show up on the Koyukuk in the face of the protocol of the miner's meeting. With hate-smouldering eyes he promised himself that some day he would quietly slip up to Myrtle and, in his own way, even up the score with the Gordons—but not yet.

The upper Yukon, policed as it was by the Mounted would prove equally unhealthy, and the Tanana hardly less so. The lower coast had been closed to him for years, so perforce, he must hit for Nome. There were plenty of natives along the coast. If he made good time he could get rid of his hooch to the Eskimos and, by judicious betting on the big race, would have a chance to retrieve the fortune he had lost on the Koyukuk.

Taking with him an Indian from Rampart, he made good time on the trail, despite the fact that, swath it as he would, his injured hand was so sensitive to the cold that it gave him almost constant pain. From Unalaklik north he managed to trade all of his hooch for fur. At Council he learned through careful inquiry that it was almost a foregone conclusion that John Johnson would win the Sweepstakes. Whereupon he placed several bets, and continued his journey to Nome.

Just beyond Soloman he had come face to face with Lou Gordon. One glance at Skookum, and he had swung wide to avoid the white fangs that had bared at sight and scent of him, and as the girl passed, the abysmal hate that had smouldered for weeks in his warped soul burst into a volcano of insane rage. Here, was the primal cause of all his misfortune. The dogs which had beaten him out of his fifteen thousand dollars—all he owned in the world except his outfit, and the single load of hooch cached at Rampart City. And here, glaring at him in all eagerness to finish a job only well begun, stood the great leader of those dogs, crouching with bared fangs. And in the brief interval before the outfit passed, it seemed as though the memory of each moment of pain that had been his since those fangs had struck, surged up within him, until as the outfit disappeared down the trail, he wiped cold sweat from his brow with the sleeve of his parka.

In Nome he learned that the Gordon dogs were entered in the race and that Old Man Gordon was to drive. In Nome, as in Council, John Johnson's team was the favorite. But Nome knew nothing of the Gordon dogs, and he,

Dalzene, did know. The Gordon dogs were a joke in Nome. They were offering ten-to-one against them—and no takers. But, they had never seen those dogs run!

The first thought that entered Dalzene's head was to take the short end of that ten-to-one money. If the Gordon dogs won, he could clean up big. But right there, the supreme hatred of his soul manifested itself. The talk in Nome was that already the stakes for the race had mounted to seven thousand dollars, and that in all probability from fifteen hundred to two thousand would be added from the proceeds of a big dance that was to be held on the night of the twelfth. If he won, so would the Gordons! All Alaska would be talking of the great dog that led the team, and of the old man who drove them—the dog that had maimed him for life, and the man who had caused him to lose his fifteen thousand dollars! No! He would bet even money on Johnson's dogs, and somehow he would put the Gordon team out of the running. He'd show 'em! They couldn't beat him out of his money and get away with it! They weren't on the Koyukuk, now! And this was only the beginning. Wait till he appeared suddenly on Myrtle—then the real squaring of accounts would come off!

For days after the return of the girl, Dalzene watched for a chance to strike. His first intent was to injure, or kill the leader. He tried to ingratiate himself with the keeper of the dogs at the hotel but the man had taken an intense liking to the girl with the dark eyes, and he cared for her dogs as though they had been his own. Furthermore, the man knew dogs, and loved them. On the day Dalzene appeared at the kennels, with the apparent intention of a friendly chat, the keeper noted instantly the actions of Skookum, who crouched on his chain with bared fangs. Noted, also, that Dalzene unconsciously shrank back from the dog, although not within several yards of him.

"Great dog you've got there," hazarded Dalzene, with a show of friendliness.

"Yeh," answered the man, dryly, as he met Dalzene's glance with a stony stare. "I'm jest about to turn him loose fer a run." As he spoke he started toward Skookum, whose smouldering amber eyes seemed to flash red lights as they fastened upon Dalzene.

"For Christ's sake—*don't!*" Dalzene's voice rose in a thin scream, and the next instant the corral gate slammed, and white faced, Dalzene stood peering through from the outside.

Advancing to the gate, the keeper spoke deliberately, "I don't know who you be—an' I don't give a damn. I do know that if you ever show up around this corral agin while that dog is here—what one of us leaves of you, the other one will finish. Now git!"

And Dalzene "got." Thereafter he sought other means of putting the Gordon dogs out of the running. He considered hiding behind an ice-hummock and taking a shot with a rifle as the dogs went past on their daily exercise run. But, decided the risk was too great in a country where there was no timber. Day after day he cudgeled his brains for a plan, and then, with the great event only a few days off he hit it. So effective, and yet so beautifully simple that the only wonder was he had not thought of it before.

Whereupon, he purchased a bottle of liquor, and bided his time until the day before the race.

Immediately after breakfast on that day Old Man Gordon visited an abandoned working at the outskirts of the town to look over a small boiler which had been offered to him at a bargain. A half-hour later from the direction of this abandoned dump, the Indian who had accompanied Dalzene from Rampart, staggered up the street, waving his bottle of liquor and howling defiance in the faces of all white men. With admirable promptitude, the hand of the law fell heavily upon his shoulder, and he was jailed. It happened that Dalzene was one of a small group of the curious who followed the officer to the jail with his prisoner, and there when questioned, the Indian stated that he had bought the hooch from an old man—a white man, and that the man was down by the old dump. Two officers, starting immediately for the abandoned dump, were accosted by Dalzene, who confidentially slipped them the word that he had happened to be passing the aforementioned dump, an hour since, and had seen a man who wore a beard, pass the Indian a bottle of liquor, in exchange for some money. It seemed like a damned shame to pinch the Injun, and he for one, would be glad to see any man convicted that would sell hooch to an Injun.

This tallied so accurately with the rather vague story of the drunken man that the officers doubled their pace, and a few moments later Old Man Gordon, fighting in righteous rage, roaring loudly his protest, was dragged to jail and locked up in a cell, after having been duly identified by the Indian.

In the meantime Dalzene had disappeared from the vicinity and, directly across the street from the hotel, came face to face with the man he had noticed very often recently in company with Lou Gordon. He knew nothing of this man, except that it was he who was backing the Gordon dogs so heavily that he had forced the odds down from ten-to-one to six-to-one. Instantly Dalzene's fingers closed about his remaining roll of bills, and abruptly he accosted the stranger. "I got five hundred that says John Johnson's dogs wins the race!" he challenged, truculently.

"The hell you have!" replied MacShane, "Well you won't have, after tomorrow. Step over here to the Malamute, an' we'll put up the dust."

The matter was soon settled, and, while MacShane strolled over and watched a game of solo, Dalzene refreshed himself at the bar. "That'll fix 'em," he muttered, "Old Man Gordon hain't on the Koyukuk, now. They'll put his bail so high he won't never be able to raise it here where they don't know him, an' I know enough about dogs to know that with their reg'lar driver out of the way, they hain't goin' to do no good in the race. The gal, she allus exercised 'em fer him, but it was the old man that druv the race that beat me out—an' it's him that's entered to drive this one." And well satisfied with himself, Dalzene quitted the saloon, a short time before MacShane left the place and crossed over to the hotel.

CHAPTER XXII
POISON

As MacShane stepped from the door of the saloon and headed toward the hotel, Lou Gordon drew swiftly back from the window of her room and sinking upon the edge of her bed, stared for a long time at the opposite wall. Quite by accident, she had happened to glance out of her window, at the moment Dalzene had accosted MacShane upon the sidewalk opposite. She had seen them converse for a few moments, and then, together, walk down the street and enter the saloon, and she had watched for an hour or more until they reappeared, separately, but within a few minutes of each other. What did it mean? Who was *Huloimee Tilakum*? And what on earth could he have in common with that prince of all devils, Dalzene? The girl pressed her hand to her breast. There was a strange lump—almost a pain, that seemed pressing upon her—weighting her down.

For more than a week this clear-eyed, handsome stranger had been her constant companion. Frankly she had admitted to herself that she liked him. Deep down in her heart she knew that her regard for him had swiftly ripened into a far deeper emotion. In her mind's eye she had compared him with other men, and she knew that he stood above them all. His very presence stirred unsuspected depths within her. When they were together the whole world sang with happiness, when they were apart, there was a void. And now, with her own eyes she had seen him apparently hand in glove with Jake Dalzene! Oh, what did it mean? In vain her shocked brain groped for an answer. "He *is* good!" she half-sobbed. "I know he is good! I can see it in his eyes—and the dogs know! Surely Skookum would know—Skookum that distrusts all men. And I have trusted him with money I brought down from Nolan, and he has worked hard in placing it all." Mechanically, as though to corroborate the statement, she produced the sheaf of receipts signed by the proprietor of the Malamute Saloon, which showed that the money was in his possession. Surely, if he had been anything but the soul of honor, he could have made away with the money, and pursuit would have been impossible—she didn't even know his name. But—why didn't she know? What possible reason could he have for concealing his identity? What possible connection could he have with Dalzene? He had told her that he had bet heavily on her dogs himself. Why, then should he have anything in common with Dalzene, who bore her only hatred?

A sharp knock upon her door brought her to her feet. She answered the knock to be confronted by a police official. "Sorry to trouble you, Miss," he said, not unkindly, "But we've got a hooch-runner locked up, an' he says he's your father, an' he wants you should come down to the jail right away an' fetch bail. But, they ain't no use botherin' with the bail part of it. Judge Cross, he's declared a holiday till after the race, an' they ain't no one else got the authority to fix the bail. You're welcome to come down an' talk to him, though. He ain't takin' his arrest none easy."

The girl stared uncomprehendingly as the man talked: "Dad! Arrested!" she managed to gasp, when the man paused, "And, for hooch-running! You're crazy! Why, if you knew dad!"

"We've got the goods on him, all right," answered the man, "I'm sorry, Miss—if you didn't know. But he done it. Sold a bottle of hooch to an Injun. Shall I wait, or are you comin'?"

"Yes, of course I'm coming! Just a minute. I'll tell you, though, you've made an awful mistake! It's the most ridiculous thing I ever heard of!"

Ten minutes later Lou Gordon stood in the corridor of the jail and listened to her father's outpouring of wrath. Stamping up and down in the narrow confine of his cell, the old man bitterly condemned the police and vociferously asserted his innocence.

"Of course, you are innocent, dad!" cried the girl. "There has been a mistake—an awful mistake—somewhere."

"'Tis no mistake!" roared the old man, "'Tis a frame-up—to make us lose the race! They locked me up because they're afraid to let me drive that race! I ain't be'n in here two hours for nothin'! I've thought it all out! A dirty trick! That's what it is—an' the judge, an' the whole town is in on it! They say I can't get bail till after the race! Don't that prove it? But—you've got to get bail—lass! I've got to drive that race! Go out an' show 'em up, lass! Surely there must be someone in the town that will stand for fair play. Go long now, an' get me out! Go to the mayor! Go to someone! Go to everybody!" he cried, excitedly, "An' tell 'em what's comin' off!"

While the old man raved, a new train of thought coursed through the girl's brain, and as soon as possible she quitted the place, promising to see what she could do. And, as she hurried toward the hotel, she smiled, and in the privacy of her own room the smile broadened, and became an audible chuckle: "Poor old dad!" she murmured, as she rearranged a wind-tossed strand of hair before her mirror, "It will be hard on him, but I guess he'll have to stay right where he is until after the race—then I'll bail him out with my own money! Whoever it was that had him arrested certainly solved my problem for me. I just know that horrible Dalzene is at the bottom of it. He thinks it will spoil our chance of winning if dad don't drive. But, why should he care? He's not in the race. Just spite, I suppose, because we beat him at Nolan. If he only knew!" and the words trailed into a silvery laugh.

Once more her thoughts turned to her tall Stranger, but instead of dwelling dreamily upon his spoken words, his easy, graceful movement of frame, or the deep, intense look that she had more than once surprised in his blue-grey eyes; they leaped at once to his meeting with Dalzene and the apparent comradery with which they had walked down the street and entered the saloon. As the picture recalled itself, a new thought leaped into her brain. Could it be possible that, knowing as he did, of her dilemma, he himself had contrived the arrest of her father? But if so, what had Dalzene to do with it? Surely, her interests were not Dalzene's, and if the stranger really had her interests at heart he could have nothing in common with the hooch-runner of Rampart. With a shrug, she gave it up. She would know soon. She must go down and have her own name substituted for that of her father in the entry book. She was to dine with the Stranger at six, and afterward they were to complete the plan for preventing her father from driving the race.

It was after dark when she returned to the hotel to find her Stranger waiting, and together they entered the dining room where the man led the way to a small table in the center of which a mass of richly-hued blossoms blazed from a glittering cut glass bowl.

"Oh!" exclaimed the girl, glancing swiftly from the riot of color into the smiling eyes of the man, "Oh, how wonderful!"

"Do you like 'em?" he smiled.

"Like them! They are the most beautiful flowers I ever saw! Where in the world did you get them?"

"There's a kind of a Dutchman that raises 'em all under glass," he explained, "I got all he had, except the ones that they've got ordered for the big wreath that they hang around the neck of the winner of the Sweepstakes. You'll be wearin' that, too—if we can figure out how we're goin' to keep your dad from drivin'. But, really, Miss Gordon, I wish you wouldn't tackle it. Let me drive the race for you. I can handle the dogs—you know that, now. You can't depend on the weather this time of year, and if it kicks up a bad storm out there without any timber to run to, it's goin' to be hell—just plain hell!"

The girl smiled at the intensity of the man's words, and as she spoke she looked searchingly into his eyes: "Don't worry about me," she said, "All my life I have lived in the North. I'm not afraid of the storms. I'm no *chechako*."

"No, you are no *chechako*" the man replied, gravely, "But, even the sourdoughs don't always pull through."

"Do you know where my father is, this minute?" Surprised at the abrupt-
ness of the question, the man met her searching gaze: "Why, no. Fooling
around with a boiler somewhere, I suppose."

"He is in jail," announced the girl, noting the genuinely shocked expression
that leaped into the man's face.

"In ... jail!" he uttered the words slowly, as though trying to grasp their
meaning. "In jail! What do you mean?"

"I mean that they have got him locked up in jail, charged with selling liquor
to an Indian."

The man half-rose from his chair: "Who has?" he cried, "It's an outrage!
Who had him locked up? But, don't you worry! Wait right here!" he was on
his feet, now. "I'll have him out in a jiffy! They've got to let him out on bail!"

The girl motioned him to be seated, and as he stared into her face he saw
that the corners of her mouth twitched into just the suspicion of a smile. "You
can't get him out on bail until after the race. The judge has declared a holiday.
It's hard on dad, but—don't you see? He can't drive the race in jail!"

There was no question about the smile on the girl's lips, now, and as the
man slowly settled into his chair, he laughed aloud: "So that's what you've
been up to, is it? But, you'd better never let him find it out. He'd be furious!"

"I had nothing whatever to do with it," answered the girl, "But, I think I
know who did."

"Who?"

"Jake Dalzene."

"Who's Jake Dalzene?"

The waiter was removing the first course of the specially prepared dinner
that MacShane had ordered with the help of the head waiter, and which included everything obtainable in Nome that was not to be found on the regular
bill of fare. The fingers that conveyed a ripe olive to the girl's lips trembled
slightly. Had she heard aright? Was the man actually feigning ignorance of
Dalzene, when, with her own eyes she had seen them together, that very
afternoon? Was it possible that he was a confederate of the hooch-runner, and
that she was being made the victim of some deep-laid scheme? But, no. For
this man knew, if Dalzene did not, that to arrest her father to prevent him from
driving the race would be playing directly into her hands. What then? As she
spoke, she was conscious that there was a peculiar tightening at the muscles
of her throat: "Don't you know Jake Dalzene?" the words were uttered with
an effort.

"Don't know him. Never even heard of him, that I know of," answered the man.

The dinner was a flat failure. Somehow Lou Gordon stuck it through, answering the man's questions she never knew how, forcing commonplace remarks by the utmost effort of will, and longing for the moment the miserable ordeal should be over with. Once or twice as she glanced into the man's face her imagination discerned something sinister in the searching gaze of his eyes. Why had she never noticed it before? She was conscious of a dull pain in the region of her heart. The last course remained before her untouched. She began to feel queer all over. The dull pain in her heart gave place to a very real pain in her stomach. Stabs of excruciating agony shot through her body. Her vitals were being torn asunder in a mighty grip. The color receded from her face, and thin beads of cold sweat appeared upon the marble whiteness of her brow. She was aware that the Stranger was standing over her, and instinctively she shrank away from the touch of his hand. The room was growing dark. She could hear voices—excited voices—far off.

When she opened her eyes she was in bed in her own room. A man stood beside the bed regarding her intently. He was not the Stranger. Beside him stood a woman whom the girl recognized as the chambermaid who took care of the room. The man spoke: "You'll pull through, all right," he said, reassuringly, "Bad case of ptomaine poisoning. If we hadn't pumped you out just when we did, I'm afraid it would have been all over with you."

"How long have I been—here?" asked the girl, surprised at the weak tones of her voice.

"About three hours. But you must be quiet, now. Don't try to talk. I've left medicine and full instructions with Kate, here. It isn't the first time we've worked together. She's as good as any nurse. A few days of quiet is all you need."

"A few days!" cried the girl, struggling to raise herself. "Why, I've got to drive the Sweepstakes tomorrow! I've got to!"

The doctor smiled: "There, there, that's all right," he soothed, "Don't get all excited, now. Go to sleep if you can."

"But—I tell you I've got to drive that race!"

"Sure, that's all right. You can drive the race, all right. But, the race don't start till tomorrow. Get a good night's rest, and if you feel like driving the Sweepstakes in the morning, why go right ahead." The girl sank back onto her pillow, and watched between half-closed lids as the man placed some queer-looking instruments into a small black bag. A few moments later he departed, and with a low moan, she turned her face toward the wall. But, she did not go to sleep.

A half-hour later the woman, Kate, answered a gentle knock on the door. Lou Gordon recognized the voice of the Stranger asking in low tones how she fared. A mighty rage surged up within her and summoning all her strength, she raised herself to her elbow and addressed him in faltering tones: "Your scheme didn't work! It almost did—but not quite. I see it all, now! When you and Dalzene found out I wouldn't let you drive and lose the race for me, you tried to poison me, after taking care that poor old dad was out of the way! But you failed! I'll drive that race tomorrow—and I'll win! All your scheming won't stop me! You've made it harder—that's all!" and with a sob, she fell exhausted onto her pillow.

Beyond the door MacShane listened to the accusations in horror. As the faltering voice stilled, he was about to answer, but with fingers to her lips, Kate motioned for silence. "She's kind of out of her head," she whispered, and without a word, MacShane made his way to the street, and with bowed head, hunted up the doctor, and later the dog keeper, with whom he held long discourse.

CHAPTER XXIII
"I DRIVE THOSE DOGS!"

IN THE EARLY DAYS of the lower Yukon, the name of Bill Ames had been a name to conjure with. Dog train freighter in winter, and poling boat freighter in summer, he had been no small factor in the development of the country. Then came the misstep that plunged him into water with the temperature at fifty below zero, a misadventure that cost him a foot and took him forever off the trail. For years thereafter he worked at various jobs along the river, until the big stampede found him a passenger on one of the first boats that landed at Nome. There, as upon the Yukon, he worked at odd jobs until his knowledge of dogs attracted the attention of the proprietor of Nome's principal hotel, who engaged him to look after the dog teams of his guests. Unlike most of the old timers on the Yukon, Bill Ames had married a white woman, and with her he lived in a log house that formed one side of the dog corral at the rear of the hotel.

Upon the door of this domicile MacShane knocked, and was cordially invited to enter. For the old sourdough instinctively liked this stranger who daily accompanied Lou Gordon to the dog corral. Bill Ames knew dogs, and loved them. And also he knew men. And with the same certainty that he had taken measure of Dalzene, he had also taken measure of MacShane. For he had been quick to note that here, also, was a man who knew and loved dogs. But there was something else that attracted him to MacShane—an indefinable something about the man that stirred vague memories. A word here, a slight trick of movement—something, that caused Ames to continually cudgel his brain in a vain endeavor to place him. He felt sure he had seen this man before—had known him—but where? The man never volunteered information as to his identity, nor did Ames ever violate the ethics of the country by asking it. Therefore, when MacShane knocked at his door he was genuinely glad to see him.

"Well, everything's set fer the big race," said Ames, by way of conversation, when the two had settled themselves into their chairs and lighted their pipes.

"Yes, I've be'n kind of keepin' cases on these other teams, an' it looks to me as though Miss Gordon's dogs have got as good a chance to win as any of 'em, provided they're handled right."

"You spoke a mouthful," agreed Ames. "Them dogs is *right*! I claim to know a little bit about dogs, an' after I'd got acquainted with 'em fer a few days, an' seen how she handled 'em I slipped out an' got me two hundred dollars worth of the short end of a ten-to-one bet—an' I ain't settin' oneasy, neither. That gal's got the dogs, an' she knows how to handle 'em."

MacShane nodded: "She does," he agreed, "But the fact is, she ain't goin' to drive 'em."

"Ain't goin' to drive 'em!" cried Ames, "What d'you mean? She told me how her old man wanted to drive, an' how she had got to outfigger him someway. But, I heard yesterday that he'd got run in fer peddlin' hooch to Injuns—an' I was damn glad of it. Did he git bail?"

"No," answered MacShane, "He didn't get bail. He ain't goin' to drive, nei-ther."

"Who is, then?"

"Well, that's up to you—an' me."

"What d'you mean?"

"It's like this. She's sick—sick as hell. Got poisoned at supper, an' the doc had to pump her out. She says she's goin' to drive anyhow. But she can't. I just come from talkin' with the doc, an' he says she won't be out of danger for several days, an' she can't even get out of bed—let alone drive the dog race. An' the hell of it is she thinks I poisoned her. She's out of her head, prob'ly—but that's what she thinks."

As MacShane talked, Bill Ames' eyes narrowed. "How come her to git poi-soned at supper?" he asked.

"We had supper together, an' I kind of wanted it to be a big feed, so I rustled up a lot of extra grub—fancy stuff—canned lobsters, and canned olives, an' a lot more stuff. The doc said it was one of them that poisoned her—ptomaine poison he calls it, an' if he hadn't got there quick an' pumped her out, she'd be dead, by now. So, seein' how I'm to blame, in a way, for her gettin' sick, it looks like it's up to me to win that race for her."

Bill Ames regarded the speaker for a full minute through narrowed lids. "It looks damn queer to me," he said, bluntly. "The old man gittin' pinched, an' the gal gittin' pizened all to onct. Facts is, I know a damn good dog driver here in Nome. Them dogs of hern has got to win. Not because I've got a little money up on 'em, but because that gal is as square, an' white, an' as game a proposition as the North ever seen—"

"Put her there, pardner!" exclaimed MacShane, impulsively offering his hand.

Ames ignored the hand. "As I was goin' on to say," he continued, still with his eyes on MacShane's face, "It would break her heart to lose this race. They trailed all the way down from the Koyukuk to win it—an' it'll bust 'em if they don't. Which thing bein' the case, I'm goin' to see that them dogs is handled by someone that'll drive 'em to win."

"I know the dogs," answered MacShane, slowly, "I can drive 'em to win?"

"You know the dogs, all right," answered Ames, without removing his gaze from the other's eyes, "An' you prob'ly *could* drive 'em to win. But—I don't know *you*! They's somethin' damn queer somewheres. They's somethin' about this here business that stinks. Mebbe you ain't it, an' mebbe you be. They was a damn skunk come nosin' around the corral a while back that that there Skookum dog know'd. He smelt him 'fore he got inside the corral, an' if I'd onchained him, he'd of et him up. This afternoon I was in the Malamute Saloon gittin' a drink, when you an' this here party comes in together. I didn't think nothin' of it then—but I do now!" Ames paused and glared, as just the shadow of a smile played at the corners of MacShane's mouth. "Mebbe you see somethin' funny about it," he burst forth truculently, "But if I know'd you pizened that gal, I'd kill you where you set—an' mebbe you'd see somethin' funny about that!"

"Maybe I would," smiled MacShane, "Because the joke would be on you. Listen here, Bill Ames!" It was the first time MacShane had addressed him by name, and the dog keeper's eyes opened in surprise. "I haven't told anyone here my name, for reasons of my own. Miss Gordon knows me only as *Huloimee Tilakum*. But, I'm goin' to let you tell me my name—tell *me*, an' no one else, either before or after the race, or I'll never speak to you again."

"What the hell you talkin' about?" exploded the man. "Me tell you yer name! You full of hooch? Er what?"

Disregarding the interruption, MacShane proceeded: "It was way back—I don't remember the year. The lower river was plugged with rough ice, an' a certain freighter thought he could figure out a new trail—up the Innoko, through the Kaiyuh Mountains, an' hit Kaltag by way of Kaiyuh Slough. It might of worked if the freighter could have got through the mountains before he run out of grub. When he was on his last dog—"

Bill Ames leaped from his chair, and stood before MacShane, staring straight into his eyes: "Just a minute!" he cried, excitedly pointing a forefinger into MacShane's face, "You tell me this, an' By God, I'll know it's *you*! What happened about a year or two after that, in a cabin at the big bend of the Anvik?"

MacShane grinned: "Why, Bill, me an' you come onto *Kultus* McCormack an' a breed girl that he'd toled off from the mission—an' we gave him—what he had comin'!"

"*Burr MacShane!* By all the gods that's swore by! Burr MacShane! You damn old sourdough! Where in hell you be'n fer the last twenty years, or so? You was only a kid, then, you might say—but you was some man! Them was the days—when I had my two legs in under me, an' the country wasn't all gummed up with *chechakos*!"

"You're right, Bill! But, do I drive those dogs? Do you think I can handle 'em?"

"That's right, damn you, rub it in! Mebbe I was a fool, Burr ... but somehow, that gal—"

"Fool—hell! You done just right."

"An' did you know me all the time? An' never let on!"

"Sure, I did," laughed MacShane, "You ain't any older than you was then, but I'm twice as old. I've never forgot you, Bill."

"All Alaska used to be talkin' about what a hell of a trail musher you was. Gosh sakes! If them other mushers know'd who was goin' to drive them dogs, they'd all quit! You'll win—but look out fer Johnson an' Scotty Allen. They're both damn good men, an' they've got damn good dogs—but you'll win. You've got to win—er you don't git the gal—"

"What do you mean?" cried MacShane.

Ames laughed, knowingly: "Go on with you! I'm fer you. An' take it from me—they ain't another woman in the North that's deuce-high with her, anyways you look at it. You're a lucky dog, Burr."

"You're crazy as hell!" exclaimed MacShane, displaying real annoyance, "If you think Miss Gordon could ever—ever care that way, for an old sourdough like me, you're a fool—an' as for me—we're just good friends—or were till she got the idea I poisoned her—an' that's all there is to it."

"All right—have it yer own way. But I've kind of had a chanct to see which way the wind was blowin' fer a couple of weeks—an' I'm tellin' it to you if you don't want to be in love with that gal, an' don't want her to be in love with you—then you're in a hell of a fix—that's all I got to say."

At eight o'clock the following morning MacShane appeared at the corral to help Ames harness the dogs. They had just concluded the operation when through the gate walked Lou Gordon. Both men stared at the figure that approached them. The girl's face was deathly white, and it was evident from her tightly-pressed lips and her slow movements that it was only by the supremest effort of will she managed to keep on her feet at all.

MacShane sprang to her side: "Miss Gordon!" he cried, "What are you doing here? The doctor said it would be several days before you would be out of danger! How did you get here? You can hardly stand!"

The girl regarded him with flashing eyes: "You should be proud of your work," she faltered, with withering scorn. "But, you should have waited until this morning. I have had a night's rest—and I am perfectly well. I will win the race in spite of you and your partner, Dalzene." She turned to Ames who stood beside the dogs. "I'll take them, now," she said, "Did you go over the harness?"

"Yes, Miss—but, you ain't goin' to try an' drive—an' you can't hardly stand on yer feet! Why, you won't even git to the startin' place!"

MacShane interrupted, his words rasping harshly, with a note the girl had never before heard in his voice. "I drive those dogs!" and as Lou Gordon stared into his face she saw that the blue-grey eyes were hard. "You—you—" she faltered, as her two bare hands clutched at her breast.

Without a word, MacShane took one swift step, gathered her into his arms, and motioning Ames to open the door of the log house, carried her in, despite her furious struggles. But the struggles were futile and short lived. The violent illness had left the girl so weak and dizzy that the exertion of dressing herself and walking to the corral had taxed her strength to the utmost. As MacShane carried her into the room her muscles suddenly relaxed, and she lay limp and lifeless in his arms while Mrs. Ames hurriedly arranged the bed which had not yet been made up for the day.

From the moment his arms closed about her, MacShane had been conscious of a strange, indescribable thrill that welled from the very depths of his being—a thrill so new, and so wonderful that he stood as one in a trance holding the girl's body close against his own until the words of Ames roused him to action.

"Lay her on the bed, Burr, an' I'll hunt up the doc while the old woman tries to fetch her around. Come on, now, it's time you got a-goin'. You got to git the driver's name changed, an' it's gittin' along to startin' time. We'll see that she's took care of."

Very gently MacShane laid the girl upon the bed, and with one long look into the pallid face, he turned abruptly and left the room.

CHAPTER XXIV
THE ALASKA SWEEPSTAKES

"Havin' a hell of a time to find a driver for those Gordon dogs," grinned the entry man, as MacShane reported the change of drivers. "First it was Stewart Gordon, then Lou Gordon, an' now they're changin' it again. What name?"

"Make it *Huloimee Tilakum*," answered MacShane.

"*Huloimee Tilakum!* Jargon for Stranger, eh? All right, down she goes: *Huloimee Tilakum.* But, if John Johnson should break his neck, an' Scotty an' Eskimo John should founder themselves on strawberries, an' you should happen to win the race, folks will be wantin' to know a hell of a lot more about you than just The Stranger. They'll be askin' 'Who is The Stranger'?"

"Well, if they ask you," grinned MacShane, "Just tell them all you know," and turning on his heel, he pushed his way with difficulty through the dense throngs that crowded about the teams of Johnson, and Allen, and Eskimo John to the point where his own team waited, surrounded by a straggling group that eyed them indifferently. "There'll be a different story to tell when this race is over," he muttered savagely to himself, "They'll be crowdin' around these dogs fit to smother 'em—an' they won't know those other teams are alive."

It still lacked fifteen or twenty minutes of starting time; and MacShane's eyes traveled up and down the street, resplendent in flags and bunting, and literally swarming with massed humanity. Never in his life had he seen so many people at one time. Indeed, he wondered whether all the people he had ever seen would equal in numbers the crowds that had collected to witness the start of the Alaska Sweepstakes, the great classic of the North. "Where do they all come from?" he speculated, "An' where do they get the grub to feed 'em all?"

The officers were clearing the street. Men, women and children surged back onto the sidewalks and lined the thoroughfare in two solid masses. In the street remained only the race teams and their drivers. Seven teams beside his own, MacShane counted, two of twelve dogs, three of fourteen, one of sixteen, and Johnson's team of eighteen. A few moments later they lined up for the start, each driver standing beside his leader. Whips were in evidence, and realizing the possibility of Skookum's running amuck amid the cracking of whips, MacShane contrived to be fumbling at the great leader's collar when the shot sounded that started the racers over the long snow-trail. As the dog teams shot away a mighty roar of applause burst from thousands of throats. For a full minute, MacShane continued to work with the collar, and then, amid a vast chorus of jeers and cat-calls he gave the word, and Skookum led his team in the wake of the vanishing racers.

At Soloman, the first reporting station, MacShane learned that Allen was leading, having made the thirty-two miles in three hours and thirteen minutes. Fred Ayer was one minute behind him, and Johnson had pulled in six minutes behind Ayer. Sapala, and Eskimo John, who drove the Council Kennel Club's entry, came in together sixteen minutes later, while Fay Delezene and Paul Kjegsted were right on their heels. MacShane's own time was three hours and forty-two minutes, twenty-nine minutes behind the leading team.

At Timber, sixty-four miles from the starting point, the order remained unchanged, Allen making the distance in six hours and fifty-eight minutes. MacShane pulled in at 4:23, and noted with a grin that he had gained four minutes on Allen. Just beyond Timber, Kjegsted came to grief with a broken sled runner and withdrew from the race. Twenty miles farther on MacShane passed Sapala, and overtook Eskimo John, and Ayer at Telephone Creek where they were resting, one hundred and twenty-two miles from the starting point. This left only Allen, Johnson, and Delezene ahead of him. Allen had reported in at 10:03, rested for ten minutes, fed his dogs, and pulled out. Johnson had pulled in twelve minutes behind Allen, and had gained five minutes by pausing only long enough to feed his dogs a handful of meal. Delezene had reported in two minutes after Johnson had left, and had pulled out without stopping. MacShane decided to do likewise as his dogs were still fresh. Eskimo John followed him out, and Ayer fell in behind him.

At the summit of Death Valley Hill, MacShane passed Delezene, whose dogs seemed to be weakening, and at Haven, one hundred and forty-six miles from Nome, he overtook Allen and Johnson who were resting. Allen had made the run in twenty-nine hours and three minutes, Johnson in twenty-nine hours and twenty minutes, and MacShane in twenty-nine hours and twenty-seven minutes. Johnson was the first to leave, resting for only fifteen minutes. MacShane fed his dogs and pulled out five minutes later, leaving Allen mending a harness.

At Gold Run, one hundred and eighty-two miles from the starting point, MacShane again overtook Johnson, pulling in five minutes after the leader. They had been thirty-three hours and thirty minutes on the trail, and each rested for ten minutes.

As MacShane pulled out of Gold Run, Allen overtook him, and without stopping, pulled out right at his heels. With hands glued to the handle bars, MacShane studied his dogs as he ran. Skookum, the superb leader, was apparently as fresh as when he started. One by one, he watched critically each dog's work, but could detect no hint of lameness or lagging. Iron man that he was, MacShane was beginning to tire. His muscles did not lag, but it was requiring a conscious effort of mind to hold them to the work. Johnson was nowhere in sight, and behind him he could hear Allen urging on his dogs. The temperature was rising, and MacShane, bathed in sweat, and conscious of a terrible thirst, sucked the first of the dozen lemons he had provided for the purpose.

He reached Candle Creek, the turning point of the race five minutes behind Johnson. Allen was nowhere in sight. MacShane fed and watered his dogs, and rolling up in his rabbit robe was asleep in two minutes. When he awoke, an hour and a half later, both Johnson and Allen had left. Johnson had rested an hour, and Allen a half-hour.

There was no hint of snow in the air as MacShane headed his dogs over the back trail. Apparently as fresh as when he started he urged his dogs to a faster pace, and at Gold Run, twenty-four miles away, he overtook Allen. He had made the two hundred and thirty miles in forty-four hours flat. Here he learned that Johnson was an hour ahead of him and going strong when he pulled out of Gold Run. He left five minutes after his arrival, and once again Allen was right at his heels. MacShane noted that Allen had taken a dog on his sled. He made Haven, two hundred and sixty-six miles from the starting point, in fifty-eight hours and thirty-five minutes. The air was full of snow, and he learned that Johnson was only forty minutes ahead of him and that he, too, had taken a dog on his sled.

As MacShane approached Death Valley Hill, the wind rose to almost hurricane violence, and the character of the snow changed from definite flakes to a fine powdery snow-fog that bit and stung the flesh of his face like a thousand needle-points. With the snow-fog came a drop in temperature. MacShane's mittens froze to the handle bars. The dogs slowed to three miles an hour. There was no trail, and try as he would MacShane could not see his leader. The wind swung the sled dangerously, and time after time MacShane nearly lost his handle bars.

Suddenly Skookum stopped dead still. In vain MacShane yelled to urge him on. One of the new dogs laid down, and MacShane took him to the sled. He hurried to Skookum and with a hand on the great dog's collar tried to start him. But the dog was immovable. MacShane walked ahead, and not ten yards away he plunged over a cliff. The fall of twenty or thirty feet did no more than give him a shaking up, as he alighted in a huge drift of the new-fallen snow, but it was a good half-hour before he managed to regain the upper level. The dogs had made good use of the interval and all were lying down in the harness. MacShane was lost! He had been lost a hundred times, but never before had it mattered. Always he had camped until the conditions that had caused his predicament had righted themselves, but now to camp meant to lose the race. Over and over, as he had frantically tried to scale the cliff, he had kept repeating to himself, "I've got to win! I've got to win!"

He reasoned that the trail lay to the westward, as the terrific wind had gradually forced them off the course. "Gee! Skookum! Gee!" he cried, "Mush-a! Mush! Hi! Mush-a! Mush-a!" This time the leader threw himself into the collar, and the whole team responded with a will. The air was an impenetrable wall of whirling, stinging fog, and gripping the handle bars, MacShane urged the dogs on, he knew not whither. On, and on, they bored through the seething smother. An hour passed—two hours, and suddenly MacShane felt the sled accelerate. He quickened his pace to keep up, and in a few minutes more he was running! There was only one explanation—Skookum had found the trail! "Go it, Skookum! Mush-a! Mush-a!" the wind tore the words from his lips and buried them in the fog—but the dogs ran on.

Suddenly, after hours of blind running, something black loomed up close beside him. Boston Roadhouse! Somehow he had missed Telephone Creek altogether, in the storm. Here he learned that neither Johnson nor Allen had been heard from since pulling out of Haven. Neither Telephone Creek nor Boston Roadhouse had seen either of them! MacShane fed his dogs and pulled out. Only one hundred and seven miles to go—and he was leading! Of course, there was a bare possibility that Johnson was still ahead, but if so, he was off the trail, and would be laboring under a severe handicap. "It was her taking the dogs over the trail that did it!" muttered MacShane, as he bored on through the storm. "Without that Skookum would never have found it. She didn't drive the race—but if we come in first, By God, she *won* it!" Two hours later the snow-fog lightened. MacShane could see all the dogs, now. It was growing colder. Again his muscles were tiring. The sweat was pouring from his body into his mukluks. He sucked lemons continually. Hour after hour he held the dogs to their work, and when he judged he had made twenty-five miles from Boston Roadhouse, he halted the team, and fed them meal and tallow. Here, also he pulled the other young dog out of the harness and replaced him with the one which had rested. "Only about eighty miles to go, boys!" he cried, after fifteen minutes of rest, "Mush-a! Mush-a! We've got to win that money!"

When MacShane staggered into Timber on the tail end of the blizzard, he had made three hundred and forty-eight miles in seventy-four hours and thirty minutes, with sixty-four miles to go.

At Timber he learned that Johnson had reported into Boston Roadhouse an hour and ten minutes after he had pulled out, and had rested two full hours. Allen had withdrawn from the race after injuring three of his dogs when his team went over a cliff in the storm. He had returned to Haven.

With a good three hours' lead, MacShane slept for two hours and pulled out with the sun shining brightly. The thirty-four miles to Topkok was made without incident, MacShane urging his tired dogs, and his tired muscles to their utmost. At Topkok he learned that Johnson, with three dogs on his sled was barely holding his own, an hour and a quarter behind. Just out of Topkok, with thirty miles to go—MacShane took another dog onto the sled. One of the big malamutes had gone lame. From that time on, he drove a terrific trail, forcing the dogs to their limit. For he knew that Johnson would gain, as with three dogs on the sled, he still had fifteen dogs in harness, while he himself, had but ten.

From Topkok on, he was forced to face the wind which tore at his exposed face and whipped the sled about so that it was with the utmost difficulty he managed to keep it from being smashed into kindling wood against the telephone poles that flanked the trail. MacShane was running mechanically, taking no thought of miles. He had used the last of his lemons and was consumed by torturing thirst. The sweat squashed audibly in his mukluks, and he ran as in a dream. A crashing explosion brought him to his senses. It was the gun at Fort Davis that announces to the waiting thousands in Nome that the first racer is in sight.

"Only four miles to go! Four miles! Four miles!" MacShane found himself babbling the words aloud. The report of the gun had put new life in his veins and he ran on encouraging his dogs to a faster pace.

Nome! From the roofs of the buildings, from the cross-arms of poles men and boys cheered him on. As he ran down the seemingly endless street the crowds thickened. Black masses of howling, yelling people lined the side-walks. And as he crossed the line the Queen of the Alaska Carnival, running at his side, hung a huge wreath of flowers about his neck.

The great race was over. The Gordon dogs had won!

"How is she?" asked MacShane, as Bill Ames, swearing great round, brag-ging oaths of pure joy, took over the dogs.

"She's comin' along. They tuk her to the horspital."

"Don't tell 'em my name—any of 'em," whispered MacShane, and the next moment he was gone.

CHAPTER XXV
HULOIMEE TILAKUM

THE GORDON DOGS WIN! The Gordon dogs win! All Nome rang with the cry. Like wildfire the words leaped from lip to lip.

Lying upon her bed in the hospital with eyes half-closed, Lou Gordon heard the boom of the signal gun at Fort Davis. "What is it?" she asked of a nurse, who at the sound had taken her position at a window that overlooked the street.

"It's the gun! The first of the racers has got to Fort Davis! It won't be long, now, till we hear the news. I'll bet it's John Johnson—he's just grand! So big and strong. But, it might be Scotty Allen. He's an awful good man on the trail, they say. I'll tell you as soon as I hear."

On the bed, the girl's eyes closed, and two big tears rolled down her cheeks. Other tears followed until two damp places appeared upon the pillow. Well—it would soon be over. She had been a fool to leave the Koyukuk. Bitterly, the panorama of events of the past few weeks floated through her brain. The high hope with which she had set out from the little cabin on Myrtle. The hardships of the long snow-trail. Her joy and wonder in the splendors of Nome. Her meeting with The Stranger, and their two weeks together, during which life had seemed to take on new meaning for her. Then—the strange premonition of evil that came over her as she witnessed his meeting with Dalzene. The arrest of the father on a trumped-up charge. Her violent illness, by means of which the plotters had eliminated her from all chances of winning the race. And, last of all—the realization that there would be no money left when the bills were paid. She vaguely wondered if there would be enough to pay the bills.

A thunderous roar of voices filled the air. Louder, and louder swelled the sound, until it seemed as though everybody in the world was trying to out-yell his neighbor. With tight-pressed lips the girl waited. What difference did it make who won? Nevertheless she found herself waiting for the words of the nurse. A young doctor charged into the room. "The Gordon dogs win!" he cried, "Eighty-three hours and three minutes! They all got lost in the blizzard—"

Lou Gordon found herself sitting bolt upright in bed. What was he saying? He is crazy! Wide eyed she stared at the white coated figure that was hurrying toward her. "Lie down! Please lie down!" His hands were upon her shoulders trying to force her gently back upon the pillow. But she resisted his efforts.

"What—what did you say?" she demanded, her fists clenching and unclenching.

"Oh, come now. If I had thought you would get so excited about it, I wouldn't have told the news. But you were the only patient in the convalescent ward, and—"

"Tell me!" the girl's voice was almost a shriek, "Tell me who won!"

"The Gordon dogs won," soothed the man, "They're a team nobody thought had a chance. Why, the odds were ten-to-one against 'em."

The girl's eyes slowly closed, and she allowed herself to be lowered to the pillow, where for some moments she lay with her head in a whirl while the voices of the doctor and the nurse sounded very far away. Suddenly, she again tried to raise herself, but the nurse held her back. "Who drove them?" she asked. "Tell me! Who drove my dogs?"

"Your dogs?" cried the young doctor, "What do you mean?"

"They're my dogs, I tell you! I'm Lou Gordon! They're my dogs! Who drove them?"

"Oh, my God!" exclaimed the young doctor, "I didn't know! Doctor Steele will murder me if he finds out I caused all this excitement. Oh, say, calm yourself, Miss Gordon! Honestly I didn't know?" The man's perturbation was so evident, that Lou Gordon despite her impatience, found herself smiling.

"I won't be excited any more—really. But—please tell me!"

"Well, that's just what everyone else wants to know," smiled the doctor. "He's entered as *Huloimee Tilakum*—and that means The Stranger. Everyone is asking 'Who is The Stranger?' You tell me, Miss Gordon? Who is he?"

The girl shook her head: "*Huloimee Tilakum*," she answered, "That's all I know," and struggled frantically to raise herself. "Go find him!" she cried.

"But—I'm on duty. I—"

"Send someone, then! Send everyone! I've got to find him. Oh, I was a fool! A fool! I'll go myself! I must find him! Oh, how can I ever look him in the face again? But, I will find him! I must!"

It took the combined efforts of the young doctor and the nurse to prevent the girl from leaping from the bed. "I'll go! I'll start a search for him!" cried the doctor in desperation, "Only, please, Miss Gordon—for your own good, as well as mine—please be quiet. I'll have him here in no time!" and with that, he was gone, as with a sigh of resignation, the girl sank back upon her pillow.

Over and over she repeated the wonderful words, "They won! My dogs won! And, *he* drove them!" The weakness that had held her listless for three days was gone. She could feel the strength returning to her body—flowing through its fibres in a life-giving current of warmth. Her heart seemed bursting with happiness, and in her brain the face of *Huloimee Tilakum* shone through a chaos of whirling thought. What would she say to him? What could she say. Would he ever forgive her?

The young doctor appeared in the doorway.

"Where is he?" cried the girl.

"No one seems to have seen him since the race," he explained, "but they'll find him. I've got a dozen men hunting for him. Told 'em to comb Nome with a fine-tooth comb until they did find him. They say you'll clean up *big!*"

"Oh, never mind that!" cried the girl, "Why doesn't he come?"

A form appeared in the doorway behind the doctor, and the bluff voice of Bill Ames rang through the room: "They win, Miss Gordon! I know'd they could do it!"

At the words the youthful physician whirled on the speaker: "Get out of here!" he ordered, "How in the devil did you get through the office?"

"Let him come!" cried Lou Gordon, "Come, Mr. Ames, tell me all about it!"

"It's against the rules!" vociferated the doctor, barring the way, and the next moment the strong arm of Bill Ames was brushing him aside.

"That's what they claimed down stairs," quoth Bill, as he stepped into the room, "An' if you don't shut up yer pesterin' young feller, I'll jist nach'ly pick you up an' chuck you through that winder, sash an' all," and, without further ado, he advanced to the girl's bed, his peg leg loudly tapping the floor.

"I know'd you'd want to hear about it, so I come—"

"But, where is he—*Huloimee Tilakum?*" interrupted the girl.

The grin broadened on the face of Bill Ames: "Oh, him—I guess he's poundin' his ear, somewheres. Eighty-three hours on the trail, an' part of it through a blizzard, calls fer a good long sleep. He was wobblin' when he crossed the finish line. They hung the big wreath on his neck, an' do you know what he done? He tore it off an' hung it on the neck of that there Skookum dog! That's what he done! An' By God, Miss Gordon, that's what I call a man! Givin' the dogs the credit. 'It was the Skookum dog done it,' he says to me, after he'd axed how was you gittin' on, 'The lead dog, an' the gal that had sense enough to run 'em over the trail. We was lost,' he says, 'An' that Skookum dog found the trail because he's be'n over it.' Them's the words he says to me, an' then he was gone. The best team won, Miss Gordon—an' the best man won. An' now all Alasky is wonderin' who is he? Why, they ain't sayin' 'Hello,' no more, down there in the streets, nor 'How be you?' It's who the hell is *Huloimee Tilakum*? But, they won't never find out from me—"

"Do you know?" cried the girl, half rising from her pillow, "Tell me! Do you know?"

"Who—me?" exclaimed Bill Ames, "Not me, Miss Gordon. I don't know nothin' about nothin'! Honest I don't. I never seen him or heerd tell of him till you brung him to the corral that day! So long, Miss Gordon! I gotta go!" And without waiting for another word, Bill Ames vanished from the room as swiftly as his peg leg would permit.

Down in the jail they rimmed Old Man Gordon's cell demanding to know who drove the Gordon dogs. The old man paused long enough in his denunciation of the police, the court, and all Nome in general, to roar his answer at them: "My daughter drove 'em! Con blast ye! That's the breed of us Koyukukers! Our women over there can beat the best mushers ye got!'Twas my wee lass of a daughter that won ye're race!"

"Hell of a lookin' daughter!" exclaimed a man in the crowd, "You ort to saw him hurlin' them dogs down the street to the finish, an' all Nome lookin' on an' yellin' their head off! Believe me, old timer! It was a he-man won that race!"

That very day they turned Gordon loose with apologies so evidently sincere that the old man's ruffled temper was completely mollified. For, upon further questioning the Indian admitted that Dalzene, and not Gordon had furnished the hooch. Whereupon Dalzene was apprehended and promptly sentenced to six months at hard labor.

The following day Lou Gordon was discharged from the hospital. During the week which they remained at the hotel for the girl to fully regain her strength both she and her father used every means at their command to locate the mysterious *Huloimee Tilakum*. But all to no purpose. The man had seemingly vanished from the face of the earth. In the prosecution of this search, Bill Ames was her most indefatigable henchman. Try as she would, the girl could not rid herself of the impression that the dog keeper knew more than he would tell. But despite her utmost endeavors to extract information, the man denied all knowledge of the vanished Stranger. And, even as he lied, nobly and desperately, Bill Ames silently cursed himself for promising silence, and bitterly he cursed MacShane for the fool he was. For he guessed rightly that no aftermath of her recent illness had caused the girl suddenly to lose all interest in life. He knew that she loved her dogs—knew her pride in them. And he knew that she should have thrilled to the heart at the vociferously expressed admiration of the crowds that came daily to visit those dogs in the corral. And knowing these things he cursed mightily under his breath as he watched her gaze upon these men in dull apathy, her eyes searching, always searching for a face that was not there.

As the miserable week wore to its close hope died within the girl's breast, for even the indefatigable Bill Ames was at last forced to admit that *Huloimee Tilakum* was no longer in Nome.

"He has gone—gone," she murmured to herself, as she stared wide-eyed into the darkness of her room upon her last night in the hotel. "And—it's all my fault! Oh, how could I have been such a fool? He is a man! The best man in all the world! I love him! I do love him! And—he has—gone!" Then the tears came, and for a long time the sound of muffled sobbing penetrated the darkness of the room.

CHAPTER XXVI
EYES IN THE DARK

BACK ON THE KOYUKUK the nightless summer dragged wearily to its close for Lou Gordon. Father and daughter had been given an ovation in Nolan upon their return from Nome. It was a great moment in the little Arctic camp, when Lou Gordon placed in the hands of Clem Wilcox bank drafts totaling in the neighborhood of one hundred thousand dollars for distribution among the men who had backed her dogs to win.

Instead of reviving her spirits, the long homeward journey had served only to increase the aching void in her breast. Even the gala day that celebrated their arrival in Nolan failed to arouse any enthusiasm in her heart, and in the little cabin on Myrtle she took up her round of duties as one assumes drudgery.

In July, when the little shallow-draught steamer transferred Old Man Gordon's "b'iler," to a waiting flat boat at Bettles, all Nolan turned out and man-hauled the ponderous piece of freight up a hundred miles of shallow water and set it in place on the Gordon claim.

"I'll show ye!" the old man had prophesied when he thanked them for their help, "Ye'd better stay an' fix up yer old cabins. For, ye'll all be back on Myrtle in the spring!"

And the men of Nolan laughed, and returned up river.

And now, as the days grew short, and the nights long, and the sting of frost was in the air, Old Man Gordon, with a huge pile of wood ready to hand, waited impatiently for the coming of the cold that would allow him to steam his way into the iron-hard gravel of the creek.

Snow covered the land—and more snow. Lou Gordon broke puppies, shot caribou, and hauled the carcasses to the meat cache. But there was no joy in the work. Life had lost its zest. Living had become simply the mechanical doing of things that had to be done.

One day in December she stood upon a long treeless ridge at noontime and, with her eyes fixed on the southern horizon, watched for the appearance of the sun. Yesterday only half his diameter had appeared for a few minutes above the horizon, and today the girl knew she would catch the last glimpse of his face for many long weeks to come. Overhead a few of the brighter stars glowed feebly through the pink radiance of the noonday dawn.

Gradually the rose-pink of the heavens deepened upon the southern horizon. Alternating bands of pink and lavender shot upward in ever widening bands that paled and merged as they approached the zenith. With startling swiftness the colors intensified, the bands of pink becoming, in the twinkling of an eye, bands of flaming crimson, and the lavender giving place to banners of purest purple. For many minutes Lou Gordon gazed upon the wonderful pageant of color. The red disk of the sun appeared above the horizon, and the next instant his yellow rays touched the glittering ice peaks with an aureole of golden glory. Only for a few moments was the segment of his disk visible, as it traveled its foreshortened arc—and was gone. The panorama of color reversed, and in the deepening twilight the big stars glowed in wan radiance.

It is an impressive sight, that swan song of the sun—that riot of flashing brilliance—that spectacular pomp of flaming color with which he bids the frozen world good night. One last blaze of glory to delight the eyes of the dwellers of the drear lone land of snow. For, until his next appearance, the land within the Circle is a dead land of black and white. Timber, cabins, animals, people that come within the short range of vision all appear a uniform dead black, against the cold dead whiteness of snow and ice.

Every winter when the heavens had been clear enough to permit it, Lou Gordon had taken her leave of the sun from this same bare ridge, and always the grand symphony of color tones had stirred her to the uttermost fibre of her being, stirred her to the very soul, heartened her for the long, long night. But, on this day there was no answering response in her heart. The sun, giver of light, and life, and warmth, had blazed his farewell from the rim of the world, and was gone. The North lay dead, as her heart was dead. Except that for the North, there would be an awakening.

She, too, had had her little day of glory. Two short weeks of wonderful pulsing life. Love had stirred her heart with the wonderful symphony of his song. Then the sun of love had set, and the world was black, and white, and toneless.

With a dull pain gnawing at her heart, the girl turned her back upon the southern horizon, spoke to her dogs, and wearily descended the ridge into the narrow valley of Myrtle.

The strong cold descended upon the land. Myrtle creek froze to the bottom, burst its ice bond, and froze again. The breath snapped and crackled as it left the lips, and men forsook the trails.

Then it was that Old Man Gordon's "b'iler" froze to its very vitals. For four weeks he had managed, by firing night and day, to keep steam in her, but as the strong cold gripped the land, it gripped the boiler, too. Unprotected by any building it froze with the fire roaring in the fire-box, and stood out under the glittering stars, a black and useless thing of iron.

With the failure of his boiler Old Man Gordon lost his grip on life. In vain Lou tried to arouse him to return to his wood-thawing. But, the old man merely shook his head and sat staring through the hours of unchanging dark, into the little squares of light that showed at the draught holes of the stove.

December passed into January of the worst winter the Koyukuk had ever experienced. Furious blizzards followed upon the heels of the strong cold, and the strong cold upon the heels of the blizzards. Snow piled to unprecedented depths, and all trails were hopelessly buried.

Not until the second week in January did Lou Gordon become really alarmed about her father. The hours when she was not busy with her dogs she spent in reading, and in trying to awaken the old man from the apathy into which he had fallen. His appetite had dwindled until he was eating almost nothing. He rarely spoke, merely answering the girl's questions with a nod, or a shake of the head.

Then came a day when she returned from the dog kennels to find the cabin empty. Her father's mukluks and parka, and his heavy mittens were not on their accustomed place. She breathed a sigh of relief. At last he had taken interest in life. Removing her outer gear, she built up the fire, and settled herself to read. An hour later she laid down her book, and leaped to her feet with a start. Where was her father? A sudden fear gripped her, a nameless terror that struck a chill to her very heart. It was one of the coldest days of the winter. The thermometer recorded sixty-six below zero. And for weeks he had hardly touched his food! Frantically she drew on her heavy clothing, and dashed out into the gloom. Tracks led toward the boiler, whose iron side showed gaunt and black on the bank of the creek above the rim of a huge snowdrift. The wind, swirling and eddying about it had whipped the ground bare of snow and left the hideous black shape in the center of a pit.

Upon the edge of the surrounding drift the girl paused and stared down into this cavity. Before the open door of the fire-box crouched the figure of her father, barely distinguishable in the darkness. She called loudly, but there was no response—not so much as a turning of the head. And with a low cry of terror she leaped into the pit and stooped over the crouching figure. One glance into the marble-white face, that showed above the grizzled beard, one grip upon the iron-hard shoulder that resisted the clutch of her mittened fingers, and she drew swiftly back. For a full minute she stood stunned, her hands pressing her breast, her eyes closed. Then with tight-pressed lips, she returned slowly to the cabin and harnessed her dogs.

It required two hours of hard labor to remove the frozen body to the cabin, and two days of thawing beside the roaring stove before the doubled limbs could be straightened—days during which Lou Gordon returned to the cabin only to wait for her gravel-thawing fire to eat into the adamantine ground. Close beside the grave of her mother, she was burning in for this new grave. Side by side they should lie deep in the eternal frost, their bodies preserved without decay until the end of time. Bravely, in dry-eyed silence she worked, and made no plan for the future.

A journey to Nolan for assistance in her grewsome labor was out of the question. Sled travel in the deep loose snow was impossible, and she had no toboggan. So she worked alone. When the body had thawed, she straightened the limbs, folded the hands upon the breast, and wrapping it tightly in a wet blanket, removed it to the wood-shed, where the strong cold converted the blanket into a shroud of iron.

It took two weeks to burn into the gravel and when the grave was finished, the girl lowered the body gently to the bottom by means of a doubled babiche line. Then she carefully filled the grave, and erected a small wooden cross, into which she laboriously burned a simple inscription, with the point of a red hot spike. Then she retired to the cabin and, throwing herself upon her bunk, gave way to an uncontrollable fit of sobbing. That night the strong cold again gave way before a howling blizzard, and in the morning when she fed her dogs the little wooden cross was buried under a pure white mantle of snow.

Days passed, days hardly distinguishable from the darkness of night. A grey cloud-bank overhung the Koyukuk, lowering and sullen and heavily burdened with snow, obscuring even the dim twilight of high noon. And with the passing of the days a deep melancholy settled itself upon the girl. In vain she tried to interest herself in her books, and the twice read magazines. But it was no use. A great weight seemed pressing upon her, smothering her. Her head felt strange, and sleep came only in short, dream-troubled snatches. Mechanically she attended to her simple duties, fed her dogs, and carried wood from the wood house.

Each day was exactly like the preceding day, and the nights were the same as the days. The eyes of the dogs glowed like live coals as she moved among them in the darkness. There was something sinister—evil, in the greenish glint of these eyes that were always upon her. Why had she never noticed it before? Why did they glare at her out of the unending night? Twenty-one dogs out there in the dark—forty-two eyes! Eyes in the dark! Always eyes! Staring eyes! Flashing eyes! And eyes that glowed with sullen malevolence! Like the eyes of Dalzene! That was it, the eyes of Dalzene—flashing with hate, when he had threatened her in the roadhouse at Nolan. Glowing with smouldering hate when he passed her that day upon the trail near Soloman. Vividly the words of the man flashed through her brain: "Myrtle's played out an' dead." Yes, Myrtle is dead—dead and forgotten—and the boiler is dead—and her father is dead—and her mother—all—all dead—dead and gone—and forgotten, as Dalzene had said.

With a shudder she recalled the leering glint of his eyes as he had begged her to throw in with him, "We'll go where we kin have some fun—down on the Yukon, or over to Nome, that's where the bright lights is." The bright lights! Well, she had seen the bright lights—had basked in their brilliance. For two never-to-be-forgotten weeks she had *lived*.

And she recalled the terrible gleam in his eyes as he had uttered his threat: "Time will come when you will talk to Jake Dalzene—an' talk pretty! Time will come when you'll learn that Jake Dalzene don't never fergit!" And his eyes had gleamed—like the eyes of the dogs in the dark.

That day, when she fed the dogs, she cast fearful, nervous glances behind her into the gloom. And, that night she took Skookum with her into the cabin. That night, also she cleaned and oiled her rifle, filled its magazine with cartridges, and stood it in the corner nearest her bunk.

Skookum was restless. Never before had he slept in a cabin, and all night long he dozed fitfully, awaking at short intervals with a start, to walk about the room. The click of his toe nails upon the floor awoke the girl, and each time she stirred in her bed the great dog would look toward her—two eyes that glowed in the dark. And, with a shudder she would turn her face to the wall—but not to sleep.

Cold fear gripped her heart. She would hit out for Nolan. Dalzene would never dare to show his face in Nolan. Tomorrow she would harness her dogs and hit the trail. But—she had no toboggan, and in the deep loose snow, the sled would be useless. No, she must stay here on Myrtle until the thaw came and hardened the surface of the snow. If she couldn't travel, Dalzene couldn't travel either. But—Dalzene had a toboggan! Pete Enright had told her of how the man had shifted to a toboggan and given them the slip below Bettles! She must go—somewhere. Dalzene would be out of jail. His time should have expired sometime last fall. He had had six months in which to nurse his hate, and to plot and plan, and three or four months since in which to carry out his plans. Dalzene never forgets! Even now he might be on Myrtle, trailing through the snow with a toboggan. There was the rifle. If Dalzene came she would kill him. Or, kill herself. Ah, that is it—no more darkness, no more gleaming eyes. No more fighting the dull pain that seemed weighting—always weighting her down. One quick flash, and then—oblivion. Sleep. Forever and forever—sleep. No eyes staring, glaring at her from the outer dark. No more fear of Dalzene. Myrtle is dead. Coldfoot is dead. Everything—everything is dead. They would bury her beside her father and her mother—the men of Nolan, when they found her in the spring—and she could sleep. And *he* would never know. Toiling, delving, far in the high North for his red gold he would never know that she wanted him. That for weeks and for months her soul had been calling, calling to his soul. He would never know that her heart cried out to him in the bright summer midnight, and in the darkness of the eternal winter night. Had he forgotten her? Some day he would find his red gold, and then—But, here on Myrtle she would be sleeping the long, long sleep.

Slowly her hand felt along the wall, nearer and nearer the corner, closer and closer it drew to the black barrel of the rifle. Her groping fingers reached it, and with a short, quick cry she drew them away from the icy coldness of its touch. In the darkness Skookum bounded to her side, and his warm red tongue brushed her cheek. Life! Splendid, pulsing life was in the two great bounds that had carried him to her side! Slowly the girl closed her eyes. *He,* too, was alive. *He* would never run away from it all. *He* would never seek the long, long sleep. He would live! Live and beat down the thing that was conquering him! For eight years alone he had been fighting the North. And he would win! He would laugh at the North, even as he gouged the red gold from its bosom! And she, too, would laugh at the North! With startling distinctness, the image of *Huloimee Tilakum* rose before her. Tall and straight, with the lithe easy movement of rugged strength he stood before her. He was smiling, the illusive, half-smile that barely curved his lips, but radiated a little fan of wrinkles from the corners of his eyes. And those eyes! The blue-grey eyes were looking directly into hers—intense, piercing—devouring. Straight into her heart they looked, and all unconsciously they were telling her what his lips had never told! Lou Gordon sat bolt upright and her two arms flew about Skookum's great neck. "I'm coming! I'm coming! *Huloimee Tilakum!* In your eyes I have seen it—*love!* Oh, I am coming to you—my love. Into the far North—beyond the timber—beyond men—we two!" She was sobbing aloud, and the words were pouring from her lips into the great lead dog's ears. "We will go to him, Skookum. Just as soon as the thaw makes travel possible. We will hunt for him on the Colville! And we will find him. And together we will find his red gold! Myrtle is dead, but we are alive, Skookum—alive! And way in the white land beyond the mountains we will live, and love, and find gold—red gold. In his eyes I have read it! Not once but many times! But—I did not know—then! Eyes, Skookum—never again will we be afraid of the eyes in the dark!"

CHAPTER XXVII
THE WORTH OF GOLD

WAY DOWN NORTH, WHERE the ice-locked Colville winds its way to the frozen sea, Burr MacShane sat upon the floor of his igloo and stared at the pile of red gold he had heaped onto a square of canvas. Beside him were many empty caribou-skin sacks. Slowly he thrust his fingers into the yellow-red pile, working them into the heavy metal until his hand was buried to the wrist.

Very deliberately he blew a cloud of blue smoke ceilingward. "'Is it worth it?' she asked, that day on the trail, 'Up here we are missing—life.' An' I said I didn't know, an' that if I found out I would tell her the answer." He withdrew his hand from the golden pile and meticulously tamped the ashes into the bowl of his pipe.

The petrol lamp sputtered and its flame grew dull. MacShane rose, filled the lamp, and stepping to the door stared out into the Arctic gloom. Then he returned to his seat on the floor. "Nothin' but cold, an' darkness, an' snow, an' ice, an' damned bare peaks—an' gold. Twenty-five years at it—twenty-five years fillin' stinkin' lamps, an' cookin' dog feed, an' gougin' gravel, an' fightin' the cold, an' what have I got to show for it? Gold! Yellow dirt! The chips in the game! You can't eat it. You can't wear it. It ain't worth a damn until it's traded for somethin' else. An' what have I ever traded it for—grub, an' petrol, an' clothing, an' dogs, an' powder—so I could go an' get more gold! I've played the game for twenty-five years, an' I've got a lot of chips stacked up. I've hit the trail when other men holed up, an' I've lived when they died like flies. I've beat the damned North! It's played all its cards, an' it's through. It's tried to freeze me with its strong cold—an' it couldn't. It's tried to starve me in its barrens, an' drown me in its rivers, an' drive me mad with its silence, an' its darkness, an' its flashin' aurora. It's done its damndest—an' I've laughed at the worst it could do! It fought for its gold, but I beat it—an' ripped the gold from the guts of its creeks. Twenty-five years—livin' like an Eskimo—like a dog—an' all for little sacks of yellow dirt hid away in iron safes!

"'Is it worth it?' she asked. I didn't know, then. But, I know—now. I promised to tell her the answer. It took me quite a while to learn it. A man can beat the North. But he can't beat—love. Yes—that's what it is—*love*. There ain't no use of a man's chasin' the devil around the stump tryin' to fool himself. He might as well come right out with it. Bill Ames was right. I wonder how the hell he knew? I didn't know, myself—then. Bill's smarter than he looks to be. What I'd ought to done the minute I saw her there on the trail, was to swing my dogs around an' head 'em hell-bent back into the North—then I could have gone on for twenty-five more years pilin' up my foolish gold. But—God, I'm glad I didn't!"

Very deliberately Burr MacShane refilled the caribou-skin sacks from the yellow-red pile on the canvas. When he had finished, he put a huge batch of dog feed to cook, and then, methodically, he moved about the little igloo selecting various articles which he made up into a trail pack. "You're a fool!" warned an inner voice, "She thinks you poisoned her. She hates you."

MacShane argued aloud: "She knows better, by now."

"But, she don't love you."

"Maybe not—but, she will. Sometimes, in her eyes, I could see—they glowed sort of soft, an' dark, an' dreamy. Damn it! Bill Ames said she would—an' he ought to know!"

"But, there's red gold in the gravel. You haven't scratched it yet."

"To hell with the red gold! I found it, didn't I? It is there—just as I figured it."

"You haven't taken out your thousand dollars to the pan, yet."

"If I get her—she'll weigh up a million to the pan."

The inner voice was persistent: "You'll be tied down. What'll you do when the long trail calls? There will be times when you will want to roam."

"God, ain't I roamed enough? But, if the long trail calls, we'll harness the dogs an' roam double."

"It's only February. The snow is deep. Wait till spring."

"I've waited too long, now. It seems like—I can hear her callin' me. An' I ain't seen the snow in twenty-five years that could stop me—with a toboggan."

His trail pack made up, MacShane sat beside the stove and smoked until his dog food had cooked, and when it was done he lashed it onto his toboggan and harnessed his dogs.

"Wait till tomorrow," urged the inner voice, "It's nearly midnight."

"Midnight, or noon, what's the difference in this God-forsaken land? It's all dark, anyhow. You might as well shut up. You lose. My hunch says 'go now!' An' I'm ridin' my hunch."

At Shungnak where MacShane arrived four days later, he entered the saloon where a dozen men were assembled. "If you want to go where you can shovel more gold out of the gravel in a day than you can here in a year, just follow my back trail," he announced. "It's red gold—under the big rock slide west of the igloo. There's a stove an' considerable grub an' some robes left in the igloo, an' a good sled, an' a half a ton of powder. You're welcome to 'em if you want 'em. But you better hit out before my trail snows under or you'll never find it."

The men looked at each other, and grinned. "No, thanks, Stranger, we don't like gravel as rich as all that. It's too heavy to shovel."

The witticism of the miner produced its roar of laughter, and MacShane shrugged, indifferently: "All right, boys, don't hurt your backs none. So long."

"Who is he?" asked someone, when the door had closed behind MacShane.

The proprietor answered: "Oh, he's be'n up on the Colville fer years, proddin' around in the gravel. He's be'n there too long. They git that way after a while. He wouldn't even come after his own grub. Used to send the Kobuks for it. The only times I ever see him was when he went down to Nome last spring, an' when he come back. He was batty then. Bet agin John Johnson's dogs, even money, an' then bet on them Gordon dogs. I give him ten-to-one, an' he took two hundred of it. When he came back through, he stopped in for to get his dust. I guess it was more gold than he ever seen before or heard tell of, an' now he thinks he's shovelled it out of the gravel."

"Don't know as he was so *damn* batty—bettin' on them Gordon dogs," opined the man who objected to heavy gravel, "They win, didn't they?"

"Sure they win, all right. But, it was a fool bet, at that. Who the hell ever heard of them dogs?"

"Maybe he had."

"Hell! He didn't even know they was a race! An' way up where he hung out he couldn't hear nothin' about nothin'."

"Maybe it was a hunch. A man ought to ride a hunch. I've got a kind of a hunch I'd maybe ought to hit out on his back trail. He might not be so damn batty. An' I never seen no red gold."

The proprietor grinned: "That's what folks always does when they make a big strike—go off an' leave it, an' tell the first bunch of strangers right where to go an' locate it. This here specimen made his real good by colorin' it red. I guess your hunch ain't workin' very strong, an' I got one that beats it all to hell. It says we ort to start a game of stud."

The miner laughed: "You win," he agreed, "Your hunch is strongest. Let's ride it!"

Out on the trail MacShane grinned as he mushed up the Kobuk. "The only stampede I ever tried to start—an' she fizzled. Men are fools!"

Instead of following down the Alatna to its mouth and up the Koyukuk, he cut northeastward across the heads of John River, Wild Creek, and North Fork, and two weeks later struck Myrtle Creek almost at its headwaters, and swung his dogs down stream. One after another he passed the deserted cabins that told the story of the creek's abandonment. What if the Gordons had gone, too? It was slow trailing, and he was very tired. The short noonday twilight had faded into night, and overhead the stars twinkled in cold brilliance. He knew he ought to camp, but doggedly pushed on. An hour later as he rounded a bend a dull square of light showed through the frosted pane of a cabin. MacShane's heart was pounding wildly as he urged on his dogs. It was the Gordon claim! There, rearing its black bulk out of the snow, was a boiler. But—it was cold! The door of the cabin opened, and MacShane paused as his eyes drank in the figure of the girl who stood framed in the doorway. It was she—the one woman in all the world—his woman! She was peering at him through the gloom. The next instant the door closed with a bang. The figure was gone.

MacShane frowned. Why was the boiler cold? Where was Gordon? And why had the girl slammed the door? The hospitality of the people of the Koyukuk was proverbial throughout all the North.

Slowly he advanced to the door. Should he call to her? Should he tell her who he was? And why he had come? He paused before the closed door. No, not yet, he decided. Then, purposely gruffening his voice, he called, loudly.

With the coming of February Lou Gordon completed her plan for the future. As soon as the spring thaws hardened the surface of the snow she would hit the trail—the long trail to the unknown Colville, and there, somewhere in those Arctic wastes she would find *Huloimee Tilakum*. Oh, why had she not interpreted the look she had often surprised in his eyes? Why had she remained blind to its meaning? She knew, now. There, in the night it had come to her—the night she had reached for her rifle—to be rid, forever, of the eyes that glowed in the dark. And there, in the high North, they two should find life—life, and love, and happiness.

She would sell her dogs in Bettles—all but the twelve great race dogs which she would keep for a trail team. And then she would hit straight up the Alatna, and cross to the Kobuk, and there she would find the Eskimos who had carried the supplies to *Huloimee Tilakum* through the long years of his exile in the land of red gold.

If only Dalzene had forgotten her. Maybe he would not dare to risk a trip to Myrtle even for the purpose of carrying out his threat, when he knew that the hand of every man upon the Koyukuk was against him. But, she dismissed this hope, as she recalled the terrible gleam of his eyes as the threat was uttered. No, Dalzene would come—sometime. She prayed that his coming should be delayed until after the snow hardened in the spring. But, Dalzene had a toboggan!

One evening soon after she had returned from feeding her dogs the sound of a voice startled her. It was a man urging on tired dogs. Stepping to the doorway she peered into the gloom. There he stood upon the creek, looking at her. For a long moment she scrutinized him as well as the starlight would permit. He was a bearded man. His shoulders drooped slightly. He was tired. He had come from the direction of Nolan, but he was no man of Nolan, that she knew. Nor was it Dalzene. She would instantly have recognized the burly form of the hooch-runner. Who was he? And why did he stand and stare at her without speaking. Possibly, some confederate of Dalzene, who had been sent ahead to see if the coast were clear. Dalzene would not risk his life lightly. With terror in her heart she slammed the door, and shot the heavy bar that she had contrived after the death of her father. Then, rifle in hand she seated herself on the edge of her bunk, and waited.

The man was approaching the door. She could hear his footsteps crunching the packed snow. The footsteps ceased and a moment later a voice called from the darkness:

"Hello, in there! Can I stop for the night?"

For a moment the girl hesitated, but only for a moment. Here was a trail-weary man, stumbling in the night upon the only cabin on the whole creek that afforded warmth and comfort, and she must refuse him! Outside, the man awaited his reply, and with an effort the girl steeled herself to violate tradition and deny him the comfort he asked.

"No. I'm sorry, but—I'm all alone. My father—isn't here." Instantly she regretted the words. What if the man were a confederate of Dalzene, and Dalzene should find that she was alone? "I—I expect him back anytime," she added, as an after-thought. "You can camp in the wood house. It is dry in there, and sheltered from the wind."

"Thanks," answered the voice, "I will."

She heard his footsteps recede from the cabin, a few moments elapsed and she heard his voice urging the dogs up the slope from the creek. Later she breathed against a frost-coated pane of the window, and when a tiny spot had cleared, she peeped out. The man was carrying an armful of spruce boughs into the wood house. He returned for another huge armful which he spread on top of the snow upon the sheltered side of the building for his dogs. "No friend of Dalzene would do that!" exclaimed the girl, under her breath, and turning to the stove, she slipped a caribou steak into the frying pan, and brewed a pot of strong tea. When the steak was done, she took the pan and the teapot and opening the door called to the man: "Here is some tea, and steak. Better get them while they're hot!" And, as his figure emerged from the wood house, she once more slammed the door. She heard him come for the food, and return to the wood house. Then she blew out her lamp and went to bed, with her rifle within reach of her hand.

When she awoke next morning and once more cleared a space on the pane and looked out the man had gone. She could see his trail where it led off down the creek.

After breakfast she fed her dogs and as she returned from the corral was attracted by the peculiar actions of Skookum, who was rushing into the wood house and out again, with short dashes down the trail of the departed trav-eler, evincing evidences of excitement and delight. He bounded to her side, looked into her face, and again raced off to the wood house. What did it mean? Skookum was no fool puppy to caper about in this manner. He was the most sedate and indifferent of dogs. Half in wonder the girl followed him to the wood house, where she found him sniffing about the pile of boughs upon which the man had made his bed. A little square of white paper attracted her attention. It was a page torn from a small note book and pinned to the wood house door by means of a sliver. There was pencil writing upon the paper, and carrying it into the cabin she held it close to the lamp, and began to read the awkwardly scribbled words. But, at the first sentence a cry escaped her lips, as with trembling fingers she turned the scrap of paper over and stared at the signature. For a moment she stood motionless her face paling and flushing as the hot blood surged from her wildly pounding heart. Turning the paper her eyes devoured the words in feverish haste:

"You asked me on Death Valley Hill if the gold was worth what it cost to get it. And if we wasn't missing life up here. I know the answer now, and I've come to tell you. I don't aim to stay around while your father is away. When he comes home I'll come back. Maybe both of us are tired missing *life*."

The last word was heavily underscored, and at the bottom of the paper were the words *"Huloimee Tilakum."*

With a wild, sobbing cry, the girl crushed the paper in her palm and thrust it into the bosom of her shirt. The next moment she was fastening on her snowshoes, and shutting Skookum in the cabin, she struck off down the creek, following the toboggan trail that was but a few hours old.

"He came to me! He came to me!" over and over she repeated the words as her feet fairly flew over the snow. "He came to me—and I didn't know him! It was his beard! He does love me. We neither of us knew it, then. We were like little children groping in the dark. He will camp at the cabin eight miles down—waiting for dad to come home. Poor old dad, he's home, now—and happy. And I will be happy, oh, so happy—with him! We will both be happy, and together we can laugh at the long night, and the strong cold." She paused abruptly and glanced back. "What if he should go on to Bettles? A hundred miles, and I haven't a bite to eat nor a blanket!" She smiled, and resumed her pace. "I can overtake him. He has got to break trail for his dogs."

Rounding a sharp bend of the creek she came face to face with a dog outfit, mushing up stream. The outfit halted and two men stood staring at her. And in that instant the blood froze in her veins. The larger of the two was Jake Dalzene! And he was eyeing her with a fatuous, grinning leer. The eyes of his companion were harder—frankly appraising.

CHAPTER XXVIII

SUNRISE

"So here you be, my pretty!" cried Dalzene. "Come down to meet me did ye?" The man's voice was thick of utterance. He was drunk.

Instantly the girl gained control of herself: "Stand out of my way! Let me pass!"

The man laughed coarsely: "Haw, haw, haw! Pretty sassy, hain't you? Well, you won't be so sassy agin you've had a chance to learn my ways."

Swiftly the girl's eyes surveyed the creek bed. The banks were high and steep. The man divined her intention: "No ye don't! No use tryin' to slip by us. Turn around an head back up the crick. I've got some business with yer pa—an' later with you."

"What do you mean?" again the deadly fear gripped at her heart.

"Remember what I told you that day in Nolan. Well, I ain't fergot. I had plenty time to think it over, back there in Nome. Six months they kep' me in their damn jail—all on account of you an' Old Man Gordon—an' now it's my turn." His voice fairly quivered with insane rage as he jerked off his mitten and extended the twisted claw that had been a hand. "An' that's what yer damn dog done! But he won't never chaw no one else up! An' Old Man Gordon won't never beat another race, neither. An' you—well—you an' me might git on all right when you come to know me better—an' then agin—we mightn't."

A cold calm took possession of the girl: "Don't be a fool, Dalzene," she said. "The man you just passed is coming back in a few minutes, and when he does, he will kill you."

"Oh, that's it, is it? That's what's goin' on up here on Myrtle? Kind of thought Old Man Gordon's b'iler would cost him about all the race money, time he got it up here. You ort to move down where they's more men."

Lou Gordon understood nothing of the man's implication, but the look in the leering eyes brought a hot flush of shame to her face. Dalzene continued: "But, you don't need to bother about him—he's through."

"What do you mean?" she shrieked the question, staring wide-eyed into the leering face.

The man laughed: "You know what yer friends would do to me if they ketched me on the Koyukuk. Well, I done it first—that's all. He's layin' back there in the snow, 'bout five mile down the crick. An' he ain't comin' back—none whatever."

A single piercing cry forced itself from between the girl's lips. *Huloimee Tilakum* was dead! And before her the man who had killed him stood and grinningly bragged of his deed. A red haze filmed her brain. Like a flash she whirled in her tracks and disappeared around the bend. In the cabin was the rifle! She would kill these two human beasts as she would kill wolves. A wild primordial fury gripped her heart—a fury that for the moment overshadowed the pain. This man had killed her man—and in red vengeance he should be killed!

With the hand of all men against him Jake Dalzene hated all men. Brooding upon this hate during the term of his imprisonment had transformed him into a veritable beast of hate. A malignant, dangerous thing of evil he was turned loose upon the North at the expiration of his term. Hating all men, he concentrated the full venom of his insane rage upon the Gordons upon whom he laid the blame for his downfall. It was Old Man Gordon who had caused him to lose his money on the Koyukuk, and indirectly had turned the whole Koyukuk against him. Over there they would kill him on sight—as they would kill a snake. The Gordon dog had maimed him for life, and Lou Gordon had treated him with supreme contempt in the roadhouse at Nolan, and later had outwitted him (as he thought) in Nome.

When he gained his freedom his one obsession was to even the score with the Gordons. He would slip over onto Myrtle, would kill the old man, and then—alone on the deserted creek with the girl—his eyes flickered with bestial lust as he thought of the girl. After that, if they killed him on the Koyukuk, they would have something to kill him for!

Dalzene was penniless. He needed an outfit, for the journey to Myrtle Creek. So he went to work on the dumps. It was there he met a fellow convict whose term had expired a month previous, and realizing that he might need help, cautiously sounded the man out. Satisfied, he laid stress upon the winnings of Gordon, and broached a scheme whereby they should visit Myrtle together, murder Gordon, divide whatever of loot there might be in the cabin.

The two pooled their earnings for the venture, and toward the middle of January, pulled out of Nome. The utmost caution had been used in the ascent of the Koyukuk from the mouth of the Alatna. Dalzene knew every foot of the country, and he was careful to detour past all camps and native villages. Once on Myrtle caution was relaxed. The deep snows of the winter had rendered it extremely improbable that there would be any travel on the abandoned creek, and the outfit held to the creek bed. The two celebrated their safe arrival on Myrtle with liberal quantities of hooch, the fiery liquor acting upon Dalzene's brain added fuel to his desire for revenge.

Upon rounding a bend they had come face to face with MacShane. The rifle and heavy six gun with which they had provided themselves were lashed to the toboggan and the man was right upon them. To attempt to release the gun would invite disaster. With a sense of vast relief Dalzene noted that the man was using a toboggan. He was not a man of the Koyukuk, and in all probability would know nothing of the edict of the miners' meeting. With elaborate heartiness, he tendered his bottle, but the other declined, and after a few words of commonplace conversation, he passed on and disappeared in the gloom.

Five miles farther on, Lou Gordon had come suddenly upon them, and all the hate of his warped soul leaped into Dalzene's brain. Helpless she was, unarmed and completely at his mercy. He took fiendish delight in taunting her. When she mentioned the man who had passed on the trail, it was his devilish ingenuity alone that prompted him to concoct the lie about killing him. He divined that it would cause her pain—so he told her the man was dead. And he had gloated as the sound of the girl's shriek rose on the air. That cry was music to the ears of Dalzene, and he chuckled all the way up the creek as his inflamed brain dwelt upon the pain that had showed in her eyes. She could not escape him. Old Man Gordon would be no match for him and his convict companion. So, as he mushed he laughed. Just before reaching the cabin, Dalzene paused, and unlashing the rifle from the sled, passed it to the other. About his own waist he strapped a belt from which dangled a six gun in a holster. Then, keeping the door in sight, they separated and cautiously advanced toward the cabin.

"Open up, Gordon!" he called, "Open up, an' we'll make a dicker." There was no response from the interior, and Dalzene drew nearer. Pausing, he examined the snow, passing completely around the cabin, and walking to the boiler. Then he returned and took a position near the door. "So that's the way of it!" he called, "The old man ain't here! He ain't be'n here since the last snow! So, yer here alone, eh?"

Within the cabin Lou Gordon gripped her rifle and answered: "I expect dad any minute!"

"You do, do you? Well, it's be'n a good many minutes since he was here, an' I guess he won't be bustin' in on our party. If he does he'll git his'n like the stranger did back on the trail."

Inside the cabin, the girl's lips pressed into a straight white line, and her fingers gripped the rifle till the knuckles whitened. If she could only shoot!

But the same log walls that protected her, protected her besiegers also. She wished now she had followed her first plan to lie in wait for them outside, but she had overestimated Dalzene's cunning. She had figured that he would divide his forces, and that she would be struck down from behind before she could kill him. The heavily frosted panes of the windows gave her no chance to shoot from the cabin.

The dog kennels attracted Dalzene's eye, and with a curse, he gripped his revolver and lurched toward them. "You kin say good bye to yer big lead dog, now!" he taunted. "I'll fix him, fer chawin' the hand off me! Damn him, he's where he can't git at me an' I'll shoot him all to pieces before I kill him." At the girl's side, in the cabin, Skookum sniffed the air suspiciously and a low growl rumbled in his throat, as the hair bristled upon his back. "Oh, why didn't you kill him, Skookum?" whispered the girl in desperation.

She could hear Dalzene moving about near the kennels. Stealthily she raised the bar of the door, and opened it just a crack, the next moment the door slammed shut and the bar crashed into place. The other man had leaped for the opening. Stepping swiftly back the girl sent a bullet crashing through the door, and the man answered with a taunting laugh. "Try it agin, sis! If you hit me you git a cigar!"

A loud cry from Dalzene brought her up, tense, listening. "Damn you, don't you kill that gal—she's mine! I'll tend to her case."

In vain Dalzene sought for the great lead dog among the dogs in the corral, round and round the fence he walked trying to single him out in the gloom. The noontime dawn had not yet broken, and as the man stepped onto a mound of snow close beside the fence for a better view of the corral, his snowshoe caught upon an obstruction and he fell heavily. With a curse, he scrambled to his feet and kicked at the obstacle that had tripped him. It was immovable, but the kick had partially dislodged the loose snow from about it. Swiftly Dalzene dropped to his knees, and with his hands dug the snow away. The object was a little wooden cross, and placing his eyes close to its surface he read the inscription burned into the wood.

STUART GORDON

Died Jan. 13, 19—.

Slowly the man rose to his feet and with lust-gleaming eyes, stood staring down into the snow, while in his brain, a new plan was born. With the journey to Myrtle accomplished and Gordon out of the way, he would have no further use for his confederate. He would watch his chance, shoot him from behind, and the loot and the girl would be his own. He glanced up. The man was watching him. He would play for time. Swiftly he walked to the cabin. "Just when was it you was expectin' the old man back?" he asked, following the words with a hoarse laugh that told the girl that he knew. She answered nothing.

Again the man spoke, changing his tactics: "Come on out, peaceable, an' we won't hurt you none," he wheedled, "All I want is you should hit up to Nolan an' fix it with the boys so they'll let me back on the river. That's all I want. Honest to God, it is. An' they'll do it if you tell 'em to." Again, no answer. "All right, I got another proposition. Throw in with me, an' we'll stay here an' work the old man's claim. They ain't no use tryin' to buck me. I got you where I want you, an' you ort to know it. The old man hain't comin' back. I jist stumbled onto his grave. How about it?"

Silence from the cabin. Suddenly into Dalzene's hate-crazed brain leaped the memory of that other day when he had talked to this girl and she had not deigned reply. It was the day of the miners' meeting. A sudden fury flared within him. And his voice raised to a bellow: "Damn you! You will come out! Come out, I say! Or, By God, I'll burn you out! Bar the door all you want to, you can't bar fire! Come out here! Damn you! Do you hear?"

Inside the cabin the girl stood gripping her rifle. Cold fear clutched her heart. She closed her eyes, and for a moment the world swam and she reeled, slightly. Fire! They would fire the cabin. Instantly she recovered herself. Well, it was the end. She would go out—when the smoke and heat forced her out. But she would go out shooting. She would never surrender! Never would that brute defile her living body with his foul touch. He might kill her, but he would never take her alive. The odds were two-to-one, but she would die fighting. She would kill them, or force them to kill her.

She could hear the enraged Dalzene ordering the man to carry spruce branches. She could hear the branches being heaped against the cabin. Then—the crackle of flames—louder and louder the crackling sounded, until it rose in a steady roar. The frost began to melt on the window panes, some chinking from high on the wall fell to the floor and the acrid smell of smoke reached her nostrils. Leaping to the window whose panes were fast clearing in the heat she saw Dalzene standing upon the edge of the creek facing the door. A cloud of smoke shot through with red flame swept past the window, concealing the figure. Stepping back the girl cocked her rifle and raising it waited for the smoke-screen to drift past.

"Wonder where they're headin'?" muttered MacShane as the two-man outfit disappeared in the darkness. "Guzzlin' hooch on the trail ain't goin' to git 'em far. The big one was plumb drunk. They'll have to camp before long. Anyway," he grinned, "They've left me a good trail!"

A half-hour later he pulled up his dogs before the door of a deserted cabin and explored its interior. "This will do till Old Man Gordon gets back," he decided, and proceeded to unharness his dogs. This done, he carried his pack from the toboggan and tossed it upon the floor of the cabin. "Wonder where the old man went an' how long he's goin' to stay?" he mused, "Nolan prob'ly. She said she expected him back any time." A slow smile twisted the corners of his mouth. "I wonder if she's found my note, yet? I wonder if she cares? Maybe I hadn't ought to put that down—about us two bein' tired of missin' life. Wish I hadn't. Wonder if she'll be watchin' for me to come back?" He paused abruptly, and stepping to the door, stared in the direction from which he had come. "I wonder if them two would bother her any?" Smiling at the thought, he returned to his unpacking. A few moments later he again stepped to the door and gazed up the creek. "Hell!" he muttered, "No one would bother a woman! But—the big one was drunk. She's a sourdough all right an' able to take care of herself. But—it wouldn't hurt to kind of mush along up that way—maybe the old man's got back." MacShane laughed aloud: "Trouble with me is I'm just naturally honin' to be near her. You can't never tell what a drunk man will do. I've got a kind of a hunch I ought to hit the back trail—an' when I get a hunch—I ride it!"

Fastening on his snowshoes he struck swiftly off up the creek. Their trail afforded good footing, and he walked rapidly.

At the point when the two-man outfit halted for the second time he paused and examined the tracks in the snow. "Someone else was comin' down the creek besides me," he muttered, "Someone in my trail—an' when he met this other outfit he turned around an'—" MacShane's words ceased abruptly as he further examined the marks left by the snowshoes where their edges over-lapped the toboggan trail. "He was runnin'," he exclaimed "What in hell?"

For an instant his heart ceased beating. Could it have been—*her*? Why had she turned back—running? The thought raced through his brain, and with a hoarse cry he dashed up the trail.

Rounding the last bend he stopped, horror-stricken. The red flare of flames confronted him. The cabin was on fire! No, it was light brush piled against the cabin! By the light of the leaping blaze he could make out the figures of the two armed men watching the cabin. The larger of the two stood upon the bank of the creek scarce twenty yards away. He caught the glint of the heavy revolver in the man's hand. MacShane was unarmed. Swiftly releasing the thongs of his snowshoes, he dropped from the bank to a strip of wind-swept ice, dashed toward the motionless figure of the man.

"Come on out! Damn you! I told you the time would come when you would talk pretty to Jake Dalzene!" The words ended in a startled cry as MacShane hurled himself upon him. The six gun, knocked from his hand, buried itself in the snow.

A puff of wind eddied the smoke-screen and Lou Gordon dropped her eye to the sights of her rifle. The man she had so long feared—the man who had, in cold blood, murdered *Huloimee Tilakum* stood as he had stood before the smoke and flames had blotted him from her sight. Her finger tightened upon the trigger. The next instant the rifle was lowered and with face pressed close to the glass the girl was staring wide-eyed through the window. Another form had leaped into view behind the form of Dalzene. The words with which the man was taunting her ended in a hoarse cry of fear—and two bodies were struggling in the snow!

A blur of motion caught the corner of the girl's eye and she turned her head to see the man with the rifle rushing to Dalzene's assistance. Crossing the room at a bound, she hurled the heavy bar aside, flung the door open, raised her rifle, and fired. The man with the rifle staggered a few steps, and regaining his balance, turned toward her, bringing his rifle to his shoulder. Again she fired and the man sagged slowly at the knees and crumpled into the snow.

As the door opened Skookum sprang past his mistress with a hoarse growl of fury.

Upon the bank of the creek the two struggling figures had regained their feet. Neither had been able to recover the six gun. At the sound of shots, they sprang apart and stared at the man in the snow.

The next instant the air was rent by a thin, shrill scream. The most blood-curdling sound MacShane had ever heard—coming as it did from the throat of a full-grown man—a cry so awful in its abandon of abject soul-terror as to cause a prickling sensation at the roots of his hair. Hardly had the shriek left the man's lips than a great tawny shape hurtled through the air and MacShane gazed in horror as The gleaming white fangs that studded the cavernous yawning mouth closed with an audible crunch upon the man's face. The great dog's momentum carried him past, as he bowled the man into the snow. Strange, inarticulate sounds came from the writhing body and MacShane, after one horrified glance turned away. The man in struggling to rise turned his head toward him and where his face had been living eyeballs bulged from their sockets and between two naked, flesh-stripped rows of teeth a living tongue writhed in audible mouthings.

The great dog sprang again—and MacShane rushed to the girl. "Quick!" he cried, "We can save the cabin yet!" and with his bare hands began to tear the blazing boughs from the wall. Side by side they worked, tearing away the brush and throwing snow on the blazing eaves. The thick logs of the cabin wall, already smoking, were easily extinguished with snow.

MacShane rubbed a handful of snow upon the last glowing coal and as he turned from the wall his eyes met the eyes of Lou Gordon—those wondrous dark eyes that were living wells of—*love!* The next instant his arms were about her and the tears from those dark eyes were wetting his cheeks.

"This is the answer to your question," he whispered, a few moments later when, with her head resting against his breast she looked up into his face.

"But we haven't missed—life! For us life is just beginning," she said.

"I sure hope Gordon will come back soon," smiled the man. And for reply, the girl pointed to the little wooden cross that Dalzene had uncovered in the snow, and together they turned away.

"And now, my woman, we'll be married," said MacShane, as they paused at the door of the cabin. The girl looked into his face with a smile. "And I will be Mrs.—*Huloimee Tilakum?*" she asked, "Do you know, dear—" the unfamiliar word hesitated upon her lips. "You have never told me your name."

"My name," he laughed, "I told you once I would some day tell you my name. It is Burr MacShane—"

"Burr MacShane!" cried the girl, staring wide-eyed into his face. "Why dad has been hunting for you for years! He wanted to apologize for—what he said—back in Dawson. Dear old dad—if he could only know!"

"Maybe he does know," whispered MacShane, softly, as his lips met hers.

"Wait!" she cried a few moments later, and darting into the cabin she reappeared with a grotesquely carved wooden doll, in a dress of faded silk. "Do you know what this is?" she asked, holding it up before him, "It has been my most treasured possession."

The man smiled, "Yes," he answered, "I gave it to you myself—years ago—that Christmas, in Dawson. I told you back in Nome it was a game—I knew you, an' you didn't know me—the biggest game of all, girl—and I won! And now I'm goin' to claim the stakes. There's a parson at Alekaket Mission," he whispered and smiled happily as the girl's face flushed crimson.

Skookum left off worrying at the *thing* that sprawled in the snow on the creek bank, and as the two stood arm in arm, he joined them, and rearing upward, placed a huge paw upon the breast of each. And as their hands stroked the great dog's neck, the smouldering amber eyes glowed softly.

An hour later the two paused for a farewell look at the little cabin on Myrtle. Beside them the worthless iron boiler reared its gaunt black sides above the drifted snow.

The girl's eyes filmed as they rested for a moment upon the little wooden cross, and as she turned away the Arctic gloom gradually lightened. She glanced upward toward the broad bands of purple and pink that shot into the zenith.

"Come!" she cried, and hurriedly led the way to the summit of a long bare ridge. "Look!" she pointed toward the southern horizon where a red disk upon the far-off rim of the world was dissipating the bands of purple and pink: "The sun! I watched it go down nearly three months ago," she murmured, softly. "And my heart was heavy and sad. I thought I had lost you, dear. I thought that for me love was dead, and my life loomed dark and cold as the long, long night that was before me. But see—now it is day!"

"Yes, girl," answered MacShane—"now it is day. It is a good omen. The sun means—life, and love, and happiness.

"I told Camillo Bill, way back in Dawson that my hunch said 'North'—an' I rode it!"

www.ingramcontent.com/pod-product-compliance
Lightning Source LLC
Chambersburg PA
CBHW011445170626
46816CB00008B/2523